Feral

Feral

Brian Knight

Five Star • Waterville, Maine

First Edition, Second Printing

Published in 2003 in conjunction with Tekno Books and Ed Gorman.

Set in 11 pt. Plantin by Christina S. Huff.

Printed in the United States on permanent paper.

Library of Congress Cataloging-in-Publication Data

Knight, Brian.
    Feral / by Brian Knight.—1st ed.
        p. cm.—(Five Star first edition speculative fiction series)
      ISBN 1-59414-065-0 (hc : alk. paper)
      1. Children—Crimes against—Fiction. 2. Murder victims' families—Fiction. 3. Washington (State)—Fiction.
4. Children—Death—Fiction. 5. Missing children—Fiction.
6. Parent and child—Fiction. 7. Feral children—Fiction.
I. Title. II. Series.
PS3611.N56F47 2003
813'.6—dc22   2003061829

Feral

Prologue

Amber heard her name called in the night and rose to answer it. She was still somewhere between dream and reality, and in her mind it was her daughter's voice.

When she saw the man's familiar face before her in the near perfect darkness, a grinning caricature of wickedness, all teeth and glaring eyes, every suppressed terror and forgotten childhood nightmare she had ever known came back to her. She had forgotten this face, but here it was again, and now she remembered.

"My sweet little Amber," he cooed. "My precious, precious thing. How you've grown."

She tried to run, but the power of his gaze kept her where she stood. She wanted to scream, but he cupped his hand over her mouth, cutting off her breath. As hard as she tried, she could not make a sound.

Then she saw his other hand and the wicked thing he held. A pair of stainless steel scissors, polished to a spotless mirror shine. They opened with a metallic hiss, making an X shape. He gripped them at the crux with his bare hand, fingers wrapped around handle and blade. They should have cut him, but did not. Weak light from outside lit the razor edges like lines of fire.

He punched through her with one extended blade and yanked upward, opening her up from crotch to sternum like one would a fish.

She felt the freezing sweat on her brow, cheeks, and chest, the odd sensation of parting skin and flesh as it hung in flaps from her midriff. Cold fire that filled her to the core, its intensity growing with each application of his weapon. There were hot, meaty splashes against her legs and feet as he gutted her.

Then, finally, her struggle for breath ended, the grinning face faded to black, and she felt nothing.

He knew she was gone. He could see the horrible understanding in her eyes die, leaving the dumb, empty gaze of a stuffed animal. He released her and she folded inward like a noiseless accordion, coming to rest at his feet.

He was drenched with her blood, painted with it, but that was fine. Just fine. He put the scissors away and rubbed his palms together in a slow, circular motion, relishing the tacky wetness between them. He closed his eyes, drew breath deep in through his nostrils, savoring her smell.

"Mommy." It was a small, fear-choked cry from down the hallway. The voice of the child he had come for. "Mommy, I'm scared!"

He opened his eyes, his smile widening, and laced the fingers of his bloodied hands together in a prayerful gesture.

"Ah," he intoned in a slow out-rush of breath. "My sweet, precious little Charity. I'm coming."

PART I
Sweet, Precious Thing

Chapter 1

Charity chanted as she ran, an endless mantra that governed the beat of her sneakers against the blacktop, concrete, and bare earth. The words kept her running through the night although she was too tired to run, kept her focused ahead when every shadow, tree limb, or mirage that she viewed sidelong transformed itself into *him*. When she was too scared to do anything but curl up in a ball somewhere and wait for him to find her, wait for her punishment, the mantra kept her moving.

> *Run, run as fast as you can,*
> *Running away from the Bogey Man.*
> *Through the light and through the dark,*
> *Running home to Feral Park.*

Charity was nine years old, and this was the third time she had run. He was neither patient nor forgiving; if he caught her again it would be over. She knew he wouldn't kill her, couldn't kill her no matter how mad he got, but he could be very mean.

She ran, keeping to the unlit streets and alleys as much as possible so no one would see her. This time she knew where she was going, and she thought if she made it, she would finally be safe.

She'd dreamed about it, the playground by the river, except it wasn't really a playground anymore. It had gone wild; the grass in the park around it, uncut for many years, supported large clusters of wild sage and thistles. The iron bars and rails that surrounded it were a blood-red color from years of rust. The swing's chains, the slides, and other metal surfaces were the same. Wooden ladders, towers, and walkways, though still sturdy in most places, were gray with age, showing signs of warping from seasons of cold, rain, and the cooking summer sun. Thick, knotted ropes used for climbing and swinging hung frayed. Some were tied into hangman's nooses.

There was a large wooden sign at the entrance that read Blackstone Park; only *Blackstone* was painted over in purple with the word *Feral*.

Feral: free, wild, returned to a natural state.

Charity understood what feral meant, the way she sometimes understood things without knowing why, upon waking from the first dream of Feral Park. The meaning touched a part of her that she thought was dead, the part that dared to hope. The part that laughed, cried, felt anything beyond the dumb, numb fear. The word, and the idea that she could be feral too, drove the numbness away. For the first time she actually dared to hate him.

Her fear of him was still there, but for the first time she realized she *needed* to escape him. The other times she had run away had been impulse, the way a dog will run from a cruel master. It doesn't think of escape, because the cowed dog does not believe in freedom. It can only hide, knowing its punishment will be great when the master finds it.

Charity was finished being his dog, his pet. This time she wasn't just hiding; this time it was for keeps.

Sometimes he wanted to kill her, burned to feel her blood in his mouth, running down his throat as he swallowed her whole. When his anger grew so big he felt on fire and the air he breathed felt like smoke in his lungs, the urge to take her was almost too strong to resist.

He could not kill her, not even now. He would punish her, though; he was going to find that little bitch and teach her not to leave him.

He remembered when he had first met her; she had awakened in the night calling for her mommy. He went to her instead, sat on the edge of her bed and asked what was wrong. He was still a stranger to her then, though she knew his face from dreams. He knew her, had come for her as he had so many others.

She had ignored him, continued to watch the door, waiting for her mother. She gave him an occasional nervous, twitching glance.

He asked her again, "Why are you crying, my precious little angel? It breaks my heart to see you crying." Again, she ignored him. The third time he grabbed her gently by the face, the V between his thumb and forefinger gripping her chin while his fingers caressed her cheeks. The blood on his fingers painted her cheeks; red streaks like the war paint on one of Peter Pan's little Indians. He eased her into a sitting position and leaned closer.

Her eyes darted, left and right, up and down. They rolled in their sockets in an effort to avoid his gaze. She was the strongest child he had ever encountered, but the force of his will was too powerful to resist.

"I had a bad dream," she said at last.

"Oh, dear Charity," his voice was soothing, offering cold comfort. "A bad dream, was it?"

"Uh huh," she said, then closed her eyes, forcing back the panic and tears. She opened them again and glanced back toward the door. She knew her mother wasn't coming. She did not cry then though, she stayed in control.

"I dreamed about the Bogey Man," she said when she had managed to kill the sobs.

He patted her head, smoothed the dark tangle of hair from her high forehead.

"There, there," he said. "Don't cry now. Close your eyes and sleep."

She nodded and slouched back against her pillow, all fear put away by the force of his suggestion. Thoughts of her mother, at least for the moment, were swept away.

He smiled and held her as her eyes slipped shut. "You weren't dreaming."

He picked her up. She lay limp as a rag doll in his arms, and he had held her like that for a long time before leaving. Instead of devouring her, as he had come to do, he took her with him.

Looking into her eyes that night, he had found something unexpected. Something he had never seen before, or thought he would ever see, in any of these sheep-like creatures. He saw something in her that would always separate her from the rest of the flock. Something strong. Something wild.

In that moment he knew she was for him, and for the first time in a long, long time, he wasn't alone. Not that being alone bothered him, but this was something new.

Now she had left him, again, and unlike before she wasn't just running to hide. She meant to escape him. He could read it in her panicked, distant thoughts.

He would not allow that. There were none like her, none who could ever replace her. Even if it meant subduing her, killing some of that wildness that made her so very special and making her more like the rest of the lambs, he would do it. If that was what it took to keep her at his side, then he would do it.

He could not lose her.

It would have to wait though. He was getting weak. It was time to feed.

14

Chapter 2

Shannon Pitcher started taking her late night walks after settling into her brother's house on Walnut Street. They had started late one evening as a walk to the convenience store for snacks, and maybe a good book to pass the next few nights with. She hadn't slept well the past few months, hadn't slept at all the past few weeks except in short, violent bursts just before dawn. She was tired of watching the midnight movie marathons, mostly B-movie rejects culled straight from the bargain basement of the trashy 1980s, and the infomercials were pure insomniac hell.

That night, an hour after starting toward the Sunset Mart, she had awakened to her surroundings and realized two things: she had no idea where she was, and she was exhausted. She could have curled up in the dew-damp grass of someone's front yard and fallen asleep right then. Instead she did a drunken about-face and walked back the way she had come.

She stopped only to read the first street sign she saw. It was the corner of Fair and 17th Street. She had walked over a dozen blocks without turning once. She wasn't used to this much street running unbroken and straight. Riverside was only a small city, but much larger than her hometown, Normal Hills.

She forgot the snacks and walked home, then crashed until late the next afternoon without the help of her hated pills.

While that long, uninterrupted sleep had been the greatest thing to happen to her in this new life, her post–Thomas-and-Alicia life, it had completely reversed her sleep cycle. Shannon found it was a change she could live with. Sleep during the day, take care of life's mundane necessities in the evening, and spend her nights in a nocturnal parody of life.

She had money, and the ability to make more when she needed it, so she was set. All she needed was a place to crash and a good movie or book to keep her company. That, and her night walks; the exhaustion and the dreamless sleep she needed to do it all over again.

Shannon heard the music before she saw the playground. It was a muffled, almost ethereal mixture of heavy metal and children's laughter. Her brother, Jared, had listened to heavy metal as a teenager.

Her taste for what their father called The Wild Stuff had never been as wide or varied as Jared's, but she recognized this tune. It was Queen's "Stone Cold Crazy," but not Queen that was playing it. Behind the heavy metal noise, and running through the fast beat and sandpaper rhythm like a scarlet thread, was the laughter of lunatic children.

Shannon knew she should turn—caution being the greater part of valor and all that shit—and go back the way she had come. Kids would be kids, she knew, and the safest thing to do when they got up to harmless mischief was to leave them alone. Just stay the hell out of their way and let them wind down.

Like I'm doing now, she thought. *Let them exorcize, or maybe just exercise, their demons and hope their better natures kick in before any real trouble starts.*

There was something fundamentally wrong about this, though. It was not the boisterous carousing of teenagers. The voices behind the laughter were too young, the maniacal tittering of grade-school lunatics on a field trip to some carnival freak show.

Can't be, she thought. *You're crazy. You're hearing things. Just turn around and walk your ass back home. It's getting early, and you're so fucking dead on your feet you're hallucinating.*

Instead, she continued along the river, ear cocked toward the odd sound of toddler metal madness. She wasn't hallucinating; there was a playground over there by the edge of the wild, where all traces of the city ended. A goddamn big one, and so old and neglected she couldn't believe any parent would let their child play in it.

The music and the laughter ebbed and swelled, ebbed and swelled.

The playground was empty.

A single voice, the voice of a haughty schoolyard queen, rose above the others. She sounded eight, maybe nine years old, Alicia's age.

Stop it, a voice in her head commanded. *We are not going there tonight. Not tonight, not ever!*

She tried to kill the thought as she approached the playground. It quieted, falling back into the denied darkness of her subconscious, but it would not die. It hung on, whimpering in the darkness where she could still hear it.

That crazy music, ebbing and swelling, and the sound of muffled laughter, distorted into something horrible.

It was *her* voice, beautiful and frighteningly familiar, singing some nonsense hopscotch song, one of many in her repertoire. Then she spoke to Shannon.

"Why did you let him do it, Mommy? Where were you when he took me away? Why didn't you stop him?" The voice, Alicia's voice, came from inside the playground, and from somewhere within her own head.

Alicia?

It can't be her, she thought coldly. *There's no way it's her, she's dead.*

You don't know that, they never found her body. You don't know she's dead.

Shannon ran toward the playground, stumbling through ankle-high grass and clumps of stinging thistles. The music, the laughter, the screams of terror that she recognized only vaguely as her own, expanded. The jumble of noise pulsed between her temples.

"Alicia!"

She passed a large wooden sign, Feral Park, and as she ran beneath the sign at the entrance that proclaimed, *The Playground of Dreams,* the noise popped like a bubble and was gone. Her momentum and the adrenaline pumping through her body carried her on. She ran through to the heart of the playground, dodging obstacles, ducking one low-hanging rope bridge strung between a pair of wooden towers. Her feet tangled in the cover of old graying wood chips and she landed, sprawled out in the sandbox a few feet away.

She lay there for a minute, not hurt, but physically and emotionally drained.

What the hell just happened to me?

She didn't understand the specifics, but the basics were clear enough. She was having a walking nightmare; she was losing her mind.

When she felt she could trust her legs, she rose and brushed the dust from her jeans. She remained as still as possible, silent, listening for the music, the laughter, or the voice, but the silence endured. She looked around, eyes and senses wide open, but among the maze of shadows, and the jungle of playground equipment that spawned them, it was impossible to know if she were truly alone. There were too many shadows, too many cubbyholes, too many hiding places.

Behind her a rusty swing squeaked, nudged by the wind, or perhaps an unseen hand. To her left, old wood groaned as if being relieved of some unseen burden. Something moved in front of her. A shadow that hadn't been there a few seconds earlier snaked across the wood-chip covered ground toward her. She stumbled away from it in horror, and something grabbed her from behind.

Hey lady! A soft young voice, faint but clear, as if someone had come unnoticed behind her and whispered in her ear.

Shannon spun around, a startled shriek escaping her lips. She tasted fear, thick and salty, in the back of her throat. She could feel, worse, could hear, the increasing tempo of her heart. It pulsed irregularly, echoed by a pounding behind her eyes.

No one was there.

Something touched her ankle.

She jerked away, striking something hidden in the darkness with her temple. The low ringing sound suggested it was metal, but the ringing might have only been in her head. For a second the playground was gone, and she was alone with the pain and a frightening sense of surrealism. Then the laughter started, like a white noise broadcast in the tender gray meat between her ears. It grew, its volume increasing like a radio that has been turned from one to ten, bringing her back to herself. She opened her eyes and looked up into the dirty face of a young boy. He was laughing too, but no sound came from his wide-stretched mouth. It was in Shannon's head with the rest of the sounds.

A second later, the face was gone.

Shannon rolled onto her knees and rose. Around her the shadows jumped, shifted, melted together like living pools of ink. Some vanished just as she caught sight of them, only to reappear in the periphery of her vision. Every swing, teeter-totter, and hanging length of rope was in motion. The rope bridges above and around her bounced and swung violently.

The noise of laughter grew and grew, again mixed with that distant music.

Shannon stood, her fists pressed to her ears, an attempt to block out the noise. It didn't help. She searched for the opening in the playground wall, the arched entrance she had come in through, found it, and bolted. She glanced back as she ran and saw something following, a long serpentine shadow. It picked up speed and size as it absorbed the smaller shadows in its path.

Now Shannon could hear screams as well as the laughter, and realized they were her own.

C'mon back lady . . . we wanna play!

Something flew past her, sailing only inches from her right ear. It might have been a brick, but she couldn't tell for sure in the dark.

Nany-nany poo-poo, stick your face in doo-doo.

Something grabbed her upper arm as she ran; it felt like tiny fingers, incredibly strong and with long fingernails that dug into her flesh like the teeth of an iron trap. She went into a rough sideways spin, stumbling over her feet and landing hard on her ass. The invisible thing lost its grip on her as she fell. She tried to rise again; the exit was only feet away. The shadow serpent, more like a shadow river now, was rushing ever faster.

She scrambled and was grabbed again, this time the tiny iron trap-hand closing around her ankle.

"Damnit, let go!" she screamed, and kicked at the invisible hand until it released her.

Ouch . . . fuckin' spoilsport.

She blundered to her feet, and was knocked down as something large and solid struck her between the shoulder blades. She made a choked *"oof"* sound and landed face first.

Get her!

She turned over onto her back in time to see the monstrous shadow stretch out wide and rear up like a cobra. It came down on her legs, and they disappeared from the thighs down. All sensation below her waist ceased.

She dug fruitlessly into the wood chips and dirt with the heels of her hands as it started to suck her in.

Catch the Bogey!

Kill the Bogey!

Cram a stick up its ass!

There was a scream, a sound of such honest terror that Shannon thought her heart might stop.

And then it was over. All was silent; all was still.

The shadow thing was gone and she had her legs back.

She turned to the exit and saw a girl, a girl who reminded her so much of Alicia it hurt, staring past her, slack-faced. The girl didn't look anything like her missing daughter; it was the clothes. Faded Arizona blue jeans, pink canvas high-top shoes, pink t-shirt, and the small heart-shaped gold locket that hung around her neck; the one with the picture of Thomas, Alicia, and herself inside it. The last time she had seen Alicia, she had been wearing those clothes. As she watched, the girl began to sag, her eyes rolling up to the whites as she collapsed before the arched entrance.

Chapter 3

Sometimes the scariest things are also funny; not funny like Bill Cosby is funny, but funny in the same sadistic way that The Three Stooges are. Like the shock on the face of a woman who has been discovered in the most personal and embarrassing of positions, or the look on the face of a man who has just been caught by his wife with his pants around his ankles and his cock in another woman's mouth.

Jared Cruse managed to stay faithful to his wife for four years, a fact that inspired an amount of awe in his friends, considering his habitually wandering eyes and his pre-marital habit of straying. That a dog like Jared Cruse could stay faithful to any one woman for four consecutive years was something worth noting. Watching him try to resist the urge of his supercharged libido whenever he caught the slightest whiff of estrogen was downright hilarious, or so his friends told him.

What wasn't funny was the thoughtlessness with which he finally broke his marriage vows, and how his wife, Anna, knew almost instantly that something was wrong. The dense cloud of denial that she lived in for the last several months of their marriage was not funny either; it was sad.

The circumstances of his first indiscretion and the person with which it happened were funny, like the X-rated version of a tacky sitcom. It was his station's dispatch, and ironically, one of Anna's best friends.

It was an unexpected liaison, but one he had fantasized about before. He'd first met her, Lillian, the week of his wedding. She was Anna's maid of honor, and he had been admiring her as discreetly as he knew how ever since. It was obvious that he was attracted to her; there were those long and lusty sideways glances when he thought no one was looking. There was his inability to look her directly in the eye whenever they spoke. He had fantasies too; nasty things that sometimes left him unable to think straight. They say that the average man spends eight hours out of the day thinking about sex, and not with their wives, Jared assumed, so he never felt guilty about his fantasies, but he did guard them. Lillian and he had carried on like friends; he had even helped her get the dispatch job when it opened up.

He never suspected that Lillian had ever once felt the same attraction toward him, at least not until he found himself alone with her one afternoon in the station's deserted evidence room.

Their *Thing*, as people called it, was sudden and explosive, and when it was over he spent the next two weeks hiding the friction burns and scratches from his wife.

They continued to meet secretly, in hotels, at her home, and at his home when Anna was away on business, for almost a year, and some people thought it was funny that they weren't caught earlier, considering how sloppy they had become.

What wasn't funny was how Anna had finally broken down and confronted them.

She had fired a single shot outside the hotel room, destroying the locked doorknob, and kicked the door in. She stood outside, the windy autumn afternoon framing her like a bad Van Gogh, screaming, crying, laughing hysterically. She was shouting something at them, but her words were impossible to decipher. She held Jared's personal revolver in her right hand; his service pistol was hidden under his jacket on the nightstand. She gripped the gun loosely, let it sway crazily from side to side, sighting in first on Jared, then Lillian, then on Jared again.

He was sitting on the edge of the bed, his pants pooled around the tops of his bare feet. Lillian knelt before him, still fully dressed, her face buried in his crotch. The gunshot had startled her, and she had bitten down, not hard enough to bite it off, but she did draw blood. She spit his withering cock out with a gurgled scream, her lips wet and red. In her horror she had transformed from beauty to beast.

Jared had enough time to raise a hand in protest, then four more shots drowned out Anna's shrieks. A pillow to his left exploded in a cloud of old gray feathers. Glass shattered behind him.

Lillian screamed again and scurried around to the other side of the bed on her hands and knees. Tufts of brown shag carpet flew up behind her as a slug tore into the floor with an ugly *crack*.

There was an explosive pain in his shoulder, like a red-hot poker pushed through flesh, and he was staring at the ceiling, screaming in pain.

Anna screamed the whole time, words having given way to nonsense.

Behind the bed Lillian had gone silent; Jared hadn't known if she was hiding or dying.

Another shot flew harmlessly into the ceiling, showering him with plaster.

Then Anna was gone.

Without so much as a sidelong glance to see if her lover still lived, Lillian rushed from the room, her hysterical sobs fading almost instantly in the growing chatter from the parking lot.

Jared had risen slowly and managed to get his pants back up before the first wave of rubberneckers arrived. Then he lay back down, ignoring the drone of questions, exclamations, and suppositions. Holding his left hand firmly over the leaking hole in his shoulder, he had waited for the paramedics. Inside his pants, his dick throbbed like a rotting tooth.

He waited for what seemed an unbelievable length of time, all the while thinking the same thought over and over again: *crazy bitch shot me with my own gun.* By the time help finally arrived, his mantra had changed to: *I fucking deserved it.*

That afternoon, post-surgery and still half-stoned from the morphine, he lay in the hospital remembering the time he had played truth-or-dare with his cousin and her friends. He was eight years old, and they in their early and pre-teens. His cousin, Terry, was spending the summer with them at Normal Hills and had been stuck with baby-sitting duty that day.

About halfway through the game he had singled out the oldest and best developed of the group, challenging her with the most embarrassing question he could think of. The alternative dare was almost as embarrassing; she would have to remove her training bra and lift her shirt over her head for exactly five seconds—enough time for all of them to get a really good look at her tits. The question, just as he had hoped, had been too much, and instead of ducking out of the game, as he had feared, she took the dare.

Red-faced with embarrassment she unhooked the bra and hoisted her faded Doors t-shirt. A few of the girls there, the ones who were jealous, Jared supposed, thought it was funny as hell. Shannon, who had refused to play the game, did not. To Jared it was serious business, and he tuned out the laughter as he studied the gentle curves and soft brown peaks of her breasts.

He spent the rest of the game terrified they would pull some equally embarrassing trick on him, but they didn't. Even if they had, it would have been worth it.

Even back then, before he had sprouted his first pubic hair, he had been fascinated with sex.

Jared knew he was a bad person, and worse yet he was also a cop, which made him a bad cop. He wasn't the sort of cop who would entrap young hotties and give them a choice between sex and jail, but he had entertained the idea a few times with some amusement.

A bad person, a bad cop, and a bad husband.

When his superior arrived that afternoon to question him, the lies came easily enough, just as they always had when he needed to get himself out of trouble. This time it wasn't his own ass he was saving.

Exactly what the hell happened back there, Cruse? Who did this to you? They were simple questions, simple and direct as the bull-faced man who asked them. Jared's answers were also simple, as the best lies often are.

Don't know, he said. *Just some bitch I met outside the liquor store. When I pick up a hump I don't bother checking identification. Who shot me? Fuck if I know. A jealous bull-dyke maybe. Your guess is as good as mine.*

Maybe Sergeant Winter had seen right through that lie. Cops spent a good deal of their time being lied to and jerked around by John Q. Public, and usually developed a good nose for bullshit. Either way it didn't matter. Winter never investigated the incident, a drawn-out investigation would have embarrassed the entire department, and Jared was terminated.

At least he didn't have to worry about being a bad cop anymore.

★ ★ ★ ★ ★

When Jared returned home from the hospital Anna was gone, and barely a week later their mail-order divorce ensued. He didn't contest it, they had no children, and she wanted nothing from him. Even before Winter fired him she was the big breadwinner of the two. He never had to face her in court; he filed the paperwork and it was over. He hadn't heard from her since.

He never heard back from Lillian either. The only lasting legacy from his fling with her, ironically enough, was the inability to fuck.

Lucky, Anna's pet name for *it* once upon a time, had unlearned all its best tricks. No more *stand up, roll over,* or *shake hands.* All Lucky did now was play dead. Nerve damage, mechanical failure, or good old-fashioned psychological scarring—it could have been any or all. Either way, it came to the same thing. No more roaming—Jared was one well-neutered old dog.

Still, after almost a year of no boom-boom, his libido had not diminished.

As he returned home from the night shift at Aljo Security, he debated: start that paperback he'd been eyeballing for the past few weeks, one of Shannon's detective novels, or watch a skin flick. By the time he walked through the front door of the house he now shared with his sister instead of his wife, he had settled on the skin flick.

All amorous thoughts vanished when he saw Shannon sitting, eyes wide and staring, in a chair in the middle of the living room. Laid out on the old sofa before her was a girl of about nine, haggard and sleeping badly. For a second Jared thought it was his dead niece, Alicia.

Chapter 4

Gordon Chambers slept, parked at a rest area alongside of Washington 95. His dreams were short little horror movies, punctuated by the sound of the occasional big rig and other infrequent night traffic. Sleep came in bits and pieces, making the short rest stretch an eternity, and when the sun rose, he felt more drained than before. He lay back in his Mazda's reclined seat for a while and watched the Cedar skyline through the car's bug-flecked windshield. It shifted from violet, to orange, to powder blue.

Oregon was behind him now; Eugene, Salem, Portland, and The Dalles, all left in his proverbial dust. Gordon had crossed the Columbia River in the black of night, scarcely aware in his exhaustion. He'd fought sleep grimly since his last pit stop outside of Portland, almost running off the road minutes after crossing into Washington. The decision to stop and rest was made grudgingly.

The rising sun slowly burned his lethargy away and the urgency of his trip returned.

He stepped out of his car, flinching at the bright flashes reflecting off its hood, and stretched as he walked to the restroom. He peed, washed his hands, his face, then stuck his head under the running water. The chill of the early June morning and the cold water did their job. He pulled a comb quickly through his thinning blond hair, and with a grimace at his reflection decided he was as ready as he would ever be.

As he walked to his car, a mini-van parked beside it and a family of five spilled from its open doors—a husband and wife, both older than him, and three children. The youngest climbed clumsily from the side door; she could not have been over three.

Gordon stopped, eyes fixed on the toddler. He watched her struggle for the ground. She made small, aggravated sounds, and let out a shout of triumph when her feet found the blacktop. He stood there, staring at her, and when her parents noticed him and exchanged anxious looks, he made himself get into the car and drive.

He drove for the next few hours with her bright face burned into his mind's eye.

He made another pit stop in Yakima—pumped gas, peed again, and drank more bad coffee. He hadn't showered in two days; he felt like crap, looked worse, and his smell was wilting. Outside, the morning air had abandoned its comfortable chill. It was oppressive, heavy, so laden with moisture you could almost drink it. By the time he made it to his car he was sweating.

One hundred and fifty miles to go.

On the highway again, Gordon let himself zone out. He saw nothing but the blacktop. Unaware, he began to rub at the long scar that ran from the top of his right cheekbone to his jaw. He saw himself doing it in the rearview mirror and forced his hand back to the wheel. It was an old scar, but deep—a jagged ashen line that roughened his profile, adding more years to his face than the three days of stubble he wore. A woman he had dated many years ago said that the scar was sexy, that it made him look like a scrapper. He had turned down her invitation to take her home that night, and had not called her again.

Gordon was all but blind to the world outside his own head, his thoughts centered on a daughter he hadn't seen in six years, and despite all his best efforts, would probably never see again.

Amber had left him six years ago and taken his baby, his Charity, with her.

He had been hosting a masked Halloween party for his father, who was fighting his last round in a nasty game called heart disease. Despite the old man's growing frailty and the certainty that that year's ball would be his last, or maybe because of that, he insisted on making it his biggest ever.

Each year, his father's Halloween parties were grander than the last, and surprisingly festive considering the caliber of snobs and blue bloods that made up the guest list. Each year the alcohol flowed, fine and expensive food was eaten, and a darkly festive mood was maintained.

Amber, his wife of five years by then, stayed home sick, a touch of whatever bug had been going around, she had said. She had canceled the baby-sitter so she could stay home with Charity. When he left she was wrapped in a wool quilt on the sofa, reading a book about feminism in the nineties with their daughter dozing beside her. On his return early the next morning they were both gone.

As it turned out she *had* been sick—sick of his snobbish family, sick of his old money (though not enough that she hadn't taken a good bit of it with her), and sick of his pretentious friends. Most of all, she was sick of him.

At first he was shocked; theirs had been a pleasant arrangement, stable and beneficial, and they had made a beautiful couple. She was poor, with a truant father and a worthless lush of a mother, but she was smart, ambitious, and stunningly gorgeous. He was young, educated, well-bred, with above-average looks, and he was rich.

She should have been content, he had thought bitterly. *She had it all, anything she could have wanted out of life. All she had to do was keep playing the part.*

She should have been content.

Then he understood. He had been an idiot, a selfish, pretentious idiot. She would never be content as his trophy wife, and though he had always been faithful and had always assured her of her equality in the marriage, in his family, and in his life, that was what she was. The fact that he *had* to reassure her of those things proved that they were a lie. There was a dignity in her contrary to her humble background that would never allow that.

After he was finished feeling foolish, he felt sad. She may have been a showpiece, barely more than a juicy piece of well-mannered eye candy, but he missed her.

And he missed Charity.

It was clear she didn't plan to come back, so he hired the best private investigator he could find to track her down. He would never be able to get her back, he knew that like he knew the earth was round and the sky was blue, but he would damn well have his daughter back. His mother had faded slowly during his childhood, eaten away by the stomach cancer that had taken her when he was eleven, and his father had died shortly after that last fateful Halloween. His baby, his Charity, was all he had left.

Amber had been resourceful, though, and would not be found. Not until she was dead and couldn't run anymore. She had changed her name to Sandra Monroe and moved from city to city, state to state, taking part-time jobs to preserve her pilfered nest egg.

His private investigator had found her in Chicago, and by the time Gordon arrived she was already in the morgue.

Charity was gone.

31

Amber's had been the last in a series of murders in the Chicago area. The victims were always the parents, or a single parent, of one or more children, and always found brutally slain. The killer never left a clue, a print, a clothing fiber, a drop of his or her own blood, nothing. The children were never found.

The killer had moved on. When a similar killing spree started up in Texas, Gordon went south.

He followed the bloody trail for three years: through Texas, Arizona, Maine, New York, and Oregon. Now Washington State. He was early this time. There were only two murders and three missing children so far. There would be more, many more, and when the killer struck again he would be near. Though he knew his chances of finding Charity were slim, he had to be there. He had to try.

If he didn't find her, maybe he would find the killer. At this point he would take whatever he could get, reunion or revenge.

Gordon entered Riverside, where the latest murder had occurred, but continued east through the south side's industrial area, passing Feral Park on his way out of town. His first stop was Normal Hills, the site of Washington's first murder.

There was someone in Normal Hills he needed to see.

He reached down for the cell phone clipped to his belt, thinking to give that someone a call, then changed his mind. There was no need to bother him just yet; they would meet soon enough.

The morning was bright and hot, too hot for June. The Snake River flowed past Main Street and Maney Park like a slow liquid sapphire. It was just past ten; by noon the air would be shimmering with heat. The ground was still moist with the morning dew but would be parched again by noon.

32

Dust would rise with the temperature, riding the warm breeze through town like a plague.

The mill on the north side of the river was a blur of activity, the log yard crawling with trucks and loaders, a constant source of white noise. The shore was a wall of stone and thistles, embraced by a bed of driftwood and flotsam.

The south shore was clean, picturesque, a mostly untouched natural shoreline fortified with hanging willows and brush. On the west end of town Maney Park faced the river, providing several small barbecue pits, a gazebo, a restroom, and a concrete footpath that stretched to the east end of town, a median between the tall wind-teased willows and Main Street.

Gordon drove another block to Little's Café on the corner of Forth Street and pulled to the curb, killing the engine. His supply of Twinkies and convenience store burritos were gone, but he was still hungry. Time for something with a little more substance.

Gordon's supply of ready cash was nearly gone as well, and most places this far west wouldn't accept a New Hampshire check unless it was at gunpoint. He had to be careful with what cash he had left until he could find an ATM machine, and he was sure there wouldn't be one in this little town.

The inside of Little's Café was as he had envisioned it: dim, rustic, faded and worn around the edges. There was a half-circle counter lined with red upholstered stools. The dark wood surface of the bar was a display of hometown pride, with a picture of the latest Normal Hills varsity football team left of the cash register, and a framed Normal Hills Chamber of Commerce certificate on the right. Three men sat at the counter eating their breakfast solemnly. A few more sat at round oak tables scattered around the country-style dining area. They watched Gordon as he made his way to the table in the farthest, darkest corner. Gordon didn't like being watched. He took a seat with his back to the wall and waited. The others quickly rediscovered their breakfasts, and he breathed a little easier with their eyes turned away from him. Charles Davis, his roving PI, wasn't there yet, but Gordon didn't worry. Charles said to meet him at ten-thirty, and it was just past ten. He would be there at ten-thirty on the nose. Gordon unfolded the menu and browsed while he waited.

A squat, balding man shuffled past his table carrying plates heaped with eggs, toast, bacon, and hash browns.

"Right with you," he said. His voice had the rough edge of a life-long smoker. He set the plates before two men sitting at a table near the door and returned to Gordon at a leisurely pace.

"G'morning," he said, looking at his note pad instead of Gordon. "What'll you have?"

"I'll take one of what they have," Gordon said, gesturing to the men by the door. His stomach ached now, as if some dormant beast inside him had awakened. "And a black coffee, please."

As the waiter turned to walk away Gordon remembered Charles, who would join him shortly. "Better make that two of each," he said.

The waiter nodded, wrote on his pad again, and disappeared into the kitchen.

Charles showed up, as if on cue, just as the food arrived. Big, well-dressed, and black, Charles stood out in this den of good old boys. Eyes followed him as he strode to Gordon's table.

"Good morning, old friend," he said, seating himself across from Gordon. His voice was as big as the rest of him. He leaned across the table, the wooden chair creaking under his weight, and snatched one of the plates. He salted the eggs heavily and dug in.

Gordon couldn't help but smile. He had only known Charles for three years but considered the driven, often dangerous private investigator a friend. Gordon wasn't an easy man to befriend and he knew it, but Charles had an earnestness about him that he had to respect, and an almost unreasonable optimism that was contagious. That, Gordon supposed, was the reason Charles was willing to keep working this case. He wasn't milking it; Gordon knew he'd been turning down easier jobs, probably better-paying ones too. He believed against all common sense that they could catch the bastard, and maybe even save his daughter, if she was still alive.

That, if nothing else, made Charles the best friend he'd ever had.

"Did you ever stop to consider that maybe those weren't for you?" Gordon asked, and sipped experimentally at the scalding coffee. He spooned a few ice cubes from his water cup into the coffee and waited for them to melt.

"Who else then?" Charles asked and shoveled another spoonful of eggs into his mouth. He chewed quickly, swallowed, and added, "You have a girlfriend here I don't know about?"

"No," Gordon confessed. "Maybe I'm just really hungry." He sipped the coffee again, found it more accommodating, and drank. The coffee was good, fresh.

"Even so," Charles countered, "you'd starve yourself before you let a friend go without a meal." He emptied his coffee in three gulps and started on the hash browns.

In minutes Charles had cleaned his plate. He briefed Gordon while the smaller man finished his breakfast at a more human pace.

"Shannon Pitcher, maiden name Cruse, lived here in Normal Hills with her husband, Thomas, and their daughter, Alicia. They divorced a few years ago, but Shannon stayed in town so Alicia could be close to her father. Thomas Pitcher is the son of Simon Pitcher, who pretty much owns this town.

"Shannon continued to work for Simon after the divorce, did the books for him. Evidently, the old man paid her well, too. From what I gather, not all of Simon's business dealings were aboveboard, so I guess he had to. Thomas was murdered a few months ago. Alicia was spending the weekend with him when it happened." Charles paused as the waiter returned to fill their mugs and recommend his wife's huckleberry pie. Gordon declined; Charles ordered two pieces. The waiter left and Charles continued in a softer voice.

"It's a sore subject to broach around here," he said. "From the early to mid-nineteen seventies, a dozen girls disappeared. Earlier this year they started finding their bodies. They never caught the killer."

"Do you think they're connected?"

"No," he said quickly. "None of the parents in the earlier cases were murdered. I don't think they're connected. The locals don't see it that way though; they think it's either the same person or a copycat, but they don't know what we do."

"So where do we go from here?"

"To see Shannon Pitcher. She's living with her brother back in Riverside. I haven't contacted her yet; I wanted you to be there."

The waiter returned with Charles's pie, two thick wedges topped with whipped cream. The sweet, tart scent of huckleberries filled their little corner of the dining room.

Charles dug in while Gordon waited for the waiter to leave again.

"How much are we going to tell her?"

"Everything," Charles said between bites. "I don't know that it will do any good, but she's all we have right now."

And that isn't much, Gordon thought, *but it's more than we started with.*

"You know we can't keep this up forever, Gordon. I've never wanted to solve a case so badly in my life, but eventually we're going to have to give it up. You need to get on with your life."

Gordon nodded, looking Charles in the eyes. "But not today," he said.

"No," Charles agreed. "Not today."

Chapter 5

The girl watched cartoons and ate cold cereal on their sofa, always keeping one sharp eye on them as they sat drinking coffee in the kitchen.

She's quick, Shannon noted mentally. *She has the reflexes of a wild animal, and she doesn't trust us. Not one little bit.*

"Would you like something to drink," Jared ventured, "maybe a soda? Or are you a coffee drinker?" He held up his mug and smiled.

The girl forgot the TV for a moment, focused on Jared, scrutinizing him. She watched him, spooning more cereal into her mouth, and spoke around it.

"Soda." It was the first time she had spoken to either of them. Shannon watched her while she kept one eagle-eye on the TV, and one on Jared.

Jared approached her slowly, knowing that if he moved too close, too quickly, he would end up hurting for it.

When she had awakened earlier that morning, it was like watching a rabid clown spring from a jack-in-the-box. She jumped from the couch with a shriek, her frail-looking body suddenly possessing a Herculean strength, a combination of panic and adrenaline. She rammed Shannon hard enough to knock her backward out of her chair, then ran around the couch toward the front door.

Jared had blocked her, and she screamed bloody hell as she tried to push him aside. When he tried to hold her back, she had kicked him in the balls.

Faint from the sudden shock of pain, the white-hot agony of an older wound, he still managed to keep her from escaping.

She was wearing Alicia's clothes, her locket. They couldn't let her get away; they had to find out how she got them. It was too weird, the possibilities mind-boggling, but here she was.

They managed to calm her down by promising food and television.

She watched Jared, and when he'd come close enough she let him know by cocking back her nearly empty bowl like a Frisbee, threatening to let loose if he came any closer. Milk and soggy kernels of cereal spilled over the side of the bowl and onto her arm, but she didn't seem to care.

Slowly, Jared set the soda can on the arm of the couch and backed away.

The girl set the bowl on the coffee table and drank the soda enthusiastically.

Jared returned to his place at the kitchen table.

"We have to take her to the police," Jared whispered. "We can't hold her like this, it's illegal as hell, and likely to get us both prison time."

"I have to find out where she got Alicia's stuff. Maybe after that. I have to know." Shannon didn't realize she'd been raising her voice until the girl looked over sharply at them, and she made herself calm down. "She might know who killed Thomas. She might know about Alicia."

"I know," Jared said. He sighed, a resigned sound, and said, "We better try then."

The girl watched them. She lurched to her feet as they neared the couch, but didn't run. Jared moved quickly around the back of the couch, to the side nearest the drawn shades of his window, and they flanked her.

"Where did you get that?" Shannon asked, her voice barely controlled, and pointed to the locket.

The girl watched her closely, but said nothing.

"It's my daughter's. Her name is Alicia Pitcher, and I gave it to her for her birthday two years ago." Her voice was steady, but it was an edge she worked hard to control. She felt like throttling the silent girl.

"It's mine," the girl said, and clutched a fist around it.

"No," Shannon said. "It's not. Have you ever looked inside? At the picture?"

The girl nodded.

"Open it up again, look at the picture," she said. "Please."

The girl did, and the recognition was instant. "It's you," she said.

"Yes," Shannon said patiently. "Me, my ex-husband, and my daughter. Thomas is dead. He was murdered, and my girl is gone." She swallowed, her mouth suddenly gone dry. It was difficult to go on, but she had to ask. "Do you know where Alicia is?"

The girl looked up from the locket to Shannon's face. The fear and distrust was gone, replaced by a look of sympathy that Shannon didn't like. "*He* got her," she said. "And he'll get me too. I have to go," she said urgently. "I have to go back or he'll get me again."

"Who?" Shannon asked, and when the girl shook her head she asked again, a demand this time.

"You won't believe me," she said. "Please let me go."

"Go where?" Jared asked. "To the river?" He spoke slowly, as if to an idiot. "He won't find you here. He doesn't know where you are."

"I think she wants to go back to the park," Shannon said.

The girl nodded, shuffled her feet. The park or the moon,

she clearly wanted to be gone, but knew she couldn't get past them.

"Park by the river," Jared said in a breathless voice. "Tell me you don't mean Blackstone."

"Feral Park," the girl said defiantly. "It's called Feral Park."

"Shit," Jared breathed, and sat on the arm of the couch. "I know what they call it now." Then to Shannon, "You didn't say anything about Feral Park."

"I know," Shannon said, remembering the insanity within those iron barred walls. "Feral Park is another story."

"No shit! In case you weren't aware, that place has a bad history. I wouldn't go there after dark on a dare. I could tell you some interesting stories. It's a bad place, Sis," he said. "I thought you knew about it."

"I didn't know, and they're not fairy stories," she talked to Jared, but watched the girl. The gold locket spun and glittered in the weak lamplight as the child looked back and forth between them. It took all her will power not to reach over and yank it from the girl's neck. "Something happened there." Then to the girl, "Why would you want to go back there anyway? You saw what happened to me."

"Because he can't see me there," she said, frustrated.

"Who is *he?*" Shannon shouted. "If you tell us who he is, we can help you!"

Slowly, she shook her head. "No you can't. He'll kill you."

"I used to be a cop," Jared said. "I can handle him."

The girl looked at him; a sad smile played across her face, but she said nothing.

"If we take you back, will you tell us who he is?" Shannon asked.

The girl considered this for a moment, then nodded. "Yes."

"Shit! I can't believe we're playing games with her," Jared said. "This is crazy."

You don't have a clue what crazy is, Shannon thought.

"Come on, Jared," she said. "I'll tell you about last night on the way, and you can tell me what I don't know about this Feral Park."

Traffic was light through town, but it was getting close to noon and would soon pick up. It was a little heavier at the northeastern end of Riverside, the industrial area. Mostly it was commercial traffic and people coming into town from the highway. The heat was a constant, but the air conditioner in Jared's Chevelle made the trip tolerable.

Shannon reported the previous night's horror with a degree of self-consciousness. She realized how crazy it sounded, but she was true to what happened. She didn't leave anything out.

Jared listened silently, caught somewhere between belief and disbelief. His sister was not an overly imaginative person, prone to flights of fancy, but the story she told was incredible. Insane.

The girl sat quietly in the back seat.

Shannon ended with how she had carried the girl home earlier that morning, praying every step of the way that no one would see them.

Jared found a parking spot at the end of the industrial area and killed the motor. The park's main entrance and parking lot were accessible only from the highway, but that had been blocked off years ago to keep tourists and passing travelers out of the abandoned park and its decrepit playground.

The dike, and the crumbling asphalt path that led to Feral Park, was a short walk away.

Jared told his sister about Feral Park.

★ ★ ★ ★ ★

They called it The Playground of Dreams, and that's what it was at first. Built in the early 1970s, it was a project one part government grant and two parts community spirit. The planning had taken years, but once they broke ground, construction was completed in a three-week whirlwind of donated time and money. The massive playground sat just outside of town, at the eastern end of Blackstone Park where the neatly manicured green gave way to wild grass, groves of old willows, then stony weed-choked shoreline. The northern border of Blackstone Park was the Snake River, flowing docilely toward the Pacific Ocean like a dark liquid giant, and a paved walkway that joined Blackstone Park to the city. Its southern border was a line of tall willows, a sound barrier for the freeway that ran past just beyond.

Blackstone Park had been developed in the 1960s as the cornerstone of Riverside's largely successful beautification project, and The Playground of Dreams was the Blackstone's pinnacle.

It was a place where Riverside's kids could go and indulge their every fantasy while parents waited, watched, or read from one of the park benches just outside the midget kingdom's iron-bared wall. Pirates roamed the deck of a tiny grounded ship, climbing up and down ladders and knotted ropes in search of treasure, imaginary enemies to run through, or a nearly forgotten soda, left in trust of a waiting parent. Brave and able knights guarded high wooden castle turrets, patrolled winding walkways like the tops of castle walls, charged down tall slides as if into battle. Sometimes the pirates and knights battled each other; sometimes they fought together, often recruiting from each other's ranks to mix up the endless battle even more. Sometimes Blackbeard watched over Camelot while King Arthur pillaged. It didn't matter; it was all one kingdom. The only enemies in The Playground of Dreams were Boredom and Reality, and inside that magical iron border they stood no chance.

Mostly though, there was no organized play; mostly it was just perfect, joyous chaos.

Then the dream ended.

In the late 1970s a girl was found beaten, almost unrecognizable, naked and violated, half-buried in the playground's sandbox. Her name was Jenny Heyworth, and she was only nine years old, a runaway.

It was like a water faucet being shut off; one day The Playground of Dreams was full of screaming, rioting children, the next it was empty.

Blackstone Park, dubbed Feral Park after years of disuse, became a different kind of playground: a playground of drinking, drugs, and teenage sex. City workers blocked the access road from the highway with a barricade and a sign reading: *Blackstone Park is closed to the public—Enter at own risk.* Someone had since crossed Blackstone out and written "Feral" above it in dripping, purple letters. Soon though, Feral Park gained a reputation as something else entirely, and even the partiers left it alone.

Sometimes the kids still found it, street kids, runaways, children of the night, and most who went there were never seen again.

Shannon and Jared walked with the girl between them, not holding onto her, but ready to grab an arm or shoulder should she try to take off. She didn't seem inclined to do so. They were going where she wanted and she seemed satisfied for now. They had no idea how they were going to get her out of there again when she told them what they wanted to know. They had both come to the same silent conclusion: they would handle that when they had to. She could kick and scream all she wanted, there was no way in hell they were leaving her there.

As Feral Park came into view Shannon asked again, "Who are you, and who gave you my daughter's locket?"

Grudgingly, as if giving up a guarded secret, she said, "I'm Charity. The man who's after me doesn't have a name; he's the Bogey Man. The Bogey Man killed your daughter." She looked away from Shannon and bit at her lower lip. "He said I needed new clothes, my others were falling apart." She looked up at Shannon again, apologetically. "He killed my mom and took me away. I think he wants to marry me," she added shyly.

Jared almost laughed aloud at the last statement, so innocent and yet obscene at the same time. It was a wonder that she had retained whatever innocence she still possessed in the custody of the killer she called *the Bogey Man*.

Shannon barely heard it. One phrase stuck in her mind like a fishbone in her throat.

The Bogey Man killed your daughter.

She knew Alicia was dead, had known since her bastard ex-father-in-law called her three months ago, but now it had been articulated and she couldn't deny it. The dark corner of her mind where that last grain of hope for Alicia lived had been upturned, uncovered.

And despite the absurdity of it, Shannon believed her. The Bogey Man *had* come in the night and taken her daughter away.

Because that is what the Bogey Man did.

Chapter 6

It was just past noon when Gordon and Charles entered Riverside. The sky was flat blue, cloudless. Charles drove his old Caddy, big and gun-barrel gray.

Gordon followed in his less impressive Mazda. His windows were down, the air conditioner having given out long ago. He listened to Paul Harvey's "The Rest of the Story," wiped sweat from his forehead with one arm. It was only June and he guessed the days were topping out at just less than one hundred degrees. This was going be a bitch of a summer.

He followed Charles's practiced route through the industrial area, through downtown, to the motel where he stayed. It wasn't quite a dump, but would never earn a five-star rating. It was called The Riverside; aptly named since it was in Riverside, and happened to look out over the Snake River. The view from Charles's room was nice if you ignored the littered gravel alley and parking lot, the dull landscape overgrown with thistle and weeds, and the crust of flotsam gathering at the river's stony shore.

The room was clean, but completely utilitarian—small, with a single bed, green shag carpet that may have been installed sometime in the late 1970s, and a bathroom that was just large enough to turn around in. There was a TV, but no cable. Only a handful of local channels came in with any clarity.

It was what Gordon expected from Charles, a man whose

philosophy was: "If I'm too comfortable, it's that much harder to leave when I have to work."

Still, it was better than the car.

Gordon grabbed a change of clothes and toiletries from his old suitcase and hit the shower. Fifteen minutes later he stepped out of the bathroom, showered, shaven, and changed. He looked like a new man, but felt like a dead one. He was bone weary, and the freshly-made single bed looked like a gift from God. He dropped into it like a lump.

Charles sat at a small writing desk, cleaning his gun, a daily ritual. When he finished with the gun, he reloaded it and slipped it into his ankle holster.

"I gotta go pay another week or the desk man will move us out the second we leave. You stay put for a while and rest your bones, okay?"

Gordon grunted a response, and by the time Charles shut the door he was asleep.

He dreamed again.

Charles let Gordon sleep and drove to Shannon's house alone. He didn't plan on talking to her just yet; he wanted to make sure she was still there before he brought Gordon along. He passed the house slowly, noting the empty driveway, and continued on for another block. Then he parked and waited for a few minutes before getting out and walking back toward the house. He watched every house along the way for signs of activity, for what he called the "neighborhood watch mentality." One concerned neighbor could put the kibosh on this little preemptive excursion.

This was not the normal order of business for him; being forward with people was his business. If he spied out every potential witness or source he used beforehand, he would never have time to *work* a case. Something was different about this one. There was a deviation to the pattern that he did not trust. His quarry always killed in waves, nothing for a few months, then several in a month's time before he moved on again. Shannon's family had been done almost as an afterthought to the Oregon killing spree. Then nothing for three months, until a few nights ago, and another one last night. Before then he hadn't even been sure it was their killer. The method fit his profile, but the timing was wrong.

Shannon Pitcher's case was a deviation, and deviations made Charles nervous as hell.

No one seemed to notice him walking down the street to Shannon's house, or if they did they didn't care. There were no curious faces pressed to living room windows, no weekend gardeners who'd forgotten about a half-weeded row of petunias. Charles guessed it was simply too damn hot to be nosy.

He turned up the walkway to Shannon's house without the slightest hesitation, and when he found the door locked, he dug in his trouser pocket for his lock pick. Charles wasn't an expert lock picker, but he could get into most places if he needed to. If the locks were old, it was usually easy. It took him half a minute to open the front door and slip unnoticed into the empty home.

Chapter 7

Charity sat alone in the playground for almost an hour, first on one of the rusty, creaking swings, then on the edge of the old sandbox, the one where they had found the girl's body.

The one I landed in last night, Shannon thought with a shiver. *Something in there tripped me; something was playing with me the way a fat house-cat plays with a mouse—not because it's hungry, but because it's enjoying the game.*

Nothing happened today though; the park was decrepit, forbidding, but not the predator that had tried to kill her the night before.

Shannon and Jared watched Charity from a bench in the weed-infested green, not knowing what to do next.

Finally, with a great and heartbreaking sigh, Charity rose and left the playground. They met her just outside the gate, the spot where Shannon had found her earlier.

"Nothing?" Shannon asked.

Charity shook her head, made a small noise, but didn't speak.

Jared, hot, hungry, out of patience with the girl, said, "What did you expect, Peter Pan and the Lost Boys to fly down and whisk you away?"

"I don't know," she said defensively. "Something was supposed to happen. I dreamed about it." She looked back into the playground, her expression a blend of fear and longing. "I dreamed about it. The kids who live there told me if I came here, the Bogey Man wouldn't be able to get me again. I think that's why they came here, to keep their bad people from getting them."

"Bullshit!" Jared yelled, startling his sister out of her thoughts. Charity was not startled, did not flinch from him. She crossed her thin arms over her chest and glared at him.

"Bullshit, Charity, or whatever your name is," he said in a softer voice. He looked to Shannon for help, but found none. "Look, I'm sorry I yelled at you, but you need to tell us the truth. Forget Bogey Men and Lost Boys, we need to know what's going on here. You need to tell us who he is so we can protect you from him. He killed my niece; he needs to go to prison."

"It's not bullshit," Shannon said at last. "Something happened to me in there last night. If Charity hadn't come when she did, I might not be alive now." She reached over and squeezed Charity's shoulder, and the girl smiled at her, a smile that reminded her of Alicia. The memory hurt her, but somehow made everything better, as well. Suddenly it was very difficult for her to speak, but she swallowed hard and did anyway. "Whatever lives in there would have had me. When she showed up, it let me go."

Shannon realized she was about to say something that made her sound just as crazy as Charity, but said it anyway. "I don't know the Bogey Man from Jack The Ripper, but I know I heard kids in here last night. And music."

"I know," Jared snapped, turning away from them and waving a hand in disgust. "Heavy metal. You told me."

Shannon said nothing more. She knew her brother well enough to recognize his bluster.

Though he didn't want to, Jared believed her.

David Trudoe, or Dirty Dave to those who knew him,

waited until they were gone, then entered the park from the trees along the highway. Once a young executive with a promising future, he was a mess of matted, filthy hair and baggy urine-stained clothes. He mumbled to himself as he walked, looking at his old, worn work boots. He didn't look up as he approached the playground, several bags of old food culled from fast-food Dumpsters clenched in his gnarled fists. A collection of tacos, burgers, and fried chicken left to the rats and cats. The smell of prepared food was maddening, but he resisted. They were not for him.

He circled the playground without looking up, entered it, ducking automatically where the playground equipment was too low to pass unscathed.

He stopped by the sandbox, and waited for a while, almost comatose in his stillness. Then he dropped the bags in the sandbox and spoke aloud to the playground.

"My children of the wild," he croaked, his voice strange and out of practice. "Be damned if you're not causing trouble again." He cackled, scratched his chin through his thick beard, and pulled something from the inside pocket of his dirty wool jacket. It was far too hot for the heavy clothing, but the jacket was like a security blanket—he never took it off.

He dropped a compact disc next to the bags and walked away.

"Be good, children," he said. "Your uncle Dave loves you."

Before he left the playground, the bags of food and the CD were gone.

Their late lunch consisted of drive-through cheeseburgers, fries, and ice water. Jared drove them to Riverside's little mall and bought Charity new clothes and shoes. Then they drove back home.

Shannon walked stoop-shouldered toward the house, the heat, the lack of sleep, and the shock of the past day dragging her down. Charity wasn't much better. She needed a shower, her hair hung in her face like strands of frayed rope. Her clothes, Alicia's clothes, were filthy and wrinkled, the shoes worn almost to rags. What she needed more than a shower and change of clothes was rest. She was a nine-year-old hag.

Only Jared seemed vital—perhaps the stress and physical demands of his previous career prepared him better for what they were going through. Or perhaps he was only better at faking it. He was alert enough to notice the tiny scratches around the lock of his doorknob. Someone had been there.

"Stop," he said, the command in his voice reminding him of a time not so long ago when he had been worthy of the respect that tone commanded. These days life seemed like a dirty joke, and he the punch line.

Charity stopped instantly, looking around nervously as if reading his thoughts. She had to yank on Shannon's arm to get her to mind.

"What?" Shannon said, looking up from her feet. She seemed half-asleep already.

"Someone's been here," Jared said. Charity squeezed Shannon's hand, worked to keep her brave face.

Good girl, Jared thought. *Tough girl too.*

He tried the door. It was locked. He fished the keys from his pocket and unlocked it.

"Stay out here," he said, handing the car keys over to Shannon. "Be ready to run if there's trouble." He mentally calculated the distance from the door to the mantle above the television, where he kept a gun hidden behind an old family picture. He could reach it in two or three seconds, and God help whomever might still be inside.

He leaned close to Shannon and said, "We're not letting this motherfucker take her again."

Then he slipped through the cracked door and raced across the room, agile as a cat despite his old wounds, leaping over the low back of the sofa and grabbing the gun from its hiding place on the mantle.

The next few minutes were tense for Shannon and Charity, but the stress relented when he returned and opened the door for them, the gun hanging ready from his right hand.

"It's clear. If there was someone here, they're gone now."

"Can I take a shower?" Charity asked, hugging the bag with her new clothes to her chest.

"Yeah, I checked the bathroom. It's clear."

She startled him with a quick hug and disappeared down the hallway.

"She's turning you into a softy," Shannon commented. Her eyes were weary, her skin ashen, but she managed a smile.

"Shut up," Jared said, but he was smiling too.

Down the block, hidden behind the tinted windows of his Cadillac, Charles watched Charity disappear into the house. When the door shut, he put the Caddy into gear and drove away.

Chapter 8

It started the same way as the dream he had often, the one that had convinced him from the start that Charity was still alive. He saw Charity standing in the dark, an almost perfect dark. She held her arms out, shouting "Daddy . . . Daddy" as he ran to her, and he seemed to run forever. This time, though, she was not the toddler he'd last seen six years ago. She was growing up so fast, he might not have known her out of this context, and that scared him more than the dream itself. She was nine now, not his baby girl anymore.

Would she recognize him if he ever found her?

In the distance between them he could see the pendant that hung around her neck; it flashed at him like a tiny star.

It was like running through water; the air seemed to clutch at him, hold him in place; moving one foot before the other became an act of frustration. It felt like the waking world was holding onto his shirttail and he was dragging it through the dark behind him.

Usually the dream went on like this for hours, until the light of dawn or his own frustration woke him, but not this time.

All around, like a part of the night itself, a familiar voice taunted.

"Ah, the little bed-wetter is all grown up now. I remember you, Gordon, the spoiled only child hiding under satin sheets. How you used to shake when I came to visit. It was only my echo, I think you knew it even then, but it was enough to make you piss your bed every time." A chuckle rippled the darkness, vibrated painfully in his ears. "How it used to anger your father." A current of scorching wind passed over his head, a living heat of violence and malice. The air groaned around it as if in pain. He could see its vague shape moving toward his daughter with purpose. "That's why I never came for you, you know. It would have been like killing my favorite pet. I enjoyed your company so much."

Charity saw the shapeless thing coming at her and screamed. The bright, star-like pendant around her neck dimmed as the dark heat took shape next to her.

He smiled at Gordon, and it was the same face Gordon remembered peeking out of his closet on those dreadful nights so long ago. It was the same face that haunted him his every waking moment as a child, and promised new terror with each sunset.

"We lost touch, Gordon," the Bogey Man said, almost apologetically. "I'm afraid it happens all the time. I have so many children, you know, and my echo only reaches so far."

Gordon ran, and though the air around him seemed to thicken further, he was getting closer. He tried to scream, but nothing came out. All words, all sound, seemed to catch in his throat, as if his breath had become solid inside him.

He focused on Charity and tried again, felt he would explode if he couldn't voice his rage, but it was in vain.

She watched him struggle toward her with a heart-sickening sadness, but did not move.

"She's a rare one," the Bogey Man said. "I've never seen one like her in all my years." He looked down at her; a smile of affection and speculation lit his eyes.

Gordon was suddenly more frightened than he had ever been, frightened for Charity. He knew the look in that old monster's eyes. He felt like killing and dying at the same time. He was closer now and could see the same sick understanding in Charity's eyes.

"We've been watching you, Gordon, we've been watching you for a long time. I've told her all about you, the good and the bad. She wants to see you again, but she knows it can never happen. She understands it is not meant to be."

One hand crept over her shoulder, around to the back of her neck, stroking her long hair. "She's a smart one. If I live to see the end of time there will never be another like her." Then he moved behind her, dark hands clutching her shoulders, holding her steady before him. "I won't let her go, Gordon." All softness had left his face; all feigned humanity fell away from him like a mask. What was left was a look of hate in its purest sense. "I've left you alone because she wants me to, Gordon; that's the only reason you live. Stop following us, leave us alone, or I will rip you apart like I did her worthless bitch of a mother."

Gordon was close enough to see the other changes in his daughter now, a distention of her belly that looked freakish in relation to her thin frame. It was not the loose flab of a portly child. It was something else.

"She was meant for me, Gordon. She's mine!"

Finally the scream came; a great inarticulate whoop of rage. Then they were gone, and he was alone.

In the receding echoes of that great, soul-rending scream he heard the laughter of children.

He awoke with her name still caught in his throat, and this time it took an act of will *not* to scream it aloud. His heart beat so fast he could hear his pulse throbbing in his temples. The dream followed him into full consciousness, clinging like the cold sweat on his brow.

After a few minutes his heart slowed and the coolness of the room dried his sweat, but the images and implications of the dream lingered. As he rose he became aware of the dampness in his crotch, and felt the absolute depth of disgust and shame. Suddenly he was the child hiding under his covers again, shaking in fear of the face in the closet, the voice that seemed to whisper to him from every shadow and unseen place in his room. He was the little boy who dreaded each coming morning almost as much as each approaching night, because his father would come to wake him and see that he had wet the bed again.

Charles knew it couldn't possibly be her, no way in hell. Cold, dead trails didn't suddenly burst into flames for no reason, and dead girls—yes, he believed she was dead—didn't walk. Cases this difficult never came to this easy a conclusion, and coincidences this big simply did not happen outside the warped minds of conspiracy theorists. It had to be someone else, a young relative or friend of the family.

Still, although the latest picture he'd seen of her was taken six years ago, it looked like Charity.

If it was her it would explain a few troubling things to Charles, like the killer's abandonment of tradition where Shannon Pitcher's family was concerned, but it opened up another line of more troubling questions.

Who are you, Shannon Pitcher? he wondered. *Who are you and how much traveling do you do?*

If Shannon, or maybe her brother, was their killer, and the girl was Gordon's missing daughter, why had they kept her around? This went back farther than Gordon's ex-wife and daughter, at least fifteen years by his estimation, maybe more. With the hundreds of missing children, why had they kept Charity?

Maybe it was another girl, their latest victim. Maybe it *was* a young relative or family friend.

Charles just didn't know.

Gordon showered and changed again, throwing his soiled pants and shirt in the Dumpster behind the motel. He called the lobby, made a red-faced request for fresh bed linen, and was grateful when the night manager didn't comment on the bundle of urine-scented sheets he took away. Gordon changed the bed himself, flipping the mattress first, and finished moments before Charles came back.

"You up for a drive, old friend?"

Gordon didn't like the look on the PI's face or the strained quality in his voice. "Sure," he said, but uncertainly. Suddenly he didn't want to know what Charles might have learned while he was away. "What's happened?"

"We need to talk."

Chapter 9

The afternoon was eventless. Shannon and Jared took turns napping on the couch while Charity sat between them, zoned out on movie matinees and commercials.

When the doorbell rang at seven o'clock Jared answered it, his gun tucked into the front of his pants and hidden by his shirttail. Shannon and Charity hid in the hallway.

"Don't worry," Charity said, giving Shannon's hand a comforting squeeze. "It's not him. He only comes when it's dark."

It turned out to be the pizza delivery guy—large pepperoni, extra cheese, and an order of bread sticks.

The sun set at a quarter to nine; Charity watched it through the kitchen's sliding glass door while she ate. Shannon and Jared pretended not to notice how her enthusiasm for food diminished steadily as she tracked the sun down the western sky, or how her face transformed in the sunset's violet glow, becoming a glowing mirror of their own fears for the night to come. By the time full dark had arrived, the fiery, bold girl they had gotten to know during the day was gone.

The half-eaten slice of pizza, which had grown cold in her hand as she watched the sun vanish, dropped on the table with a splat. Her hand, still in place above the overturned slice, elbow planted firmly on the tabletop, trembled. She groaned, a deep resigned sound, and seemed almost to shrink into herself.

"Lights," Shannon said, and they jumped up in tandem. Starting with the back patio outside the kitchen, they turned on every light in the house. Then, while Jared dug through a box of old Disney movies once kept on hand for Alicia's infrequent visits, Shannon seated herself across from Charity and grasped the girl's shaking hands.

"Don't worry, sweetheart. Remember what you said?"

"He doesn't like the light," Charity said and squeezed her hands. Then she looked into Shannon's face. "It doesn't matter. He'll come anyway. Please take me back to the park," she said. "He can't get me there."

"No," she said. "Feral Park is dangerous. You saw what it tried to do to me."

Charity glared at her silently, then lowered her head and nodded.

"We won't let him get you. If he tries, my brother will shoot him. He used to be a cop," she said, and smiled what she hoped was her most reassuring smile. "He can stop anyone."

That didn't seem to be enough for Charity. Looking into Shannon's eyes again the girl said, "Will you protect me?"

"Yes," Shannon said without hesitation. "I'll protect you."

Charity slid from her chair, raced around the table, and wrapped her in a long, aching hug. Unable to stop the tears that sprung from her eyes, Shannon hugged her back.

In the living room the movie started. They held each other, listening to the Disney anthem, a safe sound, a sound that said everything was right with the world. Good magic. The movie was *Snow White and the Seven Dwarfs*. Shannon knew how this one went. Despite all their best efforts the dwarves wouldn't be able to save Snow White, the wicked witch would get her. Only a prince could save the maiden, and Shannon was not a prince. She had promised to protect Charity, but could she? She hadn't been able to protect her own daughter.

Charity watched the movie warily, as if she did not trust the animated horrors to stay behind the screen. At length she relaxed, though, and sitting on the couch between Shannon and Jared, she fell asleep.

Shannon carried the girl, a light bundle of clothes and hair, to her bedroom. It was cluttered with dirty clothes, books, magazines, and other assorted junk. It had only been three months, but without Alicia to pick up after, housekeeping had become a lost art. Jared followed them. He stood outside the door while Shannon tucked Charity in and switched off the reading lamp next to the bed.

Shannon left her brother to watch over Charity for a few minutes, then returned with an item for the sleeping girl, a small flashlight, flat black with a small loop at the butt end. She slipped one of Charity's small hands through the loop, and when she laid it in her palm, Charity's thin fingers closed around it.

"Thank you," she whispered, looking up at Shannon. Then closed her eyes and slept again.

Chapter 10

Gordon and Charles had watched the house for over an hour but could make out nothing through the closed blinds. All the lights were on, every light in the house it seemed, and no one came out.

"I have to see her," Gordon said.

"You have to be cool," Charles countered. "It's probably not her and you know it. Charity is the last person in the world we should expect to find in there, even if one of them is . . ."

"The killer?" Gordon finished for him.

"Yes," Charles said. "Also very unlikely." He reached down and pulled his gun from its ankle holster, opened the cylinder, and checked the rounds. This wasn't a good sign for Gordon. It meant Charles expected he might have to use it.

Satisfied, he closed the chamber again and re-holstered it. "Remember," he said, "be cool. Let me do the talking. I'm the mediator here; it's one of the things you pay me for." He pulled the keys from the Caddy's ignition and stuffed them deep into his pocket. "If there's any trouble you just stand the hell back and let me handle it."

He watched Gordon with an unshakable intensity, looking for signs of potential trouble. It was clear he didn't intend to go any further until Gordon showed his complete under-standing of the rules.

"I understand," Gordon said. "Let's go."

"Good," Charles said, and stepped out into the muggy darkness. It was a half-block walk to the house, and as before, Charles took in everything around him. He checked every window briefly for that fabled Nosy Neighbor; he was alert to every shrub and hiding place along the way; he checked behind them every few seconds for some previously unseen presence. Mostly though, he watched the bright, shaded windows of Shannon and Jared's house. He couldn't shake the uneasy feeling he had that the wild card in the whole god-awful mess was about to play itself. He couldn't shake the sinking feeling that everything was about to turn to shit.

Gordon followed a step behind Charles, hands shoved in his pockets and clenched into fists. Being cool had never been so hard in his life. He had the same uneasy feeling that Charles did. Only he had a name for it, and a face. Though not a superstitious man, the dream he had earlier was now very much on his mind, nagging his every step.

They turned up the walkway, and as he mounted the steps behind Charles felt a sudden rush of warm air. Warmer than the muggy night air, it made the hairs on the nape of his neck stand and his balls draw up like small cowardly animals scenting danger. Following that warm current, a whisper so soft he thought it must be the work of his anxious mind, or a vivid fragment of that terrible dream.

Charity.

When the doorbell rang they both jumped a little, exchanging embarrassed glances that belied the brave and prepared front they tried to maintain. They waited a moment, hoping whoever it was would go away, but it rang again.

"You get it," Jared whispered. "I'll wait here."

Shannon couldn't imagine who it might be; they were not social people, had maybe a handful of good friends between them, but no close ones. She could think of no one who might have a reason to come over this late.

It couldn't possibly be Charity's Bogey Man, Shannon thought. *He couldn't know where she is, and if it were him, he wouldn't knock.*

The bell rang a third time as she reached the door. She stood there for a moment, suddenly wishing for a peephole.

"Yes!" she shouted, turning the dead bolt home with a loud click. She saw the chain lock hanging against the doorjamb, and locked it too.

"I'm looking for Shannon Pitcher," said a deep voice on the other side of the door.

"Speaking," Shannon shouted back. "What do you want?"

"Could you open the door and let us in? We need to talk to you about your daughter."

For the past three months the mere mention of Alicia was enough to bring tears. The reason she lived with Jared was because it had become difficult to fight the suicidal impulses. For all her brother's faults, and there were many, Jared had been strong enough to keep her alive through the worst time of her life. She knew the bad times, the depressions and moods, weren't close to being over yet, and maybe they never would be, but she was still alive, and stronger now than three months ago.

Tonight the mention of her daughter had a new effect on her, a galvanizing effect. "Fuck off!" she shouted. "It's too late for this shit." Grinning smugly, bitterly, at the silence from the other side of the door, she stalked back toward the bedroom.

Where Jared stood guard over the sleeping girl, there came a scream. It rang through the small house like a siren. It was a wet sound, half terror and half pain. Shannon froze, listening helplessly as it tapered off into a gurgling grunt. Then the meaty thud of a body hitting the floor.

Jared!

Whatever it was had happened quickly; Jared hadn't fired a single shot.

Shannon ran the last few feet to the open door of the bedroom, and found her brother sprawled out on the floor, in the corner by the bed. His mouth was wide open, his eyes staring at the ceiling. The gun lay beside him unused. He was cut open from crotch to chin, blood-slicked ropes of intestine slid slowly from his open stomach, covering his waist.

Charity sat upright in the bed, her face a mask of perfect fright, her hair tousled and dripping with sweat. She stared past Shannon into the hallway. Her chest rose and fell rapidly; each labored breath was followed by weak grunt, as if she were trying to scream.

Shannon ran to the edge of the bed, grabbed Charity by the shoulders and gave her a quick, rough shake. "Where is he?"

Nothing, just quick breaths and grunts. Charity pointed past Shannon.

The bedroom door slammed shut, throwing them into darkness, and when she turned Shannon saw him. A dark man-shaped outline with bright eyes and a shark's grin.

"Remember me, Shannon?" Soft laughter filled the space around them, made her skin itch like a thousand spiders' legs. "I remember you."

Shannon dropped down, squatting in a pile of her brother's insides, and searched for the gun.

The Bogey Man stepped closer. "Your girl was a peach," he said. "As long as I live I will never forget her. She brought me such pleasure."

"*You son of a bitch!*" she screamed, then found the gun and brought it up. She couldn't pull the trigger. Suddenly her hand didn't belong to her. Against her will, she stood up and put the muzzle of Jared's revolver to her temple. A burning hand, insubstantial but very real, seemed to have entered hers, wearing it like a glove.

"Should I make you pull the trigger?" he said with mild amusement, still advancing, now only a few feet away. Charity shrunk away from him to the far end of the bed, her back pressed to the wall. "Or should I do it myself?" He raised his hand above Shannon's head. His scissors were open, a wide razor jaw dripping with blood.

Charity finally found her breath.

Gordon and Charles heard the first scream, and exchanged horrified glances.

"What the hell?" Gordon said.

"I don't know," Charles said. He crouched down and pulled the gun from his holster. He pounded on the door with the heel of his other hand. "Shannon!" he shouted. *"Open the door or I'll bust the fucker down!"*

They heard her yell something, but couldn't make it out through the closed door. Charles drew his hand back for another round of pounding, then they heard the second scream, high and terrified, a girl's scream.

"Charity," Gordon whispered. He paled, looked about to faint. "That was Charity."

"Shit," Charles said, and pushed Gordon aside. He backed a few steps away from the door, as far as the small landing would allow, and rammed it with his shoulder. It shook in its frame, but the hinges and locks held. He backed up for another hit, and stopped himself. Gordon rushed to the door, pounding with one fist, working the knob futilely with the other. "Charity, baby. I'm coming!"

"Back off," Charles yelled.

Gordon ignored him. He pounded, twisted at the knob, shouted her name over and over again.

Charles drew back and slapped him, a sound like a firecracker, and Gordon hit the ground. "Stay out of my way!" he shouted, and rammed the door again.

Gordon watched from the ground, embarrassed, afraid, and swallowed by a whirlwind of emotions. Charles hit the door a third time, heard the wood crack, but it still held.

There was another scream, not Charity, not Shannon or her brother. It was like nothing they had ever heard, inhuman, full of pain and rage. It was a sound that promised death.

Charity watched him raise the scissors, the same ones he had used to kill her mother and Shannon's family, and finally found the strength to scream. The scissors stopped above Shannon's head, and he turned toward her.

"I'll deal with you soon, my sweet thing. Teach you not to run away from Daddy."

"You're not my daddy," she said, and pointed the flashlight looped to her wrist at him. She pushed the button and a small bright light burned through him like acid. His form parted around the beam, smoldering at the edges.

He screamed, a sound that hurt her all the way to her bones, but even the sudden head-sickness and vertigo that threatened to steal the strength from her could not squelch the sense of satisfaction it brought.

She had hurt him. She had hurt him bad.

Concentrating, she raised the beam and shone it in his face.

His scream faded as his face melted away. He dropped the bloody scissors and clawed at the air where his head should be.

Shannon's paralysis broke. She aimed carefully, and fired. The slug passed through the intruder's body like smoke.

"Get the light!" Charity shouted.

Ducking past the flailing headless body, Shannon did. With a fiery, sizzling flash, the Bogey Man was gone.

Charity leapt off the bed and ran to Shannon, nearly knocking her over in a fierce embrace. "You came for me," Charity sobbed. "You said you would protect me, and you did." She was crying full force now, her sobs shaking her frail body against Shannon's.

Without realizing it, Shannon started crying too. "You saved me first, Charity. Thank you."

They both heard the crack of wood as someone outside rammed the front door. "It's him again," she said with dread certainty.

"I don't know who it is," Shannon said. "Get your shoes on, quick. We have to get out of here."

With one last look back at her brother, his drained white face preserved in a permanent gape of shock, she ran through the hallway and to the kitchen. She remembered putting Jared's car keys on the table. As she passed through the living room someone hit the door from outside. The wood splintered and bulged in. The man outside hit it again, and the split lengthened.

She found the keys and met Charity back in the hallway. The girl waited, the large bloody scissors hanging from her hand, blades closed, like a small sword in front of her chest. The flashlight hung from the loop around her wrist.

"This way," Shannon said, and led her through the laundry room at the end of the hallway, through the back door, out into the darkness.

From outside they heard the front door give with a loud crack and heard someone enter the living room. They ran around the back of the house to the driveway. Jared's Chevelle waited.

"Get in," she said opening the driver's door and pushing Charity through. Charity scooted to the passenger seat and Shannon jumped in, laying Jared's gun on the seat between them.

"Stop!" Two men were in the back yard now, and closing the short distance fast.

Shannon fired up the Chevelle and laid rubber out of the driveway. Something slammed down on the trunk, and she saw a large man puffing after them in the rearview mirror.

The rubberneckers were out in force now, drawn by the shouts and gunfire. Shannon saw their blurred faces in windows and doors as she turned the corner and sped away.

Gordon reached the front just in time to see the Chevelle round the corner and disappear.

"Damn!" Charles slowed to a jog at the mouth of the driveway, stopped at the sidewalk and bent over, hands resting on his knees.

Gordon stopped behind him. "Come on," he yelled. "They're getting away!"

"They're gone," Charles said. "We're parked too far away to catch them." An old woman poked her head from an open door across the street. "Call the cops!" he shouted to her. "There's been a murder."

The old woman popped back through her door, like a reverse jack-in-the-box.

"What do we do now?" Gordon asked, near panic again.

"You calm down, and we wait for the cops." Charles reholstered his gun and sat on the curb. "The police have a better chance of finding them than we do, and if they don't know what's going on, Charity could end up getting hurt. If they think Shannon is the killer, it'll turn into a manhunt. Hell, it might be headed there already for all we know."

"You don't think it's her."

"Do you?" Charles countered.

"No," Gordon said, remembering the man in the bedroom, her brother, split down the middle like an overcooked sausage. "I don't think she could have done that."

"I don't think so either. I wondered if it was her, but . . ." Charles seemed to struggle for the proper words. "Whatever that was in there, that scream." He closed his eyes, rubbed his temples. "It didn't sound human." He laughed, a dry, humorless sound. "I'm getting too old for this shit."

Gordon sat next to him on the sidewalk. "I'm sorry," he said quietly. "I'm sorry I got in the way back there."

"You lost your head for a minute, that's all." He put a hand on Gordon's shoulder and gave it a squeeze. "Don't dwell on it, but don't let it happen again."

"Okay."

"Gordon, there's something you're not telling me. What is it?"

After a pause Gordon said, "You're going to think it's crazy."

"I already think it's crazy, old friend. It's the craziest damn thing I've ever seen. If it's going to get crazier, I want to know." He looked at Gordon. "Don't worry, I'm not flaking out on you now."

Gordon told him while they waited for the police to arrive. He told him about the terrible night frights that afflicted him as a child. He told him about the bed-wetting. He told him about the dream back at the motel room.

Gordon told Charles about the Bogey Man.

They were out of town within minutes, headed east along the highway. Charity glanced in the direction of Feral Park as they passed the old sign and the blocked-off entrance.

"No," Shannon said. "I'm not taking you there."

"I know," Charity said.

Seconds after passing the last streetlight outside of town, something hit the Chevelle's roof, hard, pushing it down in the center. They screamed in unison, and Shannon almost lost control.

"Give her back, you bitch. She's mine!"

"No!" Shannon screamed, and slammed on the brakes.

The Chevelle came to a bouncing halt. He flew off the hood into the headlight's beams, and was gone before he hit the pavement. Shannon gunned it, tearing over the spot where he should have been. Seconds later she was barreling down the highway again and he was behind them, clinging to the trunk. He punched the back window, blocking her view with the large glass spider web. He punched it a second time and it caved in to the back seat.

"Charity!" he screamed, crawling through the shattered window. *"Come back here now!"*

Charity lay curled up in a ball on the car's floor. *"No!"* she dropped the scissors and crawled onto the seat. "Go away." She shined the small flashlight again and he bellowed in pain.

Shannon turned on the dome light as he plunged in at them. She felt one of those feverish hands at her throat, skin dry as scales and light as smoke. Then he was gone.

His last words hung in the air between them like a fog as they continued toward Normal Hills.

Tomorrow night then.

PART II
Crazy Ernie's Cellar

Chapter 11

Little Andy Couldn't Sleep . . .

He couldn't, he was too afraid. He had gone to bed at nine under the threat of the belt. Dad wasn't having any more of his excuses or stories. *Everybody has nightmares,* his dad had said. *Get over it, kid, it's called growing up.* Then he had sent Andy down the hall to his room with a stinging rap to the back of his head. His dad called them love taps.

Once Andy heard his mom say love hurts, and he knew exactly what she meant. Dad gave his mom love taps too sometimes, and even when they made her bleed and cry they always ended up kissing and hugging again. Dad hardly ever hit Andy hard enough to make him bleed, but he left bruises.

When he got mad he hit harder, so Andy tried not to make him mad. That was why he had closed his eyes and pretended to be asleep after climbing into bed. That seemed like hours ago, and even though he was awake the whole time, he never opened his eyes.

Little Andy Counted Sheep . . .

Mommy was nicer about the bad dreams; she said she had them too sometimes. She said the way to make them go away was to think about good things, and if that didn't work, counting big fluffy sheep might. Andy didn't know what sheep had to do with anything, but he tried it anyway. It never worked.

What his mom and dad didn't understand was that when

he *did* sleep his dreams were usually good. Sometimes he dreamed about kissing Kimberly from next door, although he was eight and she was seven. She was pretty. Sometimes he dreamed about running away to the park by the river. He heard at school that lots of kids had run away and gone to live there, and they did nothing but play for the rest of their lives.

The nightmares only happened when he was awake. It was the man in the closet, or under his bed. Talking to him, sometimes singing to him; like tonight.

Little Andy Change Your Plans . . .

Andy was going to run away; he didn't like it here. Dad drank too much and hit a lot, and Andy didn't like the friends that he always had over. They called him cum squirt, and little shit, and they always made fun of him.

Mom was nice, but she never helped him when Dad and his friends got mean. She was too afraid.

He was spending Saturday night at Ryan's house, and he was going to leave after Ryan and his parents fell asleep. He was going to Feral Park, and he would do whatever he wanted to from then on.

Say Hello To The Bogey Man.

But the bad man was back again, singing to him in that soft and scratchy voice. Telling him to change his plans, because he would never make it to Ryan's house or Feral Park, and this time the Bogey Man wasn't hiding in the closet, or under his bed. He was standing above Andy, singing and stroking his cheek with blood-caked fingers.

When Andy finally opened his eyes he saw that shadow face, that wide crocodile smile. Ear-to-ear teeth, all white and shining. Then the teeth parted and Andy could see all the way down his throat.

Told ya, Dad, he thought. *I told you he was real.*

★ ★ ★ ★ ★

Shannon drove with the dome light on, crying silently for Jared and Alicia as she drove toward Normal Hills. She had forgotten, but she remembered now, every night spent wide-awake, she and Jared both, finding no comfort except for in each other's terrified eyes.

She cursed her mother and father for not believing them, and she cursed herself for not believing Alicia. How tired and distant she had been the last few weeks of her life, and how frustrated Shannon had gotten with her when Alicia had told her why.

How many times do I have to explain this to you, Alicia? There is no such thing as the Bogey Man.

She had even confronted Thomas, accused him of letting Alicia stay up late and watch those scary movies they both loved so much. Shannon was dead set against them, they were pointless and cliché; the only thing they were good for was giving kids like Alicia nightmares. Thomas took every opportunity he could to play the good guy with their daughter. He gave her too many presents, too much candy, and anything else her wicked mother dared to deny her.

Thomas was a hero in Alicia's eyes, but even he had not been able to save her from a nightmare come to life.

Charity slept on the car's floor, the bloody scissors stuck through the belt loop of her new pants like a savage's trophy. The little flashlight rolled and bounced on the floor next to her. It lit her face, turning every angle and shadow into a ghastly caricature.

She was chanting softly in her sleep.

Little Andy Couldn't Sleep,
Little Andy Counted Sheep,

*Little Andy Change Your Plans,
Say Hello To The Bogey Man.*

Then she jerked awake with a shriek.

"Shh, it's okay, baby. It was only a dream." This was automatic, the parental version of Pavlov's drooling dogs, and she cursed herself as soon as the words came out.

"No, it wasn't," Charity said. She picked up the flashlight and climbed onto the seat, sliding next to Shannon.

Shannon slowed the Chevelle, put an arm around Charity, and squeezed her. "I know, I'm sorry," she said. Charity clung to her arm, the little girl who just that morning had fought like a wolverine to escape them. She guessed maybe Charity had awakened from a similar dream then.

"Was it him?"

"Yes," Charity said. "Andy's dead." She began to cry again.

Shannon felt the patter of tears on her arm, and wiped them from Charity's eyes. "Who's Andy?"

"Don't know," she said. She sniffed, spent a few moments in silent concentration, and the tears stopped.

I wish I were that tough, Shannon thought.

"He's punishing me. When he's mad at me he makes me watch," she said. She stared at Shannon, and when Shannon looked into Charity's eyes she could almost see it happening inside her head. "I took his scissors, so he tore them open with his hands. I thought if I took them he wouldn't be able to do it again, but he did anyway."

Shannon squeezed her again, but said nothing. She didn't know what to say; Dr. Spock had never prepared her for this. She passed the entrance to the old Normal Hills Cemetery, and slowed.

"I need my arm back, sweetie."

" 'Kay."

She took the next right turn, a single-lane trail through the trees and brush.

"Where we going?"

"Normal Hills. I used to live there."

"We hiding?" Charity asked.

"Yes, for now," she said.

The trail went on straight for a few hundred yards then swung a sharp left toward town. The road was uneven and stony, the ride rough and slow. Shannon cringed as a low-hanging branch scraped the Chevelle's hood.

Charity watched the woods with nervous eyes. All around, the great pines pressed in, rough green walls on each side, blending into the darkness before and behind them, blocking out the night sky above.

"Almost there?" she asked.

"Almost," Shannon said. "Just ahead here." The trail ended, an old house stood in ruins in a cleared lot. In the glow of the headlights she could barely make out the faded *Condemned* sign nailed to the warped front door.

"What is this place?" Charity asked, not bothering to hide a look of disgust.

"It's my uncle-in-law's house. Crazy Ernie Pitcher, my ex-father-in-law's brother. He was kind of a weird old hermit, died when I was a kid, and his brother just let the house rot." Shannon drove slowly through the yard and around the side of the house to the back where she parked next to a long-abandoned International pickup. "When I was a kid I used to party here with my friends." She got out of the car, walked through the weeds and dust to the cellar entrance.

Charity followed warily. "I hope it looks better on the inside."

Shannon smiled in spite of herself. "Sorry, kid, what you see is what you get. Hold on." She dropped to the ground before the cellar door and searched blindly along the foundation. "Thomas wired the cellar once, tapped into the power line and ran it into the basement. If it's still here," she said, then stopped. "Here it is." She pulled the female end of a thick, orange extension cord, faded with age, from the debris around the foundation. Sticking out under the closed door like a pig's tail was the male end of a similar cord. "I hope this is still live," she said, and plugged them in.

Light shone from the edges of the warped door, weak but comforting.

Shannon opened the door, peeked in warily and, satisfied, stepped in. "Your room awaits."

Frowning, Charity stepped inside. Shannon followed her down, closing the door behind them.

As she reached the bottom, stepping on the old, loose floorboards, Shannon basked in nostalgia. This was where, once upon a time, she'd had her first drink, awaking the next morning with her first hangover. She had spent more time here between her sixteenth and seventeenth birthday than she had at home. After her mother died, home became a bad place, her father a beast whose last chain had finally broken, and in that nightmare year before she had moved in with her best friend Lacy, this had been her safe place.

She guessed that was the reason she'd come here, the old comfort. Her own Bogey Man had never been able to follow her here.

She knew that wouldn't be the case with Charity's monster, but for now it was as good a place as any, and there was light.

"You came here to escape your monster," Charity said, then looked away, almost ashamed. "Didn't you?

80

"How could you know that?" Shannon asked.

"Everybody has monsters," she said. "I'm sorry, you don't have to talk about it."

She's too wise for her age, Shannon thought. *Why do we do that to them? Why do we make them grow up before their time? Why, Dad?*

"Yes, Charity, we do." And yes, she did. Everybody had his or her personal monster, and though she had forgotten about the Bogey Man, she would never forget the monster that had driven her down here.

Crazy Ernie's cellar hadn't changed at all, except for an extra decade of rot. The same old fun room, floors and walls the color of dust, the same green vinyl couch resting against the far wall. The same Army surplus cot folded in the corner next to it. Two antique beanbags flanked a crazily-tilted end table, one of the legs missing. Some considerate young soul had donated a stack of school textbooks to hold that corner up. The beanbags were ruined; most of the stuffing chewed out and spread across the floor like white mouse shit.

An old tape deck sat on the floor next to an ancient black-and-white television, its cord chewed through by the same absent rodents. The television's power cord was in better shape. The rubber was chewed in a few spots but seemed intact. If the picture tube hadn't blown, it would probably still work.

All of this stuff, down to the abandoned textbooks, was sacred in its own way. Each brought here and left in trust to the next generation of kids who would make this place theirs. The rest of the house, ground floor, upstairs, and even the attic, she supposed, had been looted and trashed, but the cellar was a sacred place.

She wondered when this place had last been used. Had

this generation of kids forgotten about it, or simply abandoned it for a better place?

Shannon walked to the couch, ducking under the ceiling's low-hanging bulb, and took a seat on the old couch. Dust puffed up around her, making her cough. Still looking around dreamily, Charity sat down next to her.

"It's kind of like a clubhouse, isn't it?"

"Yes, kind of."

"It wouldn't be so bad if someone cleaned it," Charity said.

Shannon accepted the comment for what it was; Charity knew this place was special to her, and was trying to accept it in that spirit.

"Do you want to tell me about it?"

"About what?" Shannon asked, though she knew what the girl was talking about.

"Why you came here."

"I can't," she said.

Instead they sat next to each other, close enough to feel each other's body heat in the cool cellar. It didn't take long for Charity to fall asleep again, and when the nightmares started, Shannon held her close and calmed her.

Shannon, on the other hand, couldn't sleep. On top of the horrors of the night, the restless memories of the monster that drove her into the cellar kept her awake. Too many memories for one night, again making her wonder why the big people of the world too often forced the small ones to grow old before their time.

When she did finally sleep, those dusty memories followed her down.

Shannon was fourteen when her mom died. It was nothing prolonged or dramatic, she simply got too drunk one night, and like Jared's rock and roll hero, Bon Scott, choked to death on her own vomit while she was passed out. Barely a month later, her father, Ferris Cruse, Jr., moved her stuff into his room.

He said it was for her own good, they couldn't afford to get a house where she had her own room, and it wasn't proper for her and Jared to be sharing a room at their ages. She fought the move. She was honestly shocked that he would think such a thing might happen—they were brother and sister for Christ's sake. As was typical for him, her father took the passive-aggressive road.

"Fine," he said. "Sleep on the couch then, but your bed and dresser stay in here." The next thing he said blew her away completely. "People will start talking, you know, about you and Jared. It ain't proper for you two to be sleeping together."

Her retort, an observation on the properness of a father and daughter her age sleeping in the same room, never left her mouth. He didn't say, "sleeping in the same room"; he said, "sleeping together". That phrase said more to her than the mere sum of his beer-scented words. He honestly thought they were sleeping together; in his mind they could be doing nothing less.

When she told him she'd choose the couch, he began to cry, the oldest trick in the book, but it worked for him. He told her that he'd been so lonely without her mom, that he *needed* her; he couldn't take being alone at night. He said he would kill himself if she didn't stay with him, because she was all he had left.

As uncomfortable as it made her, she did sleep in his room. She tried to ignore the new way he looked at her, and the way Jared looked at both of them. She tried to ignore how her dad became increasingly cold toward Jared, and how he was often too warm toward her.

Two weeks after she moved into his room, she awoke in the dead of the night with his hands on her. He had crawled into her small single bed, perhaps hoping she wouldn't wake, or hoping that if she did she wouldn't mind. That was the moment he forced her to grow up before her time. When she got out of bed and left him, grabbing clothes from her drawer at random before leaving, he didn't follow. Perhaps he still had enough shame left to stop himself, or perhaps he had fallen asleep before she had awakened. She never knew, never asked.

She had gone straight to Jared's room and lain down with him, hoping her father was wrong about him. Jared woke up, and they talked. Then he had driven her out to Crazy Ernie's cellar.

Jared stayed at home for another two years, but Shannon couldn't. She spent winters on the couch in her father's house and stayed with friends whenever she could, but the rest of the year she spent most nights in the cellar.

Thomas Pitcher had been a better boy than he ever was a man.

He had known she was using his dead uncle's cellar, and made it as comfortable as he could for her. He never told his father, who would have undoubtedly kicked her out. They started dating when she was sixteen, and she lost the virginity she had saved from her father to him in this very cellar. They dated for several years before marrying.

The changes in Thomas were almost too gradual to detect, a slow Jekyll and Hyde transformation, but to his credit he never cooled toward their daughter; he loved Alicia more than anything else in life. He simply had too much of his father in him, and over the years they spent together he turned slowly from Thomas the Boy, who had once been her shining prince, to Thomas the Bastard. It could have been the stress of living in his father's extra-large shadow, both literally and figuratively, which turned him bad.

Over the years, Simon Pitcher had acquired much of the property in and surrounding Normal Hills through various means, some scrupulous, others not. While he only owned a few of the larger businesses, the grocery store, a small motel, the truck stop, and the mill across the river, he collected rent from every other business on Main Street. He held the deeds on much of Normal Hills' residential property too.

Few people actually knew how much he owned, and Shannon was one of them. Shortly after joining the family, Simon hired her on as bookkeeper. He kept meticulous records, so that part of her job was easy, but it also fell on her to *clean up* his other capital ventures.

Of course, people suspected him of being less than ethical. No one got as rich as he was from property alone, not in Normal Hills anyway, and over the last couple of years the lumber market had been poor enough that he was considering closing the mill down. The rumors of his vast drug empire were greatly exaggerated though. He was only a middleman, trafficking in bootleg liquor, marijuana, and black market cigars and cigarettes for some Back East associates. He refused to deal with the hard stuff like crack and meth; they were simply too risky.

The men fought often concerning matters of the family business, which Thomas would take over when Simon finally retired, but outside of work they were thick as thieves. When they weren't making money together, they golfed, fished, and drank. They also belonged to the Normal Hills chapter of the Masons.

After Alicia was born, Shannon saw less and less of Thomas outside the office, and when he was home their exchanges were uncomfortable at best. At the end, he became emotionally abusive, accusing her of cheating, and treating her like a whore. Finally she decided to divorce him, and his only comment on the subject was, "Good riddance."

Simon made sure their work relationship remained amiable enough, and Alicia kept them in touch on a more personal level, but from that day forward he would always be "The Bastard" to her.

The night she had left him, following The Bastard's Good Riddance farewell, she had gone back to Crazy Ernie's cellar and cried herself to sleep on that smelly old vinyl couch.

"Wake up," Charity said, giving Shannon a gentle shake. She awoke with those bitter old tears in her eyes, and was struck afresh with the realization that The Bastard was now dead. That realization had lost its ability to affect her, but with it came the memory of her last day with Alicia, and of Jared. Beyond those things though, she was struck with a sense of enveloping dread; she would likely be dead by the time the sun rose again.

"You okay, Shannon?"

"Yeah, I'll make it," she said, wiping her eyes self-consciously as she sat up.

"I'm getting hungry. Is there anything to eat here?"

"Not likely. Unless you like filet of rat," she added with a wink. She wasn't feeling light and she wasn't feeling particularly strong, but she wouldn't let Charity see it.

"Gross," Charity said, making a face at her.

Charity had turned the television on; a snowy version of everyone's favorite daytime game show played. One of Barker's Beauties, clad in an almost absent bikini, was stroking the side of a new Corvette like nobody's business.

"Will you be okay by yourself for an hour, Charity?"

"Yes."

"Good, I'll get us something to eat." Stretching the morning tightness from her muscles, she walked to the steps. She stopped at the door and turned. "Stay put."

"I will," Charity said.

The old trail was overgrown, the ground covered with dried needles and crowded by encroaching brush. The forest was slowly swallowing it up again. This, Shannon supposed, was as good a sign as any that the kids of Normal Hills had abandoned the old cellar. It was still passable though, and she found the walk calming. It was a half-mile walk to the truck stop outside of Normal Hills from this point. If she moved quickly—in for some food, pay quietly, and then out to the trail again—she might go unnoticed.

What to do about Charity?

She didn't know what to do, or if anything *could* be done. Charity was cursed, and now she was too. Or perhaps she had been from the beginning, she and Jared, from the moment Charity's monster had shown himself in that little room they once shared. If so, Alicia had been doubly cursed, for being born her daughter and for sharing Charity's build. She couldn't blame her daughter's death on Charity's need for a new wardrobe. Shannon didn't believe her daughter had been nothing more than a discount store mannequin to the Bogey Man. She had been chosen, like all of them were. She wondered if the other dead children's parents hadn't suffered the same visitations she had as a child. She wondered, if Jared had raised a child, would that child be dead now, too?

Had Charity's mother had the same curse, or her father? That thought brought her to an abrupt halt. What about Charity's father? She had told them at the park that the Bogey Man had killed her mother, but she didn't mention her father. Was he still alive, and if so, where was he?

And what about Feral Park? Where did the insanity of Feral Park fit in? It was where, by amazing coincidence, she had found the girl in her dead daughter's clothes, but it was more than just that.

He killed my mom and took me away.

Away to where?

I think he wants to marry me.

Why did he keep her when he'd simply killed the others?

The kids who live there told me if I came here the Bogey Man wouldn't be able to get me again. I think that's why they came here, to keep their bad people from getting them.

Everybody has monsters.

What to do about Charity, and what to do about the Bogey Man?

The only thing she knew was that he did not like the light, that it hurt him. But even that would not save them in the end, because the sun always sets and darkness always falls.

Charity was torn. She was hungry again, fiercely hungry, but she knew she couldn't stay with Shannon. If she did, Shannon would die, just like her brother. She had to get back to Feral Park or the Bogey Man *would* get her again. If she stayed hidden, she knew she could make it back to Feral Park before night.

She turned off the television and climbed the steps, opening the door to the bright, hot daytime world. The car was still there. Charity wished she could drive; getting back to Feral Park would be easier that way, and quicker. But she was just a kid. She would have to walk, and if she was going to walk, she would have to start now.

Instead she turned back to the old house and walked back to the cellar. She did not want to leave Shannon. She left the door open, though, and, sitting on the old sofa, stared out into the bright greens and crisp blue of the dawning day.

She had to go back. She knew why nothing had happened before, when they had taken her there.

The kids didn't like Shannon or Jared. They didn't like any grownups. If she was going back there, it had to be alone.

Chapter 12

Gordon and Charles gave their statements and after four hours of tense questioning, together and separately, their status was changed from suspects to witnesses. There had been another murder while they were in custody. There was an APB out on Shannon Pitcher and Jared Cruse's Chevelle. They said nothing about Charity. That was Charles's suggestion, agreed upon while they waited in front of Shannon's house. Sergeant Winter ordered them to stay in the area until further notice and sent them on their way.

They stepped out of the Riverside City complex and walked across the parking lot toward Charles's Caddy. Another hot day, and muggier than usual, but the gathering cover of dark clouds hinted at relief.

Neither spoke until they were in the car, driving back to the motel.

"What do you think?" Gordon asked.

"What do I think?" Charles seemed to weigh the question. "I think it's going to rain, at least I hope it does." He spoke with a terseness that surprised Gordon a little. "I think I'm hungry, and I'm pretty damn sure I'm tired too."

"That's not what I meant." Gordon tried to keep his voice as pleasant as possible; he could tell Charles was on the ragged edge right then, but damn it, so was he. After six years of searching for his daughter, he finally knew she was still alive, but they had been too late and missed her yet again.

"Well, what *did* you mean? Please be specific."

"What I told you earlier, about my dreams."

"Oh that," Charles said, feigning ignorance. "I think you're out of your fucking head is what I think." He hit the horn with the heel of his hand, yelling at the car in front of them to move it or lose it. When it didn't, he passed it and accelerated through the yellow light at the next crowded intersection. "Pardon my bedside manner, but I think you're grabbing for straws that don't exist. I don't buy into all that supernatural bullshit, and honestly I never figured you for the type that would either."

"I'm not the type," Gordon snapped back at him. "You can rationalize my dream, I'll give you that, but what about that scream, how do you rationalize that? 'It didn't even sound human' is what you said."

"Then what was it? Let's see if you can say it with a straight face. Even if you can look me right in the eyes and tell me, I still won't believe you. I quit believing in the Bogey Man when I was a kid." Charles's dark skin was deepening further, a flush of frustration.

Gordon closed his eyes and lay back against the Caddy's headrest. Part of him knew Charles was right, but most of him knew he was wrong. "So did I," he said mildly. "But now I'm starting to believe all over again." He waited calmly for Charles to explode at him, but it didn't happen

"Okay, Gordon, I'll give it to you for now. Call our killer whatever you want, but the point is that he doesn't have her anymore, Shannon Pitcher does. Arguing abstracts isn't going to get us any closer to Shannon Pitcher."

"Fine," Gordon said, and left it at that. He knew Charles was working on it, and left him alone.

Shannon hadn't gone to the police for help and she hadn't been picked up, which meant one of two things to Gordon:

she was either out of town, halfway to God-knows-where with Charity, or she had found a good place to lay low—hopefully the latter. The closer the better; she couldn't hide forever.

They pulled into the motel parking lot next to Gordon's Mazda.

"Listen," Charles said, "I need to sleep. Give me three hours and I guarantee I'll wake up with my head on straight again. We can eat and get back to work in four hours, five tops."

Gordon nodded. "I understand," and he did. He was on the brink again too, but he knew he wouldn't be able to sleep. Instead of following Charles back to the room, he dug his keys from his pocket and unlocked the Mazda.

"You should get some rest too," Charles said. "I have a feeling it's going to be a rough night."

"I can't," Gordon said. "I'll just drive around a bit. I'll be back in four hours with dinner."

"Sounds like a plan," Charles said. "Be cool. Don't lose your head again."

"I won't."

Gordon found a public library a few minutes from the motel and stopped there. He knew Charles was right: abstracts would get him nowhere now. He felt embarrassed that he had even brought the subject up in the first place, but it was an itch he needed to scratch. Using one of the library's computer terminals, he found half a dozen promising titles. He skimmed them at the shelf, and settled on one that seemed a step up from the usual campfire tales and fairy stories.

Legend of the Bogey Man: The Truth Told in Centuries
by Jeannine Carter

Centuries ago, when Christianity was new and superstition was still the religion of the masses, people believed in the Bogey, and they feared it. Thought to be an evil spirit, fairy, or demon, it was known by different names throughout Europe; Boggard, Bollybog, Bug-a-boo, or Bogle. Stories of the wicked creature's origin were also widely varied, but accounts of its evil deeds were the same. The Bogey stole children from their beds at night and took them away, never to be seen again.

Some people used charms to keep the Bogey from their children; some poured milk onto the ground outside their homes, as it was believed good fairies loved milk and would protect the house from bad spirits. Some hung open scissors over the cribs of their infants to scare the spirit thief away.

The Bogey was said to sleep with women and impregnate them. The children of such unions were shapeshifters, and would grow up to become Bogeys themselves.

Though in later times the churched population no longer believed in the Bogey, its legend continued to grow, as a fairy tale told to children to inspire good behavior through fear. All little boys and girls knew if they were not good, the Bogey Man might come for them.

Even today, the grim legend of the Bogey Man persists, and every night children lay awake, fearful of every shadow and night noise. They wait out the darkness in fear that the Bogey Man might come to take them away.

1793, a small village near Devon, England.

More than a dozen children went missing over a period of several weeks. Many of the missing children's parents were found brutally slain.

One woman, a local tavern-keeper's daughter with a less than savory reputation, claimed that the Bogle had taken the children and murdered their parents. She further claimed that the Bogle came to her in the guise of a handsome young gentleman, and slept with her. Three months later, when it was discovered she was with child, she was accused of witchcraft and burned to death by a mob in the town center.

None of the missing children were ever seen again.

Other local children, even some in neighboring towns, awoke screaming from nightmares during those bloody weeks, only to see that their nightmares had followed them back to their rooms.

1810, Dublin, Ireland.

A prominent political figure, whose name was later stricken from public records, was murdered along with his wife and one adult son. His two younger children were taken from their home that very night and never seen again.

Despite the ramblings of a superstitious house servant who claimed that a Ballybog committed the crime, the assassinations and kidnappings were believed to be politically motivated.

The courts found the servant innocent of any involvement in the crime, but committed her to an asylum, where she died a few years later.

1852, a ship carrying Scottish immigrants bound for the United States.

During the month-long journey, over half of the ship's population of children disappeared, many of their parents and older siblings were found butchered. None of the missing children returned, and were assumed thrown overboard by the killer.

A young Scottish woman reported being assaulted by a strange young man who, after satisfying himself, suddenly became very old, and withered away to nothing before her eyes.

Six months later she died giving birth to a premature but healthy baby boy. A Catholic home for orphaned children took the child in, but his fate thereafter is unknown.

The book read like a ghoul's encyclopedia. It was very matter-of-fact, and at the same time very implausible. Jeannine Carter cited cases from eighteenth-century Europe to as recent as fifty years ago in the United States. The book was one in a series of supernatural tomes, published in the spirit of *The X-Files*. Whatever the publishers thought of it, it was clear that Jeannine Carter believed.

Gordon had been there for almost three hours, time to get back.

He acquired a library card using the motel's address and checked the book out. On his way back to the room, he stopped for sub sandwiches and espressos.

When Charles woke up, his espresso was still warm and Gordon was still reading.

Charles called the detective handling the local murders to ask about Shannon Pitcher, and Gordon knew from his face that she hadn't been found yet.

"I think I made a mistake," he told Gordon. "I'm sorry, man."

"We'll find them," Gordon replied, refusing to give despair a foothold.

Charles nodded. "We'll start in Normal Hills. Her father-in-law might know where she is. Even if he doesn't, it's the logical place to start."

"Her ex-husband's house?"

"That's what I was thinking, if it's still empty." Charles pulled his gun from the desk drawer and began the cleaning ritual. "Even if she's not at her ex's place, Normal Hills is her home. She's only been in Riverside for a few months."

"If she's running, it's probably back home," Gordon concluded. "Familiar territory?"

"You catch on quick," Charles said. "You've been spending too much time with me."

"You've been spending too much time with me, I think," Gordon replied, hating what he was about to say next. "It's not like you to screw up."

Charles's mouth pulled into a frown. "Look, friend, I said I was sorry. We should have followed her."

"Don't be sorry," Gordon said. "Do me a favor and it's forgotten." He handed the book over.

Charles looked uneasy as he accepted it. He read the cover, then looked back at Gordon. "Still haven't got that bug out of your butt?"

"Just indulge me," Gordon said. "Please, I promise to shut up about it."

"Sure," Charles said, shaking his head. Finishing with his gun, he reloaded and tucked it back into its holster. "What do you want me to do?"

"See if you can find the author for me, I'd like to talk to her." Gordon braved Charles's disbelieving stare and continued. "And I'd like you to read some of the passages. I've marked the pages for you. I know you think I'm losing touch, but I think you'll be surprised."

"If I do this and I'm still not convinced, you'll leave me alone, right?"

"Swear," Gordon said.

"Fine," Charles replied and dialed his secretary back east.

"I *have* been around you too long. I can't believe I'm doing this." He cradled the receiver between his shoulder and chin, opening the book cover with obvious distaste. "Dee's going to think I've lost it."

Gordon waited silently.

"Dee, it's Charles," he said, bracing himself against her wrath. Why haven't you called, and you need to let me know what's going on, etc. "Yeah . . . I know, Dee." He rolled his eyes. Gordon knew she was an asset to Charles, but sometimes she acted like his keeper. "I know, I'm sorry. Listen Dee, I need you to do something for me." He paused, rolled his eyes again, and said, "Okay. *Please,* could you do me a favor?"

There was another pause, and he grinned and shook his head again. "Yes, I know . . . and yes, you are."

Gordon couldn't sit any longer. As foolish as it all seemed, it felt very important to him.

Charles watched him pace for a second and looked back at the book. "I need you to locate someone. Jeannine Carter, a writer, she wrote a book called *Legend of the Bogey Man: The Truth Told in Centuries.*" More silence, then he frowned. "Yeah, I know," he said, giving Gordon an annoyed look. "She may know something."

Gordon paced, feeling more foolish as Charles told Dee to make it top priority, told her to call his cell phone the second she located Jeannine Carter.

Charles said his goodbyes, promising to keep in touch, and hung up. "She's on it, my friend," he said. He threw the book onto his bed. "I'll read later. It's time to get moving."

They took Charles's Caddy and left town with the windows down. The gathering clouds had cooled the day, and the rush of wind felt good. Charles turned the radio up, listening for news of the latest murders. Listening for Shannon's name, hoping he wouldn't hear it. The police probably wouldn't release it for fear of spooking her if she heard it mentioned on the local news, but it was hard to know what these yokel cops might tell the press.

Charles saw the girl standing at the side of the road, half-hidden in the willows on the river side of the highway. Her face was a dirty oval; her hair long, brown and sticking up like a wild nimbus around her head. She was dressed like a boy, wearing small boots, a blue t-shirt, and stained overalls. She smiled at them as they approached, then tilted back and threw something large and mangled into the air. A second later it hit the windshield with a loud gunshot crack. It spread across Gordon's side with an explosion of blood and fur and a large blossoming spider web of cracked safety glass.

"Son of a bitch!" Charles yelled, struggling to regain control. The Caddy weaved, tires squealing, and he brought it to a sliding halt at the side of the road.

Gordon watched in silent shock as a mutilated cat slid toward the hood, leaving a sticky smear of blood, fur, and innards behind it. One of its eyes had popped from a socket. It lay against the windshield wiper, watching him sightlessly. Maggots squirmed from the cat's demolished head, more wiggled in the half-congealed blood on the windshield. The matted corpse looked and smelled as if it had been dead a few days. He fumbled his door open and puked in the ditch beside the car.

"Damn it!" Charles shouted, and pushed his door open. He stepped toward the highway where the girl half-hid, giggling in the trees, but jumped back as a speeding semi shot past blowing its air horn. "Son of a bitch!" Charles slammed a fist on his hood.

Gordon stumbled to his side as the truck passed. "Who the hell did that?"

"That way!" Charles shouted when the semi was past them, and led Gordon to the other side.

"Who did it?" Gordon asked again, following Charles through the bushes.

"Her," Charles said, pointing at the girl as she spun and giggled through the tall grass toward a large, dilapidated playground. "Hey you, stop!" he yelled at her.

She only laughed louder. "Na-na na-na na-na, the old fat man can't catch me."

"Damn, kid," Charles growled, and pushed himself faster.

Gordon struggled to keep up, his stomach tied in knots and his legs growing weaker with each step. Then, as if nothing had happened, the girl stopped and sat at a bench near the playground. She didn't look back at her pursuers, just stared straight ahead toward the playground's arched entryway.

Charles stopped several yards behind the bench and waited for Gordon. Together they approached the girl. She sobbed quietly, her small shoulders quaking. Gordon took the left side, Charles the right, and they stepped around the bench in front of her. Charles opened his mouth, preparing to scold, but stopped cold.

Her face was a mess of bruises and running cuts, her eyes swollen to narrow, red slits. She screamed at them, a bubbling, frothy shriek. Her bottom jaw was gone; her tongue lay like a giant, blood-slimed slug against her throat. Blood pumped from the gaping maw and ran down the front of her bare chest. She sat naked, hands folded across her lap, covering herself.

The girl's gurgling scream tapered off, her eyes closed, and she fell forward, a bloody lump, into the grass. Then she was gone. Her screams still echoed in their heads, but of the girl there was not a trace. Even the blood that had pooled on the bench where she'd sat was gone. Aside from the dust and white polka dots of bird shit, it was clean.

There was a book in the grass where her body had landed. A children's book, its cover familiar to Gordon. It had been a favorite of his.

Where the Wild Things Are, by Maurice Sendak.

Reluctantly, Gordon knelt and picked it up. Charles stood away, clutching his chest with a meaty hand. He looked as though he expected the girl to reappear at any moment to claim it.

Slowly, as if fearing the same, Gordon opened the book. *Property of Jenny Heyworth* was written inside the front cover in large, childish handwriting. He thumbed through it, noting half a dozen other such notes. On one page, drawn beside a circle of dancing monsters, was a child's rendering of a sign identical to the one by the playground. It said "Feral Park." A note on the last page read, *Leave Charity alone . . . she's one of us now!*

Dirty Dave watched from a safe distance, hidden from sight. He shook his head and frowned.

"Miss Jenny," he said. "Why do you have to torment them? They aren't the cause of your misery."

He walked toward the playground again, more bags of throwaway food hanging from his clenched fists. "I know you like to play, girl, but sometimes you play too rough." He laughed, a phlegmy chortle, as he left his offering. His penance for letting the little girl, Jenny, die all those years ago.

Chapter 13

The truck stop was quiet; a few people pumped gas outside. Shannon didn't recognize any of them. Inside, an old trucker sat alone at a table drinking coffee and studying a map. A pimply teenage boy thumbed through a rack of CDs, casting the occasional paranoid glance around or behind.

Don't even try it, kid, Shannon thought. *You're too obvious.* If the kid was caught shoplifting, she knew Simon wouldn't hesitate to prosecute him. She recognized Billy Pitcher, Simon's idiot nephew, browsing the beer cooler. Crazy Ernie's son—orphaned as a child and fostered in Simon's house with Thomas. Now that Thomas was dead, she supposed the business would go to Billy.

Keeping her face pointed away from him, she walked to the cooler and picked out four sandwiches and two small cartons of milk, one chocolate. On her way to the checkout counter she passed the automotive aisle. She saw a rack of flashlights. She grabbed two of them and a large pack of D-cell batteries. The cashier didn't recognize her. She paid quickly and made it as far as the door before Billy saw her.

"Hi, Sis!" he shouted, and came up behind her, a case of Milwaukee's Best hanging from each hand.

Asshole, she thought, and turned to greet him with a false smile. She wasn't surprised when his eyes failed to meet hers. The man was scum. He always called her "Sis," a thing that annoyed her to no end, and he never could keep his eyes off her tits.

"Hi, Billy-boy," she said. She knew he hated that nickname, and used it every time she spoke to him. "Shouldn't you be at work?" Billy worked part-time at his uncle's mill as Operations Manager and spent the rest of his time as Simon's all-purpose errand boy.

"Naw," he said. "I took a sick day. I'm going fishing today. Want to come with?" His eyes, moving spastically between her face and chest, seemed to glow at the prospect. Now that Thomas was gone, Shannon knew he considered her fair game, just another piece of family property to inherit.

He probably thinks this is foreplay.

"You know, Billy-boy, I can't today. I'm sorry, I'm really busy."

"C'mon," he said. "I miss you. Just because we're not family any more doesn't mean we can't stay close." His eyes shifted again, this time below the belt line of her jeans.

She wanted to scream. "Maybe later," she said instead, inching toward the door.

She saw the paranoid teen walking toward them, one hand tucked conspicuously inside a denim jacket that the muggy day didn't warrant.

"Hey, you, stop!" the cashier shouted, and the boy bolted for the door.

Billy saw the boy, and pushed past Shannon to stop him. The kid dropped his CD and tried to shove Billy aside. Billy stood several inches taller than the kid and outweighed him by at least fifty pounds. He had the kid pinned to the tile floor within seconds.

"Call the sheriff, and Simon!" Billy shouted.

Shannon took advantage of the lucky break and slipped out unnoticed.

★ ★ ★ ★ ★

She returned to the cellar and found Charity sitting at the edge of the steps waiting for her. The scrawny girl tore into her sandwich, eating half of it before giving the chocolate milk a vigorous shake and opening it. She emptied the cartoon in two long chugs and finished the sandwich. She voiced her appreciation with a long, raspy belch.

"You're welcome," Shannon said, and then worked on her sandwich with a little more tact.

"Sorry," the girl said shyly. "How was the walk?"

"Good," Shannon said. "Relaxing." She took another bite and washed it down with milk.

"You were gone a long time. Did you see anyone you know?"

"Yeah, I did. I'm sorry," she said. "It must be kind of scary out here by yourself."

"No," Charity said. "This place isn't scary at all. I just missed you." She shuffled her feet. "Was it a friend?"

"No," Shannon said. "He is *definitely* not a friend."

"Oh," Charity said, affecting a knowing smile. "A jerk, huh?"

Shannon smiled weakly, and remembering a favorite line from an old Douglas Adams book, said, "Yes, a real knee-biter."

Thunder boomed overhead, making them both jump. The storm was sneaking up on them. Maybe it would pass, but Shannon hoped not. She hoped it would rain like hell all afternoon long.

"Tell me about your dad, Charity."

The girl winced as if slapped in the face and glared at Shannon. "What do you know about my dad?"

"Nothing," Shannon said. "I'm just curious. You've never mentioned him." She was unsure how to ask what she really wanted to know, so she did it point-blank. "Is he still alive?"

"I guess," Charity said, then stood in a sure, swift way that Shannon envied. She paced, a girl at the end of her nerves, and continued. "I think he is. Mom left him when I was little, I haven't seen him in a long time, except in dreams sometimes." She kicked a small rock, picked it up, and chucked it side-arm into the forest. A bird squawked; a family of squirrels ran for cover.

"You dream about him?" Shannon asked.

"No, he dreams about me." She paused, and elaborated, "The Bogey Man lets me into his dreams sometimes when I'm feeling sad. He thinks it cheers me up. He tries to keep me happy. Dad's been looking for me for a long time, but he won't find me."

"And why not?" Shannon challenged, trying for at least a spark of hope in the girl's eyes. At nine, even Shannon had had hope. It was difficult to see Charity so at ease with her skepticism.

"Because if my dad ever does, *he* will kill him." Charity's voice tripped over the last words, and Shannon was sure the tears she had pushed back for so long would come now. They didn't.

"I found you, Charity. He didn't kill me." *Not for lack of trying,* she thought.

Charity gave Shannon a look that made her regret the words. *The day is still young, lady.*

"Do you know where he is?" Shannon asked hopefully. "Can you still see into his dreams?"

"No," Charity said, sitting down at the door again, staring at the ground between her sneakers. "Sometimes," she amended. "I don't want to talk about it."

"Okay, what do you want to talk about?"

"You," Charity said. "You know him, don't you?"

"Who?" Shannon asked, but she knew who Charity meant. Suddenly *she* was the one uncomfortable with the line of questioning.

"The Bogey Man," Charity said.

There was a long pause. Shannon felt small in the waiting silence, but she would not lie to Charity, and she would not ignore her. She had ignored Alicia, and Alicia was gone.

"Yes, I know him. Jared did too." She had gone most of the morning without thinking of her brother, guarding herself against the guilt and grief his memory would surely bring. If she had stayed in the room with them, he might still be alive. She tried to fight the grief now that it came, but she was not as strong as Charity. With a cry she could hardly believe came from her, she buried her face in her hands, her body gripped in a convulsion of sobs.

"It's okay," Charity whispered, playing the parent to Shannon's child. She scooted next to Shannon and pulled her head into her arms, stroking her hair, cooing at her absently.

After a few minutes, Shannon's tears tapered off. She moved from Charity's embrace and hugged her. "Thank you, sweetheart," she said wiping her red, swollen eyes.

"Tell me a story."

"What kind of story?"

"A scary one," Charity said, but without the childlike enthusiasm that usually went with the request. "It doesn't have to be about you. It can be about anybody."

Shannon knew what Charity was doing. The girl needed to know, so she obliged.

"I think I know just the one," she said, and squeezed Charity's hands as she began. "It happened in 1973, in this very town. I knew the girl it happened to very well, but we've lost touch over the years. I haven't thought of her in years, until last night . . ."

★ ★ ★ ★ ★

The brother and sister shared a room, toys, occasional daydreams of running away to Riverside, what they called the big city, and they shared a nightmare. Their shared nightmare had come back again. He lay on the floor between their beds, crooning at them, shaking the world with his soft laughter.

They stared at each other, into each other's eyes, across the threatening void between their beds. They dared not look down into the face of the Bogey Man.

"Oh . . . my children," he sang. "Seeing you tonight does my old soul good."

Slowly, their blanket moved, sliding across skin and PJs like the scales of a snake, pulled toward the floor between them by invisible hands.

"Such good children," he said with an exaggerated rasp. "How I've missed you."

And they screamed. Screamed and screamed and screamed.

When their father rushed in, still half asleep and demanding to know what the hell all the hollering was about, the Bogey Man was gone. They could hear his laughter, though, echoing in the dangerous void between them like a barely remembered scrap of nightmare.

The story ended, and for a long time neither of them spoke. Shannon picked up her sandwich, but her stomach clenched at the thought of food. She held it to Charity but the girl declined. Shannon threw the last half of her sandwich into the woods, an offering to the squawking birds and scurrying chipmunks.

"I know how that little girl feels," Charity said. "Every day of my life." She stood up, bumping Shannon's milk carton over with the tip of her shoe, and ran back into the cellar.

Shannon didn't follow right away. She watched her spilt milk soak into the dry earth like cold, white blood.

Chapter 14

Gordon and Charles rode the rest of the way to Normal Hills in silence. Gordon held the open book in his lap, reading the message on the final page repeatedly. Charles concentrated on the road. He drove slower than usual. Cautiously, struggling with what he had seen back at the park. It felt like he was losing his grip on all he understood, all the logic and practicality that made him what and who he was. He had seen some unbelievable things over the years, many of which he desperately wished he could forget, but none of his experiences had ever touched the supernatural.

The thing back at the park was no Bogey Man, but suddenly Gordon's recent craziness didn't sound so crazy. He tried to simply file the experience away as yet another life lesson, *anything is possible . . . anything,* but the image of that girl sitting naked and bloodied before them would not be so easily dismissed. Then there was the book, *Where the Wild Things Are,* and that last scribbled message. This was no side road aberration; this was part of his case now. *How the hell am I going to log that?* he wondered.

As they passed the road to the old Normal Hills Cemetery, the first blast of thunder shook the overcast sky. Gordon and Charles both jumped a little.

Gordon closed the book, set it on the seat between them, then lay back and closed his eyes.

By the time they entered town the rain had washed the remaining gore from the cracked windshield. Charles had peeled the dead cat from the windshield with an ice scraper back by the park but was unable to clean up all of the blood.

They passed the commotion at the truck stop, sheriff's deputies and a few dozen onlookers, without paying notice. They passed Little's Café and turned at the next block.

The Normal Hills Hotel was a squat brick structure; three stories tall and probably as old as the town itself. The parking lot was small and mostly empty. The hotel belonged to Simon Pitcher; it was where he kept his offices.

They ran across pitted blacktop to the lobby entrance and managed not to get too wet before they made it inside. The rain was still light, but the dark clouds overhead threatened a squall.

Beats the hell out of the heat, Charles thought as he passed through the lobby door. Gordon entered silently a step behind.

Thunder crashed again as the door swung closed.

A redheaded teenage girl sat at the front desk reading a book. She gave them a look of wide-eyed shock—caught slacking off, the look said—then set the book down and folded her hands on the counter. Charles read the cover as they approached. The kind of fiction a person read could be telling, and sometimes the insight was useful. The book was called *Bondage by Lust* and featured a Fabio-type model on the front cover, all rippling muscles and long black hair.

"Uh, hi," she said, smacking a mouthful of gum. "You want a room?" The touch of disbelief in her voice reinforced Charles's theory: this hotel was used almost exclusively by Simon's visiting "business associates." *Or maybe it's because I'm black,* Charles thought. Normal Hills had few if any blacks he guessed, and he knew that unfamiliarity bred discomfort. When he spoke to her, he used his softest, friendliest voice.

"Thank you, miss, but not tonight." He smiled and rested his arms on the counter. "I'm looking for Simon Pitcher. I understand he keeps an office here. Perchance is he in today?"

She smiled, and the discomfort, if that's what it *had* been, vanished. "I'm sorry," she said. "Simon's out. Did you have an appointment?"

"No, ma'am," he said, again flashing his winning smile. "It is rather urgent, though—it's about his ex-daughter-in-law."

"Oh," she said, and backed away a step. Her demeanor changed, seemed a little cooler.

"When will he be back?" Gordon moved up to the counter beside Charles. The question came out an impatient bark.

"I'm sorry, sir," the girl said. "I don't know. There was some trouble and he had to go."

"Trouble?" Charles asked, a conspiratorial grin stretched his face. He leaned a little closer to her. "You've got me curious now." He dropped her a wink and said, "Come on girl, give it up."

The girl considered him for a moment before returning the smile. The lobby was empty save the three of them, but she glanced around before leaning closer to Charles. "Okay," she said, "this isn't one-hundred percent for sure, but I heard Denny Buffet got busted ripping off CDs from Simon's truck stop." She giggled a little and continued, "I used to date him. I don't know why, he's so scuzzy."

Charles and the girl laughed together.

"That's a side of you I've never seen before," Gordon said on their way back to the car.

Charles gave him a sideways scowl but said nothing.

They pulled into the truck stop's parking lot just as a sheriff's cruiser carrying a gangly teenage boy pulled away. They spotted two men giving statements to a deputy. One of them, Charles assumed, would be Simon Pitcher.

Charles parked and waited.

After a few minutes the younger of the two, a big, whiskered man in flannel, loose green pants, and work boots, went back into the store. The deputy headed toward his cruiser, and the other man walked over to his truck, a monstrous Ford pickup—midnight black and shining chrome. The license plate read: *Simon #1*. He was well dressed, looking comfortable and cool in a black two-piece suit and shining cowboy boots. He didn't wear a hat; his bald head gleamed under the tarmac lights. He was deeply tanned, almost burned. He seemed to scowl at the world as he walked to his truck.

"Stay here," Charles said, stepping from his Caddy. He walked quickly and met the man at his truck. "Simon Pitcher?"

The man paused, regarded Charles with a lazy glance. "You're standing a little close for a man I don't know," he said, and climbed in.

Boss Hogg without the white suit and fat, Charles thought.

"Charles Davis, Private Investigator," he said, offering a hand he knew Simon would not take. "Now you know me." He held the truck's door open as Simon tried to close it. Simon glared down at him, opened his mouth to say something, but Charles interrupted him. "I heard you're having a bad day, Simon. You talk to me like that again and it'll get worse in a hurry."

Simon continued to glare at Charles, but something in the PI's face must have convinced him. He stepped down and held out his own hand. "Simon Pitcher," he confirmed. "A rough day to say the least."

Charles took the offered hand and gave it a pump. "Bad

days I understand," he said, and the fight was over before it started.

"What can I do for you, Mr. Davis?" he asked, his voice cold, but no longer rude.

"I'm looking for Shannon," Charles said. "Someone killed her brother last night, and they may be after her as well. She's running, but she won't be able to hide for long. I need to find her before she gets hurt."

For the first time in their exchange, Simon took notice. The look on his face did not approach fear for his ex-daughter-in-law, only a mild concern. "Who is it?" he said, and Charles heard the underlying question clear enough. *Does it have anything to do with me?*

"No one you need to worry about, Mr. Pitcher."

"That's comforting," Simon said. "I do worry about Shannon though. Do you have any proof that you're on her side?"

Charles sighed. "Fair enough," he said digging a business card out of his wallet and handing it to Simon. "Call the Riverside P.D. if you want—they'll verify I am who I say I am."

"Good enough for me," Simon said, pocketing the card after a cursory look.

"Have you seen her?" Charles asked.

"Not since she left Normal Hills," Simon said. "You think she might have come back here?"

"I don't know. Is there any place here she might stay?"

"No. Her father lives in town, but she has nothing to do with him. The man doesn't deserve a daughter as fine as Shannon."

Charles recognized real admiration in his voice and his estimation of Shannon rose. Simon Pitcher didn't appear to be a man easily impressed. "Where did she live after the divorce?" Charles asked, aware he was treading on touchy ground. But he needed to know.

Simon seemed unaffected by the question. "I gave her and Alicia a suite in the hotel." Then he surprised Charles by pulling a key from the ring in his hand and offering it to him. "She and Thomas lived at the top of Maple Road. A big white house: 614 Maple. It's sitting empty, maybe she went there," he said with a shrug of his big shoulders.

Charles had thought the same thing, but he hadn't intended to push his luck by asking for a key. Pitcher's altruistic move caught him off-guard. "Thanks," he said and pocketed the key.

"Don't thank me," Simon said, climbing into the truck. "Just find her, help her out for me."

"If you see her—" Charles started.

"—I've got your card." Simon shut the door and started the motor. The truck rumbled and he sped out of the parking lot.

"Big" was a proper description of Shannon's old white house—certainly the biggest on the block, maybe in all of Normal Hills.

No, Charles thought, *Simon's would be the biggest.*

The house was intimidating, the hillside behind it all rock and scrub, lending a wild feel to the abandoned look. The white paint was no longer precisely white, but an aged and dirty imitation. It was three stories, almost Victorian in style, but not quite. He thought the design must be original, not modeled on any pre-existing structure. It seemed half castle and half cottage. It was a shame it would continue to go empty. The large yard had gone to riot around it, grass grown knee-high and dying. A large circular driveway was littered with months of dust and wind-blown debris. Rose-threaded trestles leaned askew; once vibrant blossoms had dried to a rusty blood color.

"What are you waiting for?" Gordon asked behind him, irritation seeping through his words.

I'm waiting for another ghost, Charles thought. "Nothing. Let's have a look."

It was still furnished, the den almost inviting, the study walls lined with full bookshelves. *Mostly for show,* Charles thought. The desk was a clutter of unfinished paperwork, the culmination of a shortened life.

The atmosphere of dread lingered about them: long unbroken darkness, old dust and stagnant air, and the rusty smell of long-dried blood.

They searched every level of the house. They saw the spot where Thomas Pitcher died, the place on the carpeted floor of the master bedroom stained with his blood. More blood than could ever be washed clean. They found the room where Alicia had slept her last night.

The house was empty—only Charles, Gordon, and whatever quiet ghosts remained.

Charles's cell phone rang, startling them both.

"Hello," Charles answered testily, then his face lightened as Dee spoke. A second later his glumness returned, and Gordon knew it couldn't be good.

"We found your author," Charles said after he hung up. "She's dead, murdered ten years ago in New Orleans. She had a three-year-old boy named Jacob and a five-year-old girl named Jessica, both missing and presumed dead."

"Oh my God," Gordon said, barely a whisper.

"Let's get out of here."

Chapter 15

Though she had only slept in violent bursts the past few days, Charity was alert. The storm outside brought a premature darkness, and she knew *He* would return soon.

They had promised to keep each other awake until sunset. Then they would get in the car and drive east until daylight again, stopping only in the brightest lit places for food or gas. Charity agreed to the plan because Shannon wanted her to, but she knew better. Wherever they ran, *He* would follow, and one day he would get them. She also knew Shannon would not make it until sunset. Charity hoped exhaustion would take Shannon quickly, so she could go back where she belonged. It was the only way.

Charity felt the tug in her heart, in her head . . . *join us, Charity . . . come to us and you will never have to be afraid again* . . . and knew it was Feral Park.

The single hanging bulb burned the dark from every corner of the cellar. The television added its glow, and a comforting white noise that excused them from conversation. Shannon sat snuggled into the corner of the couch, holding her new flashlight to her chest like a talisman. Charity did the same, the smaller one Shannon had given her the night before hanging from the cord on her wrist.

She listened to the storm outside, rain giving way to a dry wind. She watched Shannon's eyes slip closed again, and begged them not to open. When they didn't, she waited, and when the telltale rapid eye movements of deep sleep started she knew it was time.

She rose slowly from the couch, careful not to disturb Shannon, then reached around her neck and unclasped the locket. She opened it again, looked at the picture, the picture of a real family, and then laid it gently on Shannon's lap.

"Goodbye," she whispered, and crept quietly up the stairs and into the darkening day.

Once away from the house, she ran. The trail into the woods seemed impossibly long, never ending, but she finally found the highway and allowed herself to rest. She stopped for only a minute, letting her aching lungs and the stitch in her side to settle, then crossed to the river side of the highway and ran along the guardrail. After a few minutes her aching legs forced her to slow, but she didn't stop. She didn't have time to rest. There were only a few hours left.

She had to make it to Feral Park before the dark came, and *He* came with it. To take her away again, to a place she knew she would never escape.

She heard the car approaching behind her before it came into view. Acting on instinct she jumped over the guardrail and hid in the bushes. A big gray car passed, and she waited until it was out of sight before she started running again.

She followed the orange glow of the falling sun to the west like a beacon.

"I want to go back to the park," Gordon said.

"I thought you might," Charles said, his distaste obvious. "You think she's going there?"

"Yes." He held the book again, but the light was getting too faint to read. He didn't know why she would be going there, but something in that park thought she was. Whatever it was, ghost or demon, had known he would be there, and had taken the time to warn him away. He didn't *want* to go back, but his desire to find Charity outweighed his fear of the unnatural presence there.

"That's where we're going then." There was no trace of skepticism in Charles's voice, no hint of disbelief. He was thinking the same thing as Gordon. Once they found Charity, and he thought now that they actually might, his job was done. The ghosts at Feral Park and Gordon's Bogey Man would not be his problem. He liked Gordon, thought of him almost as a brother, but he wanted out of the nightmare this case had become. After three years of nothing, everything seemed to be dropping on him at once, and Charles did not like what he was seeing. "Gordon."

Charles's voice conveyed a depth of solemnity that sounded strange coming from the normally lighthearted man. Gordon thought he knew what was happening, and though it made him uncomfortable, he understood. "Yes?"

"If we find her tonight, I'm done." Guilt was apparent in his voice; he usually didn't call a job finished until all the loose ends were either tied up or snipped off, but this was not his usual job. "I can't protect her from whatever ghosts and Bogey Men are chasing her. That's your job. I can only pray for you."

"I understand, Charles." And Gordon did understand. Charles had stuck with him these three years when most would not have. He couldn't blame the man for being spooked. He hoped he would change his mind, though. He didn't think he would, but hope is a helpless, stupid thing that knows no reason. It is also a tenacious thing that dies hard.

Gordon saw the one-time entrance to the park, blocked off but with enough space to park a car. "Here we are."

Charles slowed and pulled in parallel to the blockade. Gordon watched as he pulled his revolver from its holster, and it appeared at that moment a ritual akin to meditation or prayer. It was his way of crossing himself before rushing into some unknown battle.

They locked the Caddy up and stepped high over the barricade, Gordon noting the sign that said, *Feral Park is closed to the public—Enter at own risk* with some apprehension.

Why don't they just tear it down? Gordon wondered. He had a sudden image of a bulldozer and men in hard-hats milling around the park. The 'dozer advances on the playground, but dies before reaching the barred wall, sabotaged by unseen hands. He could see the workmen confused and scared as incorporeal voices taunt them.

"Let's wait down there, the bench by the trees."

"Your call, boss," Charles said.

Not *old friend,* just *boss.* In that one word, Gordon heard their three-year friendship coming to an end.

Charity walked for almost an hour but it felt like longer. Her legs hurt, her back hurt, her head hurt, and she was scared. What if she didn't make it in time? She held the larger flashlight tightly. She wanted to turn it on but didn't. Even though the batteries were new, she didn't want to waste any of their energy.

Above and to the west the sun turned violet red. She could see it glowing, a tired light behind the clouds as it touched, then melted into the horizon. In another hour it would be gone and she would be defenseless.

She watched for any landmarks that might tell her how close, or far, she was to Feral Park, but it was futile. She had cowered on the floorboard of Shannon's car leaving town, and had not seen much.

She kept running.

The sun dipped farther into the horizon; full dark would come soon. Then she saw the sign, *Riverside 2 Miles,* and felt her heart leap. She could run the two miles in time, she knew she could.

As she neared town, she saw the slope on the other side of the guardrail flatten out. The trees there were sparse enough to move through quickly. She slowed, hopped the rail, and took cover in the trees as she ran. Ahead, the trees thickened and she had to weave and duck as she passed through them. Beyond was the almost solid green wall of lush, hanging willows. Beyond them, Feral Park.

Shannon awoke from restless dreams and felt the soft pressure of a familiar object in her hand.

"Alicia . . . Charity?" In her mind, at that moment, her daughter and the strange girl had become one in the same. "Charity," she called again, but heard no answer. Charity had run.

Asleep at the wheel, she thought, and left the couch in a panicked leap. The locket fell to the hardwood floor and slid next to the little table. She stopped dead, looked at it, and for a second could not breathe. It lay face up, a tiny heart of gold, laced with a fine chain. It glowed softly under the lamplight. She bent slowly, feeling numb, and picked it up. For a second she thought she heard Charity's voice.

Goodbye.

Then the numbness departed, and she felt cold. She ran up the old warped steps and out into the open. The backyard was deserted. She ran around to the front, called out to Charity again, but there was no answer. She was gone.

Shannon sprinted back to the Chevelle and drove as fast as she could toward Feral Park.

Gordon waited as the sun set, distracted by the uncomfortable silence between him and Charles. The only sound in the hazy red afternoon was the chirping of crickets and slow rush of the Snake River. As the sun slipped away behind them another sound came into play, a phantom noise at first, barely audible, gaining volume until it drowned out everything else. Rock music; coming from the empty park.

"What the hell?" Gordon said, more to himself than Charles.

Charles only shook his head, brow furrowed in concentration as the sound of laughter drifted up to them. They searched in vain for the source of these new sounds, and their confusion grew to fear. Other than the phantom sounds, there was no sign of life in the playground below. Nothing stirred.

"Ten minutes," Charles whispered, "and I'm out of here."

"Fine," Gordon said. He didn't care anymore. Charles could drive back to fucking New York tonight and he wouldn't care. He was willing to go it alone if he had to.

Then the sun was set, the last sliver of red melted into nothing, and it was like a veil pulled from their eyes. The sounds of music and play grew louder, and the haunted playground was a frenzy of activity. Kids appeared from the shadows, a dozen or more of them. Filthy waifs, some very small, very young, a few that looked to be in their pre-teens. Most were fully clothed, some dressed in rags.

The children took up perches on the posts of rope bridges and crows' peak towers. They swung in the swings, sat on seesaws. Three of them stepped out through the playground's exit and into the wild lawn, a girl in bib overalls and two older boys, one armed with what appeared to be a long broom handle sharpened into a spear, the other with a short length of board.

It was the girl who had thrown the dead cat at them, the ghost who had warned them away. If she was a ghost—and she did appear brighter somehow than the boys who flanked her—she was the only one. The other children were as real as Gordon and Charles.

The three approached the wall of overgrown willows that separated Feral Park from the wild beyond and waited, perhaps for Charity. Gordon could only hope at this point. If the past three years had been a kind of waking nightmare to him, the last few days had been nothing short of insane. He didn't know what would happen next.

Behind them, the screech of tires and the crunch of metal broke the surreal daze they found themselves in. Below, several of the wild children took notice, but none spoke, none left their playground refuge. The three stood waiting before the wall of green, oblivious to the commotion from above.

"Stay," Charles ordered and ran back toward his Caddy. A second later his voice rose in surprise, he spoke the name that had frustrated them the long day past. "Shannon?"

"Let me go, dammit!"

Gordon ran toward the commotion, praying his daughter would be with her. She was not.

"Calm down," Charles said, holding her by the arms, straining to keep hold as she struggled against him. "Shannon, calm down. I've been looking for you. I'm here to help!"

"Let me go, bastard!" she shrieked. She freed one arm, and struck at Charles with more force than her trim frame suggested. Charles stumbled back, lost his hold on her, and she broke free. She ran toward the park and stopped just short of running into Gordon.

"Where's Charity?" he demanded. "Where's my girl?"

"Who are you?" she said, and stepped back from him.

There was recognition in her eyes. He thought she could see the resemblance, but had trouble believing it.

Charles stayed where he was, watching the unfolding drama, ready to move.

"I'm Gordon Chambers, Charity's father," he said.

The transformation was instant, her tight fearful features melted into wonder, then relief. She stumbled forward and fell against him. He caught her clumsily, and held her.

She clung to him, not crying, not laughing, but something between the two, some painful hybrid of joy and terror gripped her. "You came for her," she said. "Thank God you came."

Gordon held her for a second before pushing her away, forcing her to stand on her own. "Where is Charity?"

"I tried to stop her," Shannon said. "I wanted to protect her from him until we could find you, but she got away."

"Where?" he interrupted.

"Down there," she said, pointing to the park. "She ran away to Feral Park. We have to stop her before she gets into the playground. It's not safe."

Gordon turned and ran toward the park. Shannon and Charles followed. As he broke through the cover into the park he saw her, his Charity, emerge from the hanging willow limbs on the other side of the park. The three children met her, enfolded her in a protective triangle, and walked her toward the playground.

"Charity," Gordon screamed.

Chapter 16

He can't get you in Feral Park, Jenny told Charity, only her mouth didn't move. Her voice, cold, confident, comforting, spoke inside Charity's head, accompanied by the image of him, standing alone at the playground's threshold, unable to see or hear anything within.

"He can't follow you in there," one of the boys said, a tall wiry kid with spiked black hair. He was maybe a year older than Charity.

"We have the power here," the other boy, shorter, plumper, and blond, said. "He'll never find you inside."

"Never?" Charity asked. She knew it was true, sensed it was, but needed to hear it.

"Ever," the three said in tandem.

Welcome, Charity.

They moved around her in a triangle of which Jenny was the tip, and guided her toward the playground, their Neverland. Charity let herself move with them. She heard the crash above, broken glass and protesting metal, but the sound of the music swallowed it and the party continued.

"Wild, isn't it?" the blond boy said. "Anthrax kicks ass!"

"What's Anthrax?" Charity asked.

"It's life," he said with a grin.

"Forget him," the tall boy said. "Danzig is life."

"Hey, girl," someone said from the wooden turret that overlooked the playground. It was a young voice, high-pitched and sexless, its owner hidden in shadow.

"Rock on!" A teenage boy on a swing shouted, his deep-ening voice cracking on the last word, drawing snickers from all around.

"*Charity!*" The owner of that voice was distant, familiar but unimportant, a voice from another world.

"Charity, stop!"

Shannon?

She followed its shrill echo through the darkness and saw Shannon running through the dark toward her. With Shannon were two men. Not her brother Jared, he was dead, but a big black-skinned stranger and someone she knew.

"Who is he?" she asked Jenny dreamily. "Why do I know him?"

He's not important. He let the Bogey Man take you away. Forget him.

"She's my friend," Charity said, pointing toward Shannon. "She saved me."

We're your friends. She can't help you. Join us.

Charity turned back to the playground as the adults neared it. "If I get away, will he kill her?"

Does it matter? She's just another Bogey—if he doesn't eat you, she will.

"We hate Bogeys," the tall boy said through clenched teeth. "They come in here, we do *this* to 'em," he shifted the broom-handle spear forward and jabbed it into the ground.

"Kill the Bogeys," came a shout from the playground. "Stick 'em through their guts!"

"Kill the Bogeys, kill the Bogeys, stick 'em through the guts. Kill the Bogeys, kill the Bogeys, stick 'em through the guts," a chorus from the playground. Every child rose from their spots brandishing crudely fashioned spears, knives, hammers, and clubs. They scaled the bared wall and poured over the side into the high grass. They surrounded Shannon and one of the men she was with in a quick, deadly circle and steadied their weapons to strike.

Charity saw the look of terror in Shannon's eyes, and saw herself in it. She went cold, her heart quickened. Then she saw the man's face and her heart nearly stopped.

Daddy?

"*Daddy!*" she screamed, and broke from the triangle.

Come back, Jenny called to her.

"Stop," she screamed. "Please!"

They wouldn't; they stood in their circle around Shannon and Gordon, weapons raised. Waiting.

Kill the Bogeys!

The night exploded around them, the deafening whip-crack sound of gunshots from above. *Crack, crack, crack,* and Charles rushed the circle of homicidal kids. "*Back away or I'll blow your heads off!*"

They scattered through the grass, into the shadows, into the park, as if they were never there. The playground was empty and silence stole the night.

Shannon stayed back as Gordon rushed to his daughter, swept her from the ground in a strong and tearful hug.

A moment later Charles stood next to her, smiling, bewildered. "I'll be damned," he said. "A happy ending."

"Indeed." A disembodied voice, the voice of the night itself, filled Feral Park. It came from everywhere, from nowhere. "Charity, my precious little girl. You've been bad." He appeared in the close distance, coming from the direction of the highway, and moved toward them with purpose. "I'm your daddy now, Charity. You have forgotten."

Charity buried her face in Gordon's chest and screamed.

Shannon stumbled backward toward them and joined Charity's chorus.

Gordon held his daughter tight, gaping at the monster that approached.

"Get her out of here!" Charles shouted. He pulled his revolver, only three rounds left, and aimed it at the walking nightmare. *Stop there or I'll shoot!*

The dark man-shadow didn't slow, and Charles fired. He was a crack shot, he knew, from years of practice and a handful of altercations in his line of work, but the approaching man didn't slow. Charles fired again, and the slug passed through him like through a fog. He kept walking.

Charles turned to see the three of them still there. "Move your asses!" he screamed. "Get her out of here now!" When he turned back, the Bogey Man was upon him. He fired again, point-blank, but the monster only laughed.

Charles screamed as the thing reached through him, like smoke through a screen, then it grabbed him from the inside and began to twist. It pulled him close, his dark, sweating face touching its darker face, a black shape with burning eyes and grinding teeth. Charles could feel the hands inside him, burrowing, reaching, gripping deep within. Then it tore him in two, and his last scream echoed as he fell halved into the grass.

"She's mine!" the monster bellowed. "Give her back!"

Gordon ran blind through the stunted trees on the wild side of the park, Charity a dead weight in his arms. She had fainted. Finally back in her daddy's arms, she'd allowed herself the luxury of weakness and just let go.

Shannon fought to keep up. The growth thinned quickly as their path sloped toward the river. Soon the trail would be gone and only the treacherously rocky shoreline would remain. "The road," she yelled.

Gordon ignored her, continued to run.

She knew he would run them into the river if she let him. "The path is up there," she said, pushing hard not to fall behind.

"What?"

"The trail's ending," she said. "If we keep going this way the rocks will slow us down. If we get to the road we can go back for my car."

He held to his straight path for a few moments then veered toward the highway. "Can we make it?"

"I don't know," she said, wishing for the flashlight she had stupidly left back in Crazy Ernie's cellar. "If he followed us through the woods we might, but it's the only way to outrun him."

They broke through the last of the foliage, straddled the guardrail, and found the pavement.

Shannon saw the small flashlight still hanging from Charity's wrist and slipped it off. She tested it; the beam sliced a path before them. "This way," she said, leading them down the shoulder of the highway.

"*Give her back!*" The voice came not from behind, but from the side, somewhere in the trees. She turned the beam toward the sound of his voice as she ran, and was rewarded with a pained scream. She saw him briefly—one of a hundred shadows, as the light cut him. Then he was gone.

"*Give her back, she's mine!*"

"No," Gordon screamed, and pushed himself harder.

Shannon struggled to stay beside him.

Then he was standing before them on the shoulder. "Give me back my Charity or I'll gut you while she watches!"

Shannon skidded to a stop, slipped in the gravel, and fell against the guardrail. Gordon stopped and did nothing as the Bogey Man's gaze fell upon him.

Then the light came, and behind it the diesel roar of an eighteen-wheeler. It turned the corner, came straight at them, air horn blatting. For a moment he was a perfect silhouette, then he was gone. The truck hugged the far shoulder as it passed them, its horn giving one last angry blast as it disappeared into the night.

Shaking off the unnatural chill that had frozen him, Gordon turned and found Shannon unconscious on the shoulder, blood flowing from a cut near her temple. He knelt to see if she was breathing and out of the corner of his eyes saw a small crouched figure behind the guardrail. It stood, a crude two-by-four club raised to the sky, and after a shock of pain he fell into the deepest, blackest sleep he had ever known.

Charity awoke lying in the dirt. The blond boy stood over her.

"Wake up, pretty girl," he said. "I can't carry you all the way."

Charity rose searching, and said, "Where are they?"

The boy's face tightened into a look of disgust. "They dropped you here and ran away," he said. "They don't care what happens to you. They're not even Bogeys, they're chickens."

Charity closed her eyes, put her face in her hands, and wept silently. When the boy grabbed her hand and led her back to Feral Park, she didn't resist.

"Hurry," he said. "The Bogey Man's coming back for you. He'll get us both if we don't hurry!"

"I know," she whispered, and ran with him. In her sadness, fear became secondary. They had left her, Shannon and her daddy had left her.

As the trees thickened, her heart hardened. Shannon said

she would protect her, but she had left Charity behind to save herself. The man with her probably wasn't even her daddy. Her daddy wouldn't have left her.

Jenny was right—the wild ones were all she had now. Feral Park was her home.

"I hate you," she said to them, and though she knew it wasn't true, the words gave her strength. *"I hate you, I hate you, I hate you!"* Her new mantra, and she knew if she said it enough she could mean it. They were her feral words, and now she understood what feral really was. It was telling the world to fuck off.

Her feet pounded dirt and she broke through the last veil of hanging willow branches, her new home at Feral Park dead ahead.

"I hate you!"

"Someday you will love me," he said, and she saw him coming, a formless thing in the night, moving through the sky toward them, his heat warping the reality around him. *"Until then I will teach you to mind me!"*

"Go!" the blond boy yelled. *"Hurry!"*

Charity made it to the playground. Alone.

She turned and saw them, the Bogey Man holding the blond boy by his throat, lifting him off the ground toward his waiting mouth.

The boy kicked at him, pounded at his arms with tiny fists, then went limp as the Bogey Man stole his gaze.

The Bogey Man opened his mouth, teeth parting in an impossibly wide grin. His jaw stretched, his face tipped up to the sky, and with a final scream the boy went in, struggling, feet kicking air until he was gone.

Darkness folded around her like a blanket—warm, safe darkness. Not sleep, but something else. It swallowed her like the Bogey Man had the boy, and she was gone.

★ ★ ★ ★ ★

He couldn't see her, couldn't smell her, couldn't sense her anywhere.

Charity was gone.

The Bogey Man howled with rage at his lost prize, and all over Riverside children cried out as the thing crouching in their closets, hiding under their beds, pounced them from their sleep.

Chapter 17

The boy lay in bed, eyes wide open and staring across the room at his closed closet door. He had closed it himself before climbing into bed, latched it firmly and piled toys around its base so it couldn't swing open in the night.

A little before midnight, when he was the only one in the house still awake, it opened, just as he knew it would; as it had every night for the past few weeks.

The face inside, disembodied but undeniably real, grinned at him. A shark's grin. When it spoke, its voice seemed to come from everywhere around him.

"How's my boy tonight?" it asked, and the question sent shivers up his body. "I see you stayed up for me again. Such a good boy you are."

The boy pulled the slick satin sheets that his mother insisted he use over his head and clenched his eyes shut. Then he felt the warm spray as he pissed himself. It pooled around his butt, spreading across the expensive sheets, and soaked into the mattress. The sick ammonia smell made him gag, but he dared not uncover himself.

He began to cry, and all around him that disembodied voice that only he could hear, moaned with laughter.

Then laughter became a howl of rage, and the thing in the closet pounced.

Gordon awoke and heard the scream from his dream

echoing through the night. The face above him was a blur, and when it moved closer, he cried out, once again the little boy who peed his bed and hid under satin sheets.

"Hey," the voice of a woman said. "It's me."

"Shannon," he said. When he sat up, his head spun, vertigo overcame him, and Shannon had to hold him up. His head throbbed and burned. He felt a warm tackiness running down his face and neck. He touched the side of his head, where the kid had hit him with the board, and it came away sticky.

After a few moments his vision cleared, the spinning stopped, and Shannon came into focus. She sported a nasty cut where the kid had hit her; dried blood matted her hair. "Where's Charity?" she asked, giving Gordon a little shake to make sure he was still awake.

"I don't know," he said, sweeping her hands from him. "The kid who whacked us must have taken her back to the park."

They stood together, helping and holding each other until they were solid on their feet. Shannon remembered the flashlight and searched near the guardrail. She found it and whispered her relief when it worked.

"That way," Gordon said, pointing into the trees.

Shannon led the way, flashlight glaring, casting grotesque shadows, and Gordon followed. They found the club the boy had used against them only a few feet down the trail. They followed the trail, scanning the trees around them. Above them, distant, the sound of thunder, and several seconds later a flash lit the sky. Rain fell, patters on the leaves all around them, like tiny footsteps. They ran, finally breaking through into Feral Park. It too was empty.

"Where did she go?" Gordon whispered hard in frustration.

"In there," Shannon said, and pointed the beam into the playground, creating more shadows, shadows that seemed to shift and merge while she watched.

"It's empty. She's not there!"

"It's never empty," Shannon said as she walked toward it. She dug into a pocket with her free hand and pulled her daughter's locket out by the chain. "Watch."

Gordon stepped close to her and watched without comment. He had no skepticism left.

Shannon stepped to the entrance of the park and tossed the locket inside. It landed in the old wood chip path and lay there. Above it the rope bridge shifted, its shadow moving with it. The shadow covered the locket, and when it withdrew, the locket was gone.

Something flew out at them, landing at Gordon's feet. A wallet. He picked it up, opened it, and saw Charles's face staring up at him from the picture on his driver's license.

Go away!

A voice from inside the park, but not spoken aloud. Shannon looked at Gordon, found him looking back. They had both heard it.

"What *is* this place?"

"I don't know," Shannon said. "I think she's safe in there, though. That's why she came."

Distantly, they heard the sound of sirens.

"Let's go," she said, and pulled him away from the playground.

Though the danger was over for now, their night had barely begun.

PART III
Feral Park

Chapter 18

Charity had to blink repeatedly before she believed what she saw around her. It was the playground, but not as it was from the outside. The darkness within the playground was deeper than the darkness without. A single bright torch burned, lighting the inside unevenly. The torch was set into the sandbox, the bright flame dancing with an inner life. It did not burn the wood it surrounded, as if sustained from some other fuel. The girl who had met her at the edge of the park sat beside it, close enough that the heat should have burned her.

The flame did not cast her shadow.

"He got Jesse." In here she had a voice. It was soft, sure, and emotionless.

Charity nodded her head. She didn't know what to say.

"I guess he was too slow this time. I should have sent Toni."

The tall, dark-haired boy with the spear appeared, like a bodyguard. He stood next to the girl, smiled, and nodded. Pointing at Charity's belt, he said, "Nice."

Charity looked down and saw the bloody scissors still slid through her belt loop, tucked snug under the belt.

"Did you take those from him?" The girl looked at the scissors, her tone flat but inquisitive.

"Yes," Charity said, putting a guarding hand over them. "I took them. Why?" She backed away a step, suddenly afraid they would take them from her, her one small victory over the Bogey Man who had taken everything away from her.

"We won't take them," the boy, Toni, said. "I'm just impressed is all. I mean . . . wow!"

"We know who he is," the girl said. "He's King of the Bogeys. He's come through here before, I've seen him." She stepped away from the sandbox, toward Charity, and the bright glow the torch cast on her went with her, clinging to her like a cloud of bright dust. "We can see him, but he can't see us. He's blind to us in here."

"Motherfucker doesn't have a clue," Toni said. "But he doesn't like it here." He laughed, a sound calculated to sound tough and carefree. Charity thought he was trying to impress her. "The Big Bad Bogey was too chickenshit to follow you in."

"He's vulnerable here, he felt it." The girl took another step toward Charity, and in the blink of an eye they were standing face-to-face.

Charity flinched but didn't back away. She didn't feel any threat from this girl. She felt almost like a sister.

"I'm Jenny," she said. "I'm glad you came back." She turned away and, taking the torch from the sand, walked past the sandbox, past the swing set, past where the playground should have ended. The iron bar wall that surrounded the park from the outside was gone. There was only darkness above them; where there should have been a sky was a blank nothing. There was no background; the park was gone, the river was gone, the monstrous willow trees and the highway and mountain beyond, the nocturnal glow of Riverside, all gone. There was nothing outside the torchlight but a black absence, as if the light of the flame sustained this place, and if it were to burn out, the playground would fade away.

A narrow path marked by the glow that surrounded Jenny

like a nimbus led through the darkness, to a place she couldn't see.

"C'mon," Toni said urgently. "Let's go." He grabbed Charity's hand, and exhausted as she was, sad, and hurt, and totally overwhelmed, she felt her heart quicken at his touch. She saw him smile awkwardly, as if he felt the same thing.

Charity let him lead her, running until they caught up with Jenny. When they slowed, she turned around. No playground. There was only darkness. She raised a hand gingerly, reached out to where Jenny's glow ended, and Toni grabbed her arm.

"Don't do that," he said gently. "You fall into the Never and you won't come back."

"Oh," she said. "Okay." She kept her hand close to her side, the other one still holding Toni's. Jenny walked silently in front of them; even her movements were perfectly silent. Where Charity and Toni's feet made soft scuffing sounds against the dirt, Jenny's did not.

They walked for a few minutes, before them nothing but the flat darkness that Toni called "the Never." A second later they stepped into a vast cavern of light. The strange, fast music and a din of loud conversation slammed her ears. All the kids from the park were here, and when they saw Jenny leading Charity and Toni into their midst, everything stopped. The song they listened to ended in mid-chorus, and they waited.

Torches lit the inside of the cavern, the high stone walls, and the dirty stone floor. The torches were everywhere, probably close to two dozen, Charity guessed, spread out so their even glow touched every surface. Most were stabbed into the ground, supported by small mounds of stone; some were stuck into crevices in the wall a few feet up from the ground. There was no ceiling, just another great blank spot. At the far end of the cavern was an opening, a narrow cave. Torchlight touched it enough to see a foot into it, where it ended abruptly. Beyond was more of the Never.

Most of the activity centered around one torch, its flame extinguished. It sat at the left hand of a strange rock formation at the base of the wall. It looked like a throne to Charity, with two smaller seats on either side of it. On the right another torch burned brightly. Toni let go of Charity's hand and walked to the right of the throne, standing next to it.

Jenny walked to the throne, the crowd of filthy children parting quietly around her. She set the end of her torch, which burned brighter than the others, into a niche at the front of the throne, and sat down. When she was seated, Toni sat down too, and the rest of the kids gathered around Charity.

They watched her, intense stares making her squirm. After several awkward moments Jenny spoke. "We have a new friend today. You gonna say 'hi' or what?"

Cheers broke out at that, and Charity was pummeled by dozens of patting hands. The cave erupted in a gale of laughter and welcomes. The music started again, an old song she recognized because her mother had liked it.

Hello! Hooray! Let the show begin, I've been ready!

Then the chanting of a single word filled the cavern.

"Choose, choose, choose, choose!" It went on for several seconds. Feet stomped in time. Boards, spears, and knives were thrust into the air for punctuation.

Jenny stood, held up a hand, and the cave quieted again.

"Who will sit at my left hand?" she asked.

Several names rang through the cave, but one rang out above the rest, the name Ginger.

"Ginger," Jenny said. *"Come on down!"*

A broad, dark-haired girl burst from the crowd, whooping

aloud and waving her weapon in the air—a gun, taken from the black man they had found torn apart in the grass. She stopped before Jenny's throne and faced the crowd, her freckled face flushed with excitement. "I got the gun!" she yelled.

There were cheers from some in the crowd and silence from others. Ginger glared at several of the silent in the raggedy throng until their unenthusiastic cheers joined the others.

"It has to be a choice," Jenny said. Her words had the ring of formality, or ritual. Other names were tossed out, though with less enthusiasm. At Jenny's right hand, Toni stood suddenly and his voice rose above all.

"Charity!"

Gasps, silence, disbelieving looks. The crowd drew back from her.

"Her?" Ginger looked Charity up and down with a frown. "She's new! She doesn't even have a torch yet. She's not one of us!"

"Look at what she has," Toni shouted to the crowd, ignoring Ginger. He pointed at the blood-crusted scissors under her belt.

There were a few "ohs," a few pointing fingers and admiring stares. Most still looked doubtful. Charity wanted to go but she was frozen, pinned down by the dozens of scrutinizing eyes. She pulled the scissors out and slid her hand through the cold grip, squeezing.

"What?" Ginger said, and laughed. "So she swiped some scissors from her mom's sewing box. Who gives a shit?" She waved the gun over her head again. "Look what I have!"

"You took it from a corpse," Toni said. "Charity took those from the King of the Bogeys."

The smile on Ginger's face vanished, her thunder stolen.

Suddenly no one was watching her. All eyes were on Charity, and one by one they drew closer to her, staring at her like she was some kind of Super Kid.

My very first fan club, she thought.

"Charity, come on down," Jenny said. When she didn't move, those behind her pushed her forward. She stumbled to a stop beside Ginger, who had tucked the gun back into her pants and stood pouting with her arms folded across her chest.

"You've been called out to replace the one we lost earlier," Jenny explained.

Charity thought it was strange the others hadn't asked about Jesse, the blond boy who evidently sat at the left hand of this ghostly child queen. Jenny wouldn't even speak his name now; he was just *The One We Lost.*

"Do you know why you were picked?" Jenny asked.

Charity said nothing, felt incapable of speech, just shook her head no.

"Because you kick ass," someone shouted from the crowd, and the cheers started again.

"Because, like Ginger, you are strong," Jenny said.

"I don't want to be picked," Charity said to a dozen startled gasps, and stepped back from the throne. She gave Toni a questioning look, and he stared down at his feet.

"But you are," Jenny said, as if that settled it, and Charity supposed it did.

"But she's not one of us yet," Ginger yelled at the girl on the throne, her face flushed with anger.

There were more gasps from the crowd of kids, followed by silence. Jenny looked down at her, and in a tone that invited no argument, she said, "She will be!"

Ginger went pale, nodded, and was silent. From his spot at Jenny's right hand, Toni smirked and looked away.

"Tomorrow we will tell her about Feral Park, and us. Toni will teach her," Jenny said to silent nods of approval. "When she *is* one of us, she and Ginger will decide who sits with me." There were more nods, a few murmurs, gleams of excitement in the eyes of the children.

"Decide," Charity said uneasily.

Ginger smiled at her and patted the stock of the gun jammed into her pocket. Then she stepped into the breaking crowd, kids drifting to every corner of the massive cavern, and Charity stood alone.

For the next few hours she was something of a curiosity, and though it made her uncomfortable, Charity tried to be nice. Some asked her questions about her life, and about the Bogey Man, who they called *the King of the Bogeys*. She didn't like that term; it implied that all adults were like him, only lesser monsters. She supposed it was correct, though. Shannon and her father, her own father, had abandoned her to the Bogey Man. The kids here had saved her; Jesse had died trying to save her. Jenny, whom Charity thought of as Queen of the Brats, had lost her left-hand man, or boy, saving her. Maybe she was supposed to be picked then, maybe she owed it to them. She didn't want to. She had finally escaped, but into what?

At length the kids, starting with the younger ones, wandered each to a torch, *their* torch she assumed, and laid down to sleep. She didn't have one yet, maybe because she wasn't officially one of them. She grew cold, having no torch to lie down next to, so she found a spot and lay down alone, shivering.

She was almost asleep when Toni appeared next to her.

"C'mon," he said, and grabbed her arm, helping her up from her cold, granite bed.

"Where are we going?" she asked.

"Over here where it's warm," he said.

Charity pulled her hand from his grasp and crossed her arms. "No thanks, I'll stay over here." She gave him a cold look, then turned around and walked away.

"Hey," he said, indignant. "What's up?" He caught her arm again, and flinched a little when she turned and looked him in the face.

"I'm mad at you," she said, and pulled her arm back. "I just got here and I'm already getting into trouble because of you!"

Kids glanced up from their resting places, watching the two speculatively.

He shook his head and smiled. *The crooked grin of a born troublemaker,* she thought. There was something about it, though, and she couldn't stay mad at him. He grabbed her hand, gently. "We need to talk about it, and I'd rather do it over there away from everybody."

Charity let him lead her. They walked to his stone ledge seat beside Jenny's throne, and he lifted the light from its holder with his free hand. About ten feet farther down the wall they stopped. He wedged the butt of his torch into a crack where ground and wall met, then sat. Charity sat beside him.

This part of the cavern was empty; no kids camped out along the wall where the queen sat. They were as alone as they were going to get.

"Okay," she said, "what's going on?"

"I can't tell you yet," he said. "That starts tomorrow. I can tell you about Ginger, though, and why I picked you."

Charity crossed her arms over her chest again, wanting to be mad at him, and mad at herself because she couldn't be. "I'm listening."

"Nobody much likes Ginger, but a lot of the other kids are afraid of her." He peeked over his shoulder, making sure no one was close enough to listen. "I guess that's why they picked her. We may be free here, but only as free as we allow ourselves to be, and a lot of them still think authority should be scary."

"Yes," Charity prompted, still unsure where she fit in.

"She's more than scary, though, she's mean, and not very smart. If she ends up being Jenny's left hand, things down here could get bad."

"But why me?"

Heads turned toward them from across the room. Jenny watched the exchange with detached interest.

"Shh," Toni said with a grimace. "Because you're stronger than she is. You escaped from the King Bogey. And," he added, his face reddening slightly, "you're nicer than she is."

"You don't know that," Charity said. "You don't even know me."

"Yes, I do," he said. "I know you enough. I trust my instincts about you." He looked at her now, deep into her eyes as if probing, and she looked away.

She saw Ginger sitting next to her own torch, the gun tucked into the front of her pants, glaring at them. She tapped the stalk of the gun with anxious fingers.

Maybe I'll get lucky and she'll shoot herself playing with it, Charity thought. "She's gonna shoot me, Toni. Stupid or not, she has the gun."

"Can you count?" Toni asked, more than a hint of sarcasm showing.

"Yes, I can count!"

"Good," Toni said. "Do it then!"

"What do you mean?"

145

He shook his head. "I can't say any more. It's against the rules. You're smart," he said. "You'll figure it out."

For a while they said nothing, and though she was tired she didn't want to sleep yet. Toni was tired as well; his eyes slipped shut every few minutes. The broken conversation in the cavern dissipated as the kids dropped off. Even Ginger slept, her hand resting on the gun in her lap.

"I'm sorry about Jesse," Charity said softly.

At once Toni was wide-awake, his eyes blazing. He grabbed her arm and pulled her so close his lips nearly touched her ear. "Don't say that name again," he whispered harshly. "His flame burned out. He doesn't exist anymore."

"Okay," she said, a little embarrassed, and suddenly a little scared. "Sorry." She looked around nervously, but no one else had heard.

He released her arm, frowning. "I'm sorry," he said. "It's just bad luck—to talk about the dead, you know."

"Toni?"

"Yes."

"Why did you come here?"

There was a long pause, long enough to make her think she had crossed another unknown line, that there would be no answer. Then he spoke.

"Maybe later," he said. He rested against the wall and drifted off.

She scooted against the wall next to him, careful not to touch him, and let her eyes close. She was too tired to fight it now. Sleep would have her, and no matter how safe from *Him* she was here, she didn't know where her dreams would take her tonight.

Sometime later she awoke from dreams of running and she heard quiet sobbing echoing through the cavern. She opened her heavy eyelids, turned her head with an effort toward the sound, but Toni was in the way. It was coming from their left, from the rock throne where Jenny sat.

She turned her head again and saw a few of the others had awakened. They watched the throne with wide eyes. A few were crying themselves, silent tears. Ginger was awake too— she lay on the ground, head resting on a balled-up coat, and watched Jenny without emotion.

She wanted to awaken Toni and ask him what was going on, but hated to disturb him, he slept so peacefully. She turned toward the throne and tried to sit forward, but didn't have the strength. After a few moments she gave up. The noise that had awakened her fell to the back of her mind, and her eyes slipped shut. Soon she dreamt again, of running— and crying.

When Charity awoke it was dark as before, but the growing bustle of activity made her think it was morning. Her stomach cramped with hunger. That was when she first considered the very real problem of her survival down here, and what she was going to eat.

Toni was nowhere near. After scanning the cavern Charity found him with a group of six kids on the other side of the room. He saw her coming and waved. The others looked. Some hid grins behind cupped hands; others didn't bother to hide their grins. With a few parting words that she couldn't hear in the growing commotion, he met her halfway.

"Morning," he said with a smile.

"Is it?"

"I think so." He shrugged. "Guess we'll find out soon anyway."

What did that mean? she wondered. *Are we going out?*

"I'm kinda hungry," she said, hoping it didn't sound too

much like a whine. Her stomach tightened again, and she clamped her hands over it.

"We're going out on a food run. Wanna come with?"

She was about to say *sure,* but Jenny was suddenly standing beside them. "No," Jenny said. "She's not ready to go out yet."

Toni looked thoughtful for a moment, then conceded silently with a nod that was almost a bow.

Charity did not. She looked back and forth between Toni and Jenny, her face reddening. "Excuse me," she said. "I've been a prisoner for as long as I can remember. I won't be locked up again!" She expected this to anger Jenny, possibly get her kicked out. She was beginning to worry about this place and her strange company, but she didn't want to get kicked out. As strange as it was, it was a safe place. It was a place the Bogey Man couldn't see or reach. Still, she couldn't help but be upset as these two casually made decisions about where she could go and what she could do.

Jenny reached out and brushed Charity with a cold hand. "We are not your keepers," she said gently. "We're your friends."

"And friends look out for each other," Toni finished. "Jenny's right. It was stupid of me to ask."

The group of kids Toni had been talking to were restless, ready to move. "Hurry it up," a skinny blonde girl with a tie-dyed shirt urged.

Charity looked between Toni and Jenny again, shrugged her shoulders and sighed. " 'Kay," she said, resigned. "How long am I *stuck?*"

"Not long," Jenny said, her attention to the subject fading. She drifted away to another part of the cavern on whatever strange business she had next.

Toni stepped closer and whispered, his lips almost touching her ear. "We'll talk later. I promise."

As the group walked toward the path which led to the playground, Toni leading the way with torch in hand, Charity saw Ginger watching her. Clutched in her hands like a trophy was a small black item, something Charity recognized from the first time she had run from the Bogey Man. She had seen people walking by her on a sidewalk punching buttons and talking to other people through it. A cell phone, probably taken from the same dead man as the gun. Ginger didn't seem to know what it was. She glared at Charity, the look in her eyes promising pain and humiliation.

Charity pulled the Bogey Man's scissors from her belt loop, gripped them like a dagger. She didn't want to hurt anyone but if Ginger tried to hurt her, she would rip the big girl's guts out.

She thought she understood now what Toni had meant when he asked her if she could count. She hoped her memory, and her count, could be trusted.

Chapter 19

Dirty Dave watched from his usual hiding place as the kids appeared at the playground's exit like dirty little genies from a bottle. They didn't usually come out in the daylight, it was too dangerous for them, but last night's bloodshed had kept them from going far. They would need food, so he had brought them some. He had also brought them another gift, a copy of Ozzy Osbourne's *Tribute* CD. He thought they would like that. He watched them as they approached his hiding place in the bushes, heart beating a little heavier as the distance between them shrank. They knew it was dangerous coming out in the daylight, but they were in more danger than they knew. They didn't know Feral Park was under the eyes of the police following the events of the previous night. Dirty Dave did. He couldn't let them go any further. When they were close enough that he could almost touch them, he stepped out of the bushes. He held the bags of scavenged fast food and the CD out to them like an offering.

They stopped. The boy, one of Jenny's boys, in the lead, watched him warily. He knew they knew him, but that didn't change their distrust. They danced the line between fight and flight for several moments before their leader spoke.

"What do you want, *Old Bogey?*"

Dave was not used to speaking; for years he had spoken to no one but himself. The first thing he had discovered about himself was that he was not good company. It was several seconds before he found his voice.

"I brought food," he gestured with the bags. "And music too." He crouched slowly, his arthritic limbs complaining all the way down, and laid the bags at his feet. He pulled the CD from the plastic bag and held it out to the boy in the way old men at the waterfront park in town held out pieces of bread to the half-tame marmots.

The boy's eyes lit up; all their eyes lit up.

"Cool," one of them whispered. "Ozzy!"

Their leader watched him uncertainly for a moment, then stepped forward and took it. "Thanks," he mumbled, almost against his will it seemed. The others rushed forward and scooped up the bags of food, grinning at their good luck.

Dave felt the tension loosen and grinned himself. It had been a long time since he had expressed that particular emotion, and it pleased him.

"Hey, you down there!"

The kids were frozen for a moment, all big eyes, out of their element and terrified. A dark, wet spot appeared and grew down the pant leg of one of the younger boys in the raiding party. Then they were off, and before Dave even turned to see who had shouted at them, the kids were halfway to the playground.

Dave didn't need to turn to know who it was. The police. He ran too, stiff legs pumping awkwardly, back complaining at the sudden jarring. His head pounded with the aftereffects of the previous night's dinner, half a bottle of Thunderbird. He ran toward the river, hoping to draw the cops away from the playground, also hoping to make it to the woods on the other side of the park where he had a chance of losing them.

"Freeze, motherfucker!" The cop was close behind, making up ground fast. As Dave climbed the slope to the levee, he saw two more cops running down the crumbling asphalt trail from town.

"Stop!" one of them yelled.

He ignored them and kept running. Sweat poured down his face, stinging his eyes. He reached the top where sun-baked grass turned to dirt and small chunks of stray blacktop, where he found the trail and continued on. Seconds later he felt a hand on his shoulder, fingers digging for a hold on the dirty green fabric of his jacket, then slipping away.

"Stop, old man!" They were too quick. Dave knew he couldn't outrun them, but he couldn't stop. He screamed. It was a high meaningless noise of frustration. A second later a hand grabbed the collar of his jacket and yanked him to the ground.

"Fucking pervert," one of the young cops said under his breath, just loud enough for him to hear. He felt something long and smooth and hard come down on the top of his head, splitting his shaggy scalp down the middle. It made a sound like a metal pipe hitting wood, and there was a dull ringing in his head. The pain was so much and so sudden he could taste it. He struggled against the hand that held him, and there was another blow on the side of his head, above the temple.

For a second there was perfect darkness, then his face pressed against the blacktop. The taste of pain mingled with the salty taste of blood. It felt like they had busted his head wide open; he was sure if he tried to stand up his brains would pour out onto the trail. Blood ran down his face, into his eyes.

"You dirty son-of-a-bitch," the cop on top of him said with real venom. "What did you plan on doing with those kids? Huh?" He punctuated the question with a wilting blow to the side, just below the ribcage where it was tender.

Dave groaned in pain. He hadn't the strength to scream. He felt the world swirling away fast, like bloody water down a drain.

"Enough, Harris," another voice said. "That's enough, damn it. Go find the kids. They went toward the playground."

After that there was nothing but rolling waves of blackness. There was no pain, no sound, and no sensation. For a short time Dirty Dave thought he was dead, and the only thing he knew was rest.

The feral kids watched the cop from inside the playground on perches of wood and rusted metal; they could see him but he could not see them. This cop had beat the old man who brought them food and music.

"Wait," Toni growled from his place atop the rope bridge. "Let him come." They had left their weapons in the playground when they went out, in the sandbox next to Toni's torch. Now they had them again.

The cop trotted through tall grass and thistles, nightstick in hand, and stopped inside the playground entrance. "What the hell?" he said, scratching the back of his neck with the nightstick.

Toni walked the rope bridge, rocking it, and stopped above the cop. "Hey, Pig."

"Huh?" The cop looked up sharply, his expression puzzled. Toni grinned and stuck his tongue out. This guy might be a cop, but he was still a Bogey. He rocked the bridge, kept the cop looking up, searching above in confusion. He was close enough that Toni could read the plastic nametag pinned above his breast pocket, Harris, but the Bogey couldn't see him.

The others gathered slowly, morning shadows closing around the cop.

Toni let the rocking bridge settle, then stop.

Harris looked around, behind, but saw nothing.

"Kill," Toni shouted, and the shadow circle closed in. They covered Harris like a blanket. The cop's scream rang out for an instant, and then he was silent.

With a savage howl Toni dropped into the center of the shadow circle, his spear leading the way.

A few minutes later the shadow broke up, dissolved in the sun. The kids were gone. Officer Harris was gone. The wood-chip-covered ground was soaked in blood.

Dirty Dave heard the brief scream from the playground. It broke through the thin crust of sleep, bringing back the pain in his head and the feel of dirty pavement pressed to his cheek. His eyes opened slowly, the lids tacky with blood. He saw the other officer's feet pounding away from him.

"Where are you, Harris?" he called. "What's going on down there?"

The man disappeared down the dike's grassed slope toward Feral Park, and Dave was alone. He tried to rise but his hands were cuffed tightly behind his back, and he was too weak to fight his way up.

Time passed. Dave turned his head so he could watch the calm waters of the Snake River. More time passed, not much, but it seemed long because he couldn't move. He became drowsy and let his eyes slip shut. He thought he probably had a concussion; if he fell asleep he might not awake, but he didn't care.

If the river is the last thing I see, I'll die blessed, he thought.

Then someone kneeled down next to him, leaned over him. There was a jingle of keys and a metallic *snick* as the lock turned and the cuffs released his hands. He let his arms fall to the pavement, waited with gritted teeth for the sudden cramping in his shoulders to relax.

"Thanks," he said, but got no reply. He turned his head, though it hurt like hell to do so, and watched the boy disappear down the slope. A pair of police-issue gun belts hung low on his hips.

Dave saw the officer's blood-streaked badge laying on the blacktop inches from his face. His hand moved slowly toward it, closed over it.

The blood was still warm.

After a few minutes no one had come—not many people came by this blighted place anymore. He worked up the will to stand, and staggered off into the woods to lick his wounds.

He felt a pang of pity for the two officers but it was fleeting. Mostly he was grateful that he hadn't shared their fate. He had watched those kids for a long time and he knew that their sizes and ages didn't mean a thing. They had gone feral, like a pack of abandoned dogs. They might have been human once, but now they were animals.

They were merciless.

Chapter 20

"Is that all then, Mrs. Pitcher? Nothing else?"

"Nothing else," Shannon said with a sigh. "Look, I'm tired, and we've been through this already. If there isn't anything else, I'd like to get some rest."

She endured the lingering, come-hither-scumbag look that Sergeant Winter gave her until she could stand it no longer. Then she endured it some more. She wasn't under arrest—he had made that fact clear early into their interview. He had also made it clear he didn't believe she was telling him everything, and that her tentative freedom could easily disappear. They were in his office, not the interrogation room; Sharon figured she rated that much at least, being the sister of an ex-cop. She knew he didn't like her, mostly because she was her brother's sister and Winter had hated Jared.

The office was small and had no windows except for the single large pane that faced the bullpen. Its shades were drawn. The hard fluorescent lighting and white walls made the room uncomfortably bright, every speck of dust seemed magnified as it moved about on subtle currents.

"Are you positive there isn't anything you would like to add, Mrs. Pitcher?" he asked again, his tone unabashedly sarcastic. "You know, expound upon?" He drummed his fingers against the surface of his cluttered desk. A cup of coffee sat forgotten at one corner. A dead fly drifted across the surface of the dark liquid.

He kept his eyes on her, never looking away, never seeming to blink. He was waiting for her to screw up and change the story. He had offered to let her bring in a lawyer before the questioning, but she declined. She didn't want to prolong the informal interrogation, and a lawyer would have cost her time. She knew she hadn't screwed up; the story she and Gordon agreed upon in the park as the police arrived was simple and fell in line with what he had told them earlier. She knew what Winter was trying to do. Jared had explained the technique to her; wear them down with hours of repeated questioning, exhausting the interviewee until they couldn't remember their own middle name.

"Nothing," she said. "My story isn't going to change, Sergeant Winter. It's the truth." She pointed to the cup at the edge of the table, an exhausted grin touching her lips. "You're not drinking that, are you?"

Sergeant Winter looked into the cup, grimaced, and looked back at her. "Nothing else," he said with a wave of the hand. "Get out of here."

Shannon was happy to oblige.

"Don't leave town," he said as she opened the door.

She nodded and closed it behind her with an immeasurable sense of relief.

Gordon waited on a bench in the lobby, slouched, hands cupped behind his head, eyes closed. He had talked to Sergeant Winter before Shannon, but his interview was shorter. Outside the office the lights were dim, easier on the eyes. The walls were also white, but cleaner, the desks tidier, the faces friendlier.

She weaved through the bullpen traffic, office personnel and a few street cops. The dispatch, Lillian, Jared's nearly fatal fling, gave Shannon a wary look as she rushed toward Sergeant Winter's office. "Bitch," Shannon muttered. She heard a few scattered snickers as she crossed the lobby. They all knew Lillian had been fucking her brother. Shannon wondered who she was fucking now.

"Wake up," she said, giving Gordon's shoulder a squeeze.

Gordon's eyes popped open, foggy white orbs shot with red. The heavy rise and fall of his chest belied his comfortable position. His face went pale until he looked up at her and remembered where he was. He had been having a nightmare.

He sighed, a soul-deep sound, and stretched. "We finished?" he asked.

"Yeah," she said. "Let's get out of here."

Jared's car, Shannon's car now, sat in the parking lot in a row next to parked police cruisers. She supposed she was lucky they hadn't impounded it. Though they couldn't pin a specific crime on her, they could have impounded her car for illegal parking the night before. Charles's car had been impounded. It was in a fenced lot behind the station. She could see it as she unlocked her car door, sitting between an old white station wagon and green spray-painted jeep. The front quarter panel was bashed in where she had hit it the night before. The Chevelle was in better shape, the bumper dented and grill twisted out of shape, but it still ran like a champ. She unlocked the passenger door and Gordon climbed in.

"Where to?" she asked, starting the car.

"The Riverside. You know where that is?"

"Yeah."

She drove silently. It was a short trip through town, the morning traffic light. She looked over at him a few times, stealing quick glances. His gaze alternated between his lap and the sidewalk. He opened his mouth a few times as though to speak, but closed it again and continued his study of the downtown foot traffic.

She turned into the Riverside parking lot.

"Back there," Gordon said pointing to the gravel back alley lot. She whipped right into the alley and parked next to a lone car, an old, gray Mazda.

"Yours?" she said.

"Yeah. It's ugly but reliable," he said.

"How long will you stay?" she said.

"The room's paid for the rest of the week, I think." He moved to open the door, stopped, played with a piece of lint on his pant leg. "It's Charles's room, but . . ." he broke off into silence.

"How long?" she repeated more forcefully. She watched him. An old scar, a jagged white line that ran from temple to jawbone, contrasted sharply with his tanned face. His eyes met hers and she saw through the exhaustion, to the heart of the strength that lay beneath. The look in those eyes told her she should have known better.

"Until I get my Charity back," he said.

She nodded and averted her eyes, studied the moldy bricks on the motel's back wall, waiting for him to ask his question.

"Will you stay with me?" he asked, not a proposition, but a plea.

"Yes," she said. "I will." The question was a formality, but it had to be asked. They were in it together; with Jared and Charles dead, each was all the other had. They were all Charity had.

"I'm going to find her," Gordon said, and when Shannon regarded him, she saw that his eyes were focused on the dirty brick wall in front of them, or perhaps on nothing at all. He was talking to himself, trying to reassure himself. Or maybe it was an oath.

"We will," she said, and killed the engine.

★ ★ ★ ★ ★

Shannon took a shower, long, hot, and relaxing. She felt better when it was over, as if some psychic dirt from the past few days had been washed away. Her clothes seemed to have retained the residue of fear and pain along with the marks of sweat and dirt. Dressing in them seemed a step backward; she would have liked a fresh change, but couldn't bring herself to go back to the house. That would be even worse.

She stretched out on the room's single bed while Gordon showered, and was asleep ten minutes later when he stepped out of the bathroom in clean clothes, still toweling the water from his hair.

Despite the exhaustion her sleep was light. She retained a dreamy awareness of everything that happened when Gordon lay down next to her. He didn't touch her, but scooted close, taking comfort in her presence. When he was still, his breath a slow and barely audible rhythm next to her, she rolled toward him and put an arm around his waist, holding tight, feeling his heat, his essence. It calmed her into a deeper sleep.

When he took her hand, his fingers curling through hers, she responded with a squeeze. The warmth and strength of his hand was the last thing she felt before sinking into a sound and blessedly dreamless sleep.

Gordon had awakened when she curled into him, at first startled and confused, but not uncomfortable. It had been years since he was this close to a woman, and Shannon was a beautiful woman. Beneath the tangled hair, dust-caked and sweat-slick skin, and even in the darkness where he had first seen her, she had been beautiful. He hadn't known how beautiful she was until she had come from the bathroom clean, except for the old clothes she wore. He knew that under her clothes she was clean too.

When he had reached for her hand, he expected her to pull away and deny him the small comfort of her touch, but she did not. Whether conscious or not, she had returned the gesture.

This was the woman who had saved his Charity from the Bogey Man, and for that he already loved her. He knew it was foolish, dangerously distracting, but he hoped. If he had believed that there was a God above who listened to the thoughts and hopes of a man like him, he would have prayed that maybe he could hold her like this after, if, he found Charity. He knew it was a fool's dream, but as he fell into the darkness again, he dreamed it anyway.

"Tell me about yourself," Shannon said pouring them coffee from the room's small pot. Her heart jumped a little, her breath caught in her throat as Gordon stepped behind her, brushing her, and accepted his cup.

God, has it been that long?

"Not much to tell," he said with a shrug, brushing off the question.

Shannon turned, sipped coffee, and watched him as he walked to the shaded window and peeked outside. Gray sky, overcast and bloated with barely-held moisture, peeked back in at them. Inside was cool, outside would be hot and muggy, the air like a thick, wet blanket.

She watched as he stared into the fading daylight, perhaps seeing Charity's face in the contours of the clouds, perhaps hearing her voice in the whisper of the wind. He sipped absently at the coffee in his right hand, traced blindly along the jagged scar running up his jaw with the index finger of the left.

"How did you get that scar?" As soon as the question came out, she regretted it. She cringed as his hand stopped midway up the length of the ashen line. He stiffened and turned to face her. His face was unreadable, but his eyes looked hurt, embarrassed.

"I'm sorry." She found she couldn't hold that sad gaze, her eyes turned to the cup she held. She sipped at it again, could feel those sad eyes still on her.

"It's okay," he said. "I guess I was calling attention to it."

"I just want to know about you, is all." She dared a glance toward him and found him staring out the window again.

For a while he didn't respond and she let it drop. She finished her coffee but it did nothing for her weariness. When she lay down on the bed and closed her eyes again, he had not moved. As she neared sleep, his voice broke the cold silence, startling her to awareness.

He started in a crisp, measured voice, a tone calculated to filter out any sign of emotion. As he spoke, the dispassionate quality of his speech faded, the mask of detachment disappeared, and his words reflected the pain in his eyes.

"My father was born wealthy, and throughout his life managed to take his old money and generate a good deal of new money with it. He was an investor, an investment capital gambler. He did well. You could say that I was born rich, too. We weren't the Rockefellers or the DuPonts, but we did very well."

Gordon couldn't believe he was telling her this, a story he had never told anyone, not even his ill-fated ex-wife. He supposed he was closer to Shannon than he had been to her, though. Their fear, for themselves and Charity, the binding by a secret they could never share in polite society, made them close. Their mutual nightmare made them closer.

It was her story too.

"My mother was sick a lot. She died later, it was cancer, but she was still alive then, though not with us very much.

She was in the hospital for a few months when it happened, my only mementos from her were the slippery satin sheets she had bought for me during her last remission. For some reason she insisted I have silk sheets." Gordon barked a dry, humorless laugh and shook his head.

"Father really didn't approve of me sleeping in girl's sheets, as he called them. They bothered him more than a little. I wasn't too happy about them either, partly because he hated them, but we obliged my mother. When someone is dying it's hard to tell them no; even the little things take on greater meaning, and it seemed inhumane to take even that small thing from her.

"I was eight, I think, when the Bogey Man first came to me. It wasn't really him, just a foreshadow of him, a projection. Like the preview of a scary movie that you know will be in your town soon enough."

While Gordon spoke, visualizing the night moment by moment, he found himself rubbing the old scar again. This time he did not make himself stop. He let his fingertips explore the scarred terrain of his cheek while his mind explored the scared terrain of his childhood. He hadn't let himself think of these things in a long time. Now they came back with a vividness that was startling, almost as if the simple act of blinking might take him back to the very time and place.

"I would lay in bed just waiting. Sometimes he would come, sometimes he wouldn't. Some nights I didn't sleep at all, and when I did sleep it was only when exhaustion took me.

"One night I woke to the sound of someone opening my door, and when I saw the silhouette against the light in the hallway I screamed . . . and I pissed myself." The last he spoke quietly, as if whispering the words would make them less real. He glanced nervously at Shannon and saw her eyes were closed. She lay on the bed, pillows propped under her head, hugging herself. Not sleeping though—her lips were pursed, her expression one of dismay. Tears spilled silently out of the corner of her eyes as she relived her own private hell through his memories. He saw this and his shame vanished.

"Mother referred to my bedwetting as my 'little problem,' like the night terrors. My 'little problem' made my father foaming mad; he thought my bedwetting was simple laziness, and the Bogey Man nightmares were a fiction I used to get out of trouble when I did it."

Outside, the moisture-heavy sky finally let loose. The rain started sparingly, and within a few seconds was pouring. Gordon could almost taste the electricity in the air. A storm was coming, and watching it depressed him more. He let the curtain fall over the window and sat on the edge of the bed, lightly as not to disturb Shannon.

"I saw him standing there, and I pissed myself. Then he stepped inside and turned the light on. It was my dad. He drank a lot when Mother wasn't there—I could smell it on him, the usual mix of rum and pipe smoke. I learned later that he had a cocaine problem, so he may have been high too, but I don't know.

"When he turned on the light and saw what I had done, he went insane. He threw his bottle across my room. It shattered against the wall by my headboard. Then he dragged me out of bed and hit me." He tapped the scar with an index finger. "I woke up on the floor the next morning and had this cut on my face from the broken glass. I don't know if it happened when he knocked me down or if he did it himself. I never asked."

He felt the bed shift underneath him, turned and saw Shannon's eyes were open again. She was sitting a little closer to him now, her back against the wall, her eyes red and swimming. "I'm sorry," she said.

Gordon didn't know why she had apologized: if she was sorry for what his father had done, or for having reminded him. He didn't have the energy to ask.

"It never happened again. He never hurt me after that night, but he didn't talk to me much either—not until Mother died. I don't know if it was because he was ashamed of what he had done, or if he was ashamed of me. Probably both.

"He told my mother I did it playing at shaving with his straight razor. I never told her any different."

A long, uncomfortable silence followed—neither spoke, neither moved.

Nothing like a little pleasant conversation to break the ice, he thought, and laughed. "You sorry you asked now?" he said, not caring for the tone of his voice. The words sounded harsh, like the bark of a cranky old man.

"No," she said. "I'm not sorry you told me either."

He jumped a little, startled as her hands slipped around his waist. She pulled herself closer to him, and as he turned to face her, he felt the silk touch of her lips on his cheek, on the scar. He realized he was shaking, a nervousness he had not felt in a long time making his movements unsteady. Tentatively, clumsily, out of practice and unsure, their lips met and lingered, and they kissed.

Across the room the phone rang.

Gordon and Shannon pulled away from each other. They stared at each other, embarrassment and fear coloring their cheeks. Gordon rose and answered on the third ring.

"Gordon Chambers," he said, and paused, his face darkening. "Yes, she's with me . . . no." He cupped a hand over the phone and whispered to Shannon. "Sergeant Winter."

She was off the bed, standing next to him an instant later, leaning close to hear the conversation.

He could smell her, not the chemical sweetness of perfume or deodorant, not the acrid scent of her sweat-stained clothes. A smell that was all her, that made his heart quicken and his face burn.

"We were going out," he said, "to eat." There was another pause, and his face flushed with anger. "Yes, to look, too. What of it?" He was silent again for almost a full minute, Shannon watching him closely, trying and failing to read his expression. "Sure," he said at last. "We'll be here." Then he hung up.

"What?" Her voice was urgent, almost panicked. "Did they find her? What's going on?"

"No," he said. "There were two more disappearances. Winter is on his way over to talk to us again."

"Oh no." Her face went ghost-white. She stumbled backward a few steps, striking the edge of the bed and falling to a sitting position. "Were they . . . ?" She seemed unable to finish, but she didn't need to.

"No, not kids. Two cops keeping an eye on Feral Park, and in the middle of the day." Though he knew the words sounded ludicrous, he spoke them aloud anyway. "It wasn't the Bogey Man." He didn't need to finish. They both knew.

Feral Park had its own Bogey People.

Little ones.

Chapter 21

Charity thought the dead man's gun was a six-shooter; she was almost sure of it. Almost sure. She sat alone in a shaded niche next to the small cave at the far end of the giant den, as alone as she could be in this cavernous dome full of raggedy children, anyway. A few had come and gone, carrying torches into the tunnel and disappearing. She thought it was the place, or maybe led to the place, where they went when they needed to be alone. It wasn't an option for her yet. *Until I have my own torch,* she thought, *stepping into that darkness would mean a quick end.*

It was a six-shooter, she thought. *But how many times did he fire it?* She counted the reports over and over in her mind. *Three to scare the kids away, and three at the Bogey Man. Or maybe it was only two.*

Music played as always in the background, but it had a watery quality to it. She thought the batteries in their stereo might be going dead.

Five shots at least, maybe six.

The harder she tried to remember, the foggier the memory became.

Another set of feet approached, but instead of continuing into the tunnel they stopped in front of her. She looked up and saw a younger girl dressed in black denim and a leather jacket. Tangled blonde hair stuck up from her head like a fright wig.

"Who do you like?" she asked.

"What?"

"Who do you want to listen to, who do you like?"

"I . . . I don't know," Charity said. She didn't know what the choices were, let alone have a preference. Then she remembered Jesse, the blond boy who had died the night before. *Anthrax is life,* he had said with his goofy grin. "Anthrax," Charity said.

The girl smiled and ran off. A few seconds later the music started again, a bass-heavy tune, slow at first, then speeding up as the drums kicked in. She felt a surge of adrenaline when the guitar started—a heavy, scratchy rhythm. She closed her eyes and took it in. When the singing started, she couldn't make out the words very well, but she responded to them, her heartbeat sped up to match the beat. It sounded like the pounding of war drums.

She was beginning to understand why they liked this music so much. It was energizing.

When she opened her eyes, she saw some of the others dancing like jungle savages around the entrance of the cavern—spinning, jumping, bumping chests and shoulders. Toni and the group he left with were there, the center of activity. His spear was gone now. Two gun belts hung crisscrossed low on his hips. The guns slapped against his thighs as he danced. His hands were covered with blood. A shiny badge hung crooked from the front of his old t-shirt.

A cop, Charity thought. *He killed a cop.*

She stood warily, afraid. The truth came to her then. They were killers, all of them, and if she was going to stay, she would have to become just like them.

She walked toward them, slowly, clutching her scissors in front of her chest like a crucifix. They seemed to warm in her hands. Around her the children began to settle, kids standing

alone or in clusters watched her expectantly, sensing something to come. She felt it too, a tension in the air that hadn't
been there a few moments before. At the mouth of the tunnel
the dancing continued, but seemed to slow, like a magic trick.
She realized that the dancing had not slowed at all, her per-
ception of it had sped up. She felt her senses open all the way:
her skin itched, her mouth felt dry, her head began to pound,
and every sound was suddenly too loud.

It's time.

Jenny's voice drowned out everything else, but the Brat
Queen had not spoken aloud. It was in Charity's head.

She saw Ginger in the crowd, the only body not spinning
and slamming in the slow-motion frenzy. Ginger lifted the
gun toward Charity, a smile on her pudgy face, and pulled the
trigger.

Nothing, the gun was empty.

Around them, the others realized what was happening and
stilled.

Thank you, Charity thought. The gun was empty; she had
counted right.

The sly smile didn't leave Ginger's face. She dropped the
gun and lunged at Toni, snatching a gun from his low-hung
holsters and shoving him aside. She raised the gun toward
Charity and fired.

There was a deafening *twang* as the slug hit stone behind
Charity and ricocheted, sending shards in all directions.

Toni shouted, lunged at Ginger, but the others held him
back.

There was another loud report and Charity heard the
whine of the slug as it passed her. Strangely, she also saw it
from the corner of her eye as it passed. Another bang, distorted, like a record played on its lowest speed, and she saw
the ball of lead flying toward her. She ducked and watched it

fly over her head. It seemed everything had slowed except for her. When she looked back to the crowd she saw Ginger standing alone, her mouth hanging open in disbelief. Gun still raised, she fired again, and again.

Charity dodged them easily and charged with a cry of rage. She held the scissors over her head like a dagger.

The cavern became a blur of gray stone dotted with staring pink faces and the sluggish dancing of torchlight. All sound melted together into a low, liquid buzz. Only the sounds of her enraged shrieks were real. At some point, Charity's feet left the ground, but she didn't notice. The only thing she saw was the round, freckled face of the girl who was so casually trying to kill her, eyes wide and fearful, mouth hanging open in a dumb O of surprise.

Charity saw this through a shrinking tunnel of gray before the sound of Ginger's cries of pain brought everything back into sharp focus. For a second everything froze, and then in an instant the rest of the world caught up with her.

There was total silence, no music and no dancing. Ginger screamed again, and this time it was a red, bubbling sound. Blood dribbled slowly from the corner of her open mouth. She looked down, and Charity followed her gaze to her own hand. She still clutched the scissors, stabbed to the handle into Ginger's chest.

Ginger screamed again, this time feebly, barely audible, and fell away. The scissors pulled from the wound with the scrape of metal against bone. She fell and rolled across the stone like a rag doll, and lay motionless.

No one spoke and the room went darker as Ginger's torch flickered and died. A second later the cavern brightened again as a new torch appeared—Charity's torch.

Charity stood over Ginger's body, wanting to feel happy that she was alive, wanting to feel angry that the others had let this happen, wanting to feel horrible about what she had done. But she felt nothing. She bent down slowly, switching the bloody scissors to her left hand, and searched Ginger's coat pockets. She found the cell phone and put it in her own pocket. Now she was a killer too, and she realized she didn't care.

I guess I'm one of them now.

She rose to her feet and the others moved away. Even Toni stepped back from her a little fearfully.

Charity left them without a word, walked toward her new place by Jenny's throne. Her torch burned with an angry intensity before her stone seat. She picked it up and ran to the far end of the cavern, through the tunnel, to where she did not know, but away from all the staring eyes of her new family.

She found nothing unusual in the narrow tunnel, just rock and shadow. There were several openings in the wall along the way, low to the ground so she would have to get on her hands and knees to crawl in to explore them. After several minutes of running, the tunnel did not narrow. It did not turn or peter out. When she tired of running, when she felt enough distance between her and the others, she slowed, and finally stopped. A few feet ahead of her to her right, low to the rough floor, was another of those dark egresses.

She wiped the scissors across her shirt and stuck them through her belt loop again. The shirt was new a few days ago, but now it was ruined by dirt, grass stains, and blood.

She crouched before the opening and stabbed the torch in, lighting a small, amorphous room. It was empty so she crawled in on her hands and knees. She propped her torch—which should have burned her with its radiant heat in such close quarters but did not—between a pair of large stones, and rested against the wall.

She wasn't hungry anymore; the thought of food made her want to puke, even though her stomach was empty. She had killed a girl, had done so without a second thought. She had done it as easily as one would squish a spider, even though Ginger had a gun and she did not. *How* had she done it?

"What's happening to me?" she asked aloud.

She closed her eyes and played the murder back in her mind, over and over like something she had watched from outside her body. She had seen another kill like that—with the speed and thoughtlessness of a natural, or supernatural, predator.

She pulled the Bogey Man's weapon from under her belt and regarded it dourly. She cast it into the shadows at the other end of the room. It landed, blades open and shining in the torchlight.

"Charity!" The sound of Toni's voice startled her.

She considered whether to answer him. Toni was her only friend down here, and he had tried to help her when Ginger pulled his gun on her. He didn't give her the time to decide. She saw the flicker of his torch in the passage a second before he poked his head into the opening.

"Room for two?" he asked, and crawled inside without waiting for her answer. "You kicked ass," he said. "How did you do that?"

"You sound happy about it," she said. "You wanted me to kill her, didn't you? Is that why you chose me?"

Toni recoiled, a look of surprise plain on his young rogue's face. "No," he said. "I didn't want her dead." He settled against the wall across from Charity, his gaze turning briefly to the gleaming crimson blades of the scissors, then back to her face. "She started it, though. She didn't have to take the contest that far, so it's her fault."

He was a terrible liar. He knew Ginger would take the contest deadly serious, and even though he said he didn't want to see her dead, he didn't answer Charity's other question. Charity knew he liked her, had a crush on her almost the same way the Bogey Man did. He had wanted to see her kill, and was thrilled at how good she was at it.

She tried to ignore him, pulled the cell phone from her pocket and played with it. She found the Power button and turned it on, its sudden green glow painting the walls around her. She read the menu displayed on the glowing screen with a forced indifference. She had never been to school, and no one had taught her to read. Like other things, she had just picked it up somewhere along the way. The way she knew lots of things, like her father's name being Gordon.

She scrolled down to the contact sub-menu and pushed Select. There were close to a dozen entries in his contact list. *Gordon's Cell #* was second down from the top. She thought her father's number might be there—it was his friend's phone after all. But actually seeing it there, and knowing she could talk to him and Shannon with the push of a button made her heart flutter. She wanted to talk to them again, but she was mad at them for abandoning her.

"What's that?" Toni asked, scooting toward her for a closer look.

"Nothing." She pushed the Power button again before he could get closer and shoved the palm-sized phone into her pocket.

"You have to go back, Charity. They're all waiting for you. Jenny is waiting for you."

"Do I?" she asked indifferently. She looked away from him, eyes searching for her bloodied weapon. The scissors were gone; Toni had taken them while she was playing with the phone.

Good, she thought. *He can have them. I don't care.*

But she did. She hated them, hated the way they warmed instantly to her touch, hated the way they had helped her kill. But they were hers.

"Don't be mad," Toni said. His voice was reproachful but laced with guilt.

"I am," she said simply, then grabbed her torch and crawled for the exit. "C'mon," she said. "We don't want to keep them waiting."

When Charity and Toni stepped back into the main cavern, it was as if nothing had happened. The children talked and played. They ate hamburgers and tacos from a cluster of bags on a small stone pedestal next to the radio, and despite Charity's previous disgust, the sight of food made her stomach gurgle. The radio was silent; she guessed the batteries had finally run out.

Ginger's body was gone, and so was her extinguished torch.

Where did they put her body? she wondered, and realized she already knew. Where they had put the body of her father's friend and the cop Toni had killed. In the Never. She wondered what the Never really was, what might be inside of it.

You fall into the Never and you'll never come back, Toni had said.

Some of the others saw them coming, Toni leading the way toward Jenny's empty throne. There was no sign of Feral Park's Brat Queen. Charity knew that meant nothing; she was there somewhere, watching.

Toni walked to his lesser throne to the right of Jenny's and slid the butt of his torch into the niche at its foot. He motioned Charity to do the same, and she did.

"Munch time," he exclaimed rushing past her and scooping up a bag next to the dead radio. He reached in, pulled out a fistful of thin tacos, and held them out to her. "C'mon," he urged. "You said you were hungry." He smiled brightly, but the smile faded quickly when Charity didn't return it. "You should be nicer to me." He was pouting now, face set into a petulant frown as he chowed down on his first taco.

"How old are you?" she asked, and bit into her taco. She expected her stomach to turn at this but was happy when it didn't. It seemed that she was starting to fit right in here. Sure she had killed someone, the blood was still fresh on the front of her shirt, but even that didn't bother her much now. Like most things, once it was over it wasn't so bad.

Toni was silent for a moment. He seemed to weigh the question, then said, "I don't remember. I was ten when I came here, but that was a long time ago." He went back to chewing his food with a troubled look on his face. She was about to ask if he was okay when she realized he wasn't upset, only trying his hardest to remember. He stuffed the remainder of his food into his mouth and walked over to the radio. There was a stack of CDs next to it. He dug through them, searching. Then he pulled one from the tumbled stack with a grin and brought it back to her.

"Metallica," he said with a triumphant grin. "I watched a video to a song from this a few days before I ran away." He turned the plain black CD face around and scanned the fine print on the back. "This was made in nineteen ninety-one, so that's when I came here, and I was ten years old then."

Charity added the numbers in her head several times before giving up. She knew she could count, and she knew what they added up to. She just couldn't believe it was all. Standing here in front of her was a twenty-some-year-old man in a kid's body, and he didn't even know it.

Toni must have read something wrong in her face. "What year is it now?"

"Charity," they all heard Jenny's voice that time, it echoed through the cavern like a voice through a bullhorn. The room quieted at this, and though the others didn't stop eating, or playing, or standing around in clusters doing nothing, they remained respectfully quiet.

Jenny appeared, dirty coveralls, stringy brown hair hanging against cotton-white skin, feet bare. She stood in front of the tunnel to the playground, waiting.

Charity handed the remainder of her breakfast to Toni, grabbed her torch, and went to her queen.

Jenny grasped Charity's free hand and stared into her eyes while speaking to the rest of the room. "She's one of us now."

Cheers rose to that, a few wolf whistles, and somewhere from the large gathering a hearty, "Hell yeah, sister!"

"Tonight she'll be my left-hand sister," Jenny said. "Anybody have a problem with that?"

"Nos" all around, with a few "hell, nos" and giggles thrown in to keep the meeting from becoming too ordered.

"We're gonna take off for a while," Jenny said. "Be good." She pulled Charity toward the tunnel to the playground.

Charity looked back once before stepping into the darkness; Jenny's glowing form and supernova torch leading the way.

Toni was seated, the rest of his food laying forgotten in his lap. He held the foldout from the CD in his hands and studied it. Perhaps he was reading the lyrics to the song that had come out on video right before he ran away. Maybe he was trying to remember how long he had been there.

All at once the darkness fell before Charity's eyes like a curtain. She turned back around and there was just the glow of their flames, Jenny's own strange radiance, and the barely lit path stretching on through the Never.

Chapter 22

Sergeant Winter arrived in the rain with two other officers, one a street officer and one in plain clothes. He told Shannon and Gordon about the missing cops. They had been down at the old park keeping an eye on things, and after reporting spotting a suspicious man, had vanished.

"You're not suspects," he said. "It happened while I was interviewing Shannon." He explained that the plain-clothes officer was to be their shadow, for their protection.

Shannon frowned at this. It would make looking for Charity harder.

"It's not necessary," Gordon said, eyeballing the officer with a little annoyance. "We'll manage on our own."

Mr. Plain Clothes said nothing, just measured Gordon and Shannon with eyes hidden behind dark glasses and shaded by the bill of a Seattle Seahawks cap. He was clean-shaven with an unremarkable face.

"It's necessary," Winter said, and that was that. Then they excused themselves, Mr. Plain Clothes giving Gordon a last, long glare from behind his shades as he stepped out behind Winter. As the door swung shut, a peal of thunder boomed overhead. It was still raining.

Get soaked, Shannon thought.

Gordon said nothing for a while. He drank more coffee. Finally, with an energy that hinted of decision, he jumped up from his seat and crossed the room to where Shannon sat on the edge of the bed. He took both her hands in his, squeezed them, and kissed the side of her mouth. "Do you like movies?"

"What?"

The Marquee Cineplex was only a short drive away but the streets surrounding it were crammed with parked cars and pedestrians. One of the old Cineplex's three theatres was playing the latest *Star Wars* movie, and predictably enough it looked like a full house. That was good, though it meant having to park the car and walk over a block, getting soaked in the process. A crowd would make this easier.

Featured in smaller letters beside the *Star Wars* flick, almost like an afterthought, was an animated kids' movie called *The Princess's Shoes* and the latest cookie-cutter romance: big names, big hair, and a paper-thin plot. They waited in line for ten minutes, mostly hiding beneath a series of storefront awnings. When they reached the ticket booth the rain had become a light drizzle, but the occasional flicker of lightning and low, moaning thunder threatened worse.

Gordon and Shannon scanned the line behind them frequently, searching for their shadow. They spotted him in the thinning crowd several yards back, just as it was their turn.

"Good evening. Welcome to the Marquee." The ticket vendor was a teenage girl with punky red hair and numerous facial piercings.

"Two for *The Princess's Shoes*," Gordon said in a low voice.

The punky redhead paused for a second, rolled her eyes toward him without looking up from keyboard. "I'm sorry," she said. "Two for what?"

"*The Princess's Shoes*," he repeated.

"Two for *The Princess's Shoes*," she repeated, again in her robot servant's voice. "That's fourteen dollars." She took his money, and gave Shannon a sympathetic look as she handed them the tickets. *Some hot date, huh?*

Gordon scanned the crowd behind them as he led Shannon through the door and past the ticket taker.

Mr. Plain Clothes was no closer than before, waiting his turn in line to see a movie the city would have to reimburse him for. He had no way of knowing which movie they were headed to, but he seemed unconcerned.

Gordon figured his chance of their shadow choosing the wrong movie was fair, but some doubt in his hastily constructed plan lingered. He supposed there was also a fair chance the cop would flash his badge and ask which show the blond guy with the scared face and his date had gone to see. Even so, the crowd was thick; they might have a chance.

"Popcorn?" Shannon smiled as she said it and gave him a feeble tug toward the concessions.

"No thanks, I'm watching my figure." He watched her smile widen, and responded, leading her through the crowd toward theatre #2 and *The Princess's Shoes*, hopefully the last place Mr. Plain Clothes would expect. Like his decision to try the Cineplex, his choice of movies had been on the spur of the moment, a decision based on logic that might or might not be faulty.

If Mr. Plain Clothes thought they were out on a date, he would expect them to chose the romantic film, and if they were trying to lose him, *Star Wars*, with its easy-to-disappear-in crowd, would be the best choice. Or he might see right through the whole scam, which was most likely.

We have to lose him, Gordon thought. It was getting dark already, the premature dark of a stormy night, and they had to get to Feral Park. If they ditched him and somehow made it to the park before one of Riverside's boys in blue caught them, they wouldn't have very long. It wouldn't take long at all for Winter to figure out where they had gone, but it was their only chance.

Maybe we should just keep him around. He might not stop us from going there. Hell, he would come in handy if there was trouble. He considered this for a moment, but dismissed it. If the Bogey Man came for them, Mr. Plain Clothes, cop or no, would die just as easily as Shannon's brother had. Just like Charles.

As they stepped into the darkness of theatre #2, Gordon realized they had forgotten to replace Shannon's broken flashlight. He glanced back toward the lobby and didn't see Mr. Plain Clothes.

Shannon paused at the sudden darkness within, then led the way down the last row of seats. They rook the two last seats, closest to the wall and deepest in shadow.

They watched the entrance while previews and commercials played. People trickled in, mostly small flocks of children led by one or two harried adults. The seats closest to the screen filled up first; Gordon and Shannon were alone. Mr. Plain Clothes stepped through the entrance a few minutes later, stopped just inside, lifted his dark glasses, and scanned the theatre.

"Damn," Gordon hissed.

Shannon squeezed his hand.

Mr. Plain Clothes found them, tipped his hat cockily, smiling a big *"gotcha"* smile, and took the seat at the end of their row, next to the door.

"What now?" Shannon said in his ear.

"I don't know," Gordon said, feeling like an idiot. "I haven't planned past getting caught." He offered her a weak smile. "I'm thinking," he said. "Meantime, how about that popcorn?"

"Might as well," she said. "A cola too?"

"At your service, milady. I'll be back directly." He squeezed her hand before rising, and walked the littered aisle toward the cop.

Mr. Plain Clothes watched him with a cocked head. His shades were off now, and Gordon could see amusement in his eyes and the crooked smile on his lips.

"Popcorn?"

Mr. Plain Clothes said nothing, just shook his head once and kept watching him with that amused grin.

Asshole.

The line for popcorn and soda was long. Five minutes after stepping to the end of it, it was finally Gordon's turn. He was about to order when a scream broke the peace of theatre #2.

Chapter 23

Jenny walked slowly and Charity followed a few steps behind. Neither spoke. The path seemed to go on forever, then it ended abruptly as it had on her trip to the cavern; one second a dimly lit path through the darkness, the next they were in the playground. They weren't completely there, though. The degraded playground equipment was visible in the energetic torchlight, but beyond the rusted iron fence was pitch black.

Charity wondered how they got out when they made their raiding party visits to what she now thought of as *The Other World*. Through the exit, she supposed, and even as the thought occurred to her, the darkness of the exit lit up with light from the outside. The small wooded area beyond appeared like a picture in a television set.

Jenny stood motionless by the sandbox for a moment, her silence enduring. She stabbed the end of her torch into the sand and stepped away from it. The dancing lunatic glow of its flames brightened as if feeding from the sand. She motioned for Charity to do the same, and she did, stepping away quickly as hers flared up, too. She shielded her eyes from the combined brightness.

"There was a girl who liked to play here," Jenny said.

Charity moved her hands from her eyes. The glow had evened out and weakened, the torchlight replaced by the pale gray light of a full moon and the phantom glow of Riverside.

"She used to sneak out on nice summer days and on the

weekends when she was in school. She came here because it was the only good place to go. There were lots of other kids to play with, and grown ups who didn't hit."

Charity had an image, brief but powerful, of the playground in its heyday, full of screaming, laughing children and playground equipment still shining new. The wood-chip floor was clear of litter and the grass in the park was a short and healthy green. Then the image vanished; the mellow glow of the full moon and lights from Riverside returned.

There was something in the sandbox, mostly buried. She thought she knew what it was, had seen enough of them in her short life to recognize it by the shape and shadow of what little was visible. She felt her stomach tighten as she neared the sandbox. Her heart thumped uncomfortably in her chest and the air suddenly tasted nasty, like the wind blowing off something long dead.

"She liked this place so much she came here the night she ran away, and she never left." Jenny's voice was distant. She wasn't there—an echo from another reality.

The shape in the sand was a naked torso; only one arm visible, the other lay buried up to the shoulder. It lay at a crooked angle in the sand, dappled and smeared with drying blood. Her head lay against the partially submerged shoulder. The hair was pulled out in clumps, blood seeping from several places on the scalp. Her eyes were bruised, swollen half-shut. Her nose was a bloody lump in the center of her ruined face. It had been busted into a surreal new shape. Her bottom jaw was missing; where it should have been gaped a large red and black hole. The tongue hung out, far too long, resting in the sand.

A feast for the bugs—flies, ants, and beetles teemed around her, wondering in their insect drone where to start first.

"No," Charity gasped, covering her face with cold hands. She tried to close her eyes against the grisly spectacle, but they would not mind her. She stared, unable to look away.

Then, in one powerful, spastic jerk, the dead girl moved. Her arm shot up into the air, hand groping, reaching for Charity. The eyes fluttered like tiny, dim strobe lights. The tongue rolled over in the sand, pulled back into her wide-open face like a snake slithering backwards, and she let out a horrible, gargling scream.

Charity jumped away with a shriek, and the dead girl was gone. She turned and ran from the playground, stopping dead outside the arched exit. She tried to scream again but all that came out was a feeble whimper.

They were coming at her, hundreds of them. From the woods, from the crumbling walkway on the dike, and down the tall, dead grass of the slope. They came from the tall willows by the highway, and from everywhere else.

"They're all Bogeys," Jenny said in a low, angry voice. "Even the ones who pretend to be your friends, especially them. They'll hurt you again. That's all they know how to do."

The tall shadow people ambled slowly toward her. Charity couldn't see their faces, but when the closest ones spoke to her, she knew their voices.

"Charity," her dad said. "Come on, baby, let me take you home now." His voice was a parody, his words dripped with cruel intention. "I want to make up for lost time." He cackled like a fairytale witch, then raised his face toward the moon and howled.

Beside him, Shannon spoke. "You troublesome little bitch!" She spoke with sincere hatred, her words as painful to Charity as the barbs of a hook. "Look what you got me into. Come here, I'll teach you what happens to little brats who cause trouble."

"No!" She backed away from them and screamed as someone grabbed her from behind. Large hands gripped her thin shoulders; meaty fingers bit in like the teeth of a trap. They spun her around hard enough to whip her head to the side. The pain was fast and bright, making strange colors and stars appear in her vision. When they cleared, he was there, staring down at her, all smiling teeth and shining eyes in a vague, dark shape.

"My sweet, precious little Charity," he said, his voice the whisper of scales on dry leaves. "How I've missed you."

Charity opened her mouth, and this time found the strength to scream. She screamed and screamed until all her strength had flowed out through her mouth. She screamed until the world went a perfect black.

When she opened her eyes she stood where she had before, several feet back from the glowing torches in the sandpit. Nothing had changed except for the glow of the flames, which had dimmed. Jenny stood beside her, and her glow had grown pale too. She was almost transparent.

Charity felt wrecked. Physically, nothing seemed to be wrong, but her head hurt and she felt sick.

The experience had weakened both her and Jenny.

After a few seconds, Jenny looked better, more there. Charity's sickness passed, but her head still pounded.

"That's why we all came here. They're all monsters."

Charity was silent. Her feelings for Shannon and her father were mixed—she hated them for abandoning her to the Bogey Man, yet was helpless not to love them. It was a residual attachment, she knew; it would fade.

Jenny took her torch from the sand and started down the path through the Never again. Retrieving her torch, Charity followed.

★ ★ ★ ★ ★

When they got back to the cavern, Jenny replaced her torch at the foot of her throne and quickly vanished into the crowd.

When Charity replaced her torch at her new place by Jenny's throne, she found a surprise waiting on her seat. The scissors she had abandoned in the small den. Toni had not meant to keep them. They lay slightly open in the middle of her seat. Menacing. Next to them lay a small heart-shaped locket on a fine gold chain. She picked the locket up with trembling hands and opened it. From inside, Shannon and her dead family smiled at her.

They came back for me.

"I found it outside," Toni said behind her.

She tensed at his voice. Her nerves were on the ragged edge. "Thank you," she said. Her mouth was numb, clumsy, her tongue thick and dry.

Jesse lied to me. Toni and Jenny lied to me. They came back. Dad and Shannon came back!

She closed her eyes, closed her hand around the locket, and could almost visualize them. Standing alone, staring into the playground hopelessly. She saw Shannon take the locket and toss it in to her, even though they both knew she was already gone.

They came back for me!

When she opened her eyes again, Toni was still there, watching with a shy smile, waiting. A killer with a hero's face.

"I thought you would like it," he said, and looked away.

"I do. Thanks." She slipped the chain around her neck and let the locket slide between her shirt and skin. It lay close to her heart, and for the first time since coming here, she felt warm.

"Wanna go for a walk?" Toni asked, suddenly all business.

"No," she said. "Not right now."

"We have to. I have to tell you some stuff."

"Okay." She picked up the scissors and shoved them into their place under her belt. They felt warm too, but unlike the locket near her heart, it wasn't a comforting heat. It was a sick heat, like a fever.

Toni grabbed her hand and led her toward the tunnel at the other end of the cavern.

She followed listlessly. She watched the guns bounce against his hips as he led her through the dark. They walked for several minutes without stopping; Charity recognized her den as they passed it. Toni's torch lit the walls with an unsteady light that made her feel a little woozy, like seasickness. She realized with a momentary prick of fear that she had left her torch. It didn't matter, though; no one would touch it.

"Where are you taking me?"

"You'll see," he said.

Finally, they reached the end of the tunnel. There were screams—not of pain but fear. Crying and a surrealistic landscape that could only be the product of some troubled imagination.

They stepped from the cramped tunnel into a wide-open nightmare.

Chapter 24

The single scream, a child's scream, echoed through the hall joining the Cineplex lobby to theatre #2. There was a second of stunned silence. Everything stopped; pale faces surrounded him. Then more screams, the screams of adults and children mingled.

Gordon pushed his way back through the disorganized line and ran.

It's not dark yet, he thought furiously. Then on the heels of that, *It is in there.*

"Everybody down!" The voice of a lone adult sounded out. Gordon thought it might be Mr. Plain Clothes but wasn't sure. Then a gunshot, followed by two more, and a scream of pain.

When Gordon pushed through the swinging door into the theatre, shoving past an exodus of screaming children and their parents, he saw Mr. Plain Clothes hanging limp from the outstretched arm of the Bogey Man. The cop was already dead, entrails hanging from his torn gut to the popcorn-specked floor.

The Bogey Man stood at the end of the front row next to where the cop had been seated. Sans his usual weapon, he was ripping the dead man's guts out with his bare hands. He noticed Gordon standing by the door only a few feet away, and his shark's grin broke the shadowy darkness of his face.

"Daddy," he said, dropping the gutted body to the floor.

"I told her I would kill you if she tried to run away." He took a step toward Gordon, stopped, took another step, and stopped again, like a groom practicing his walk down the church aisle.

As he neared, Gordon saw beyond the shadow of his face for the first time since the fevered nightmares of his childhood. He looked into the demon eyes, and couldn't move. He was stuck, frozen in place, could only watch helplessly and prepare to die.

"No!" Shannon shouted, standing at the end of her row.

The Bogey Man stopped and faced her.

Gordon felt the hold on him loosen as the Bogey Man focused on Shannon.

"You bitch, you took her from me!" There was a sick squelching sound as he walked through the dead man's guts and started down the row toward Shannon. *"I'll tear your guts out through your thieving cunt!"*

"Stop!" Gordon screamed, but the monster didn't stop. He walked toward Shannon with slow and deadly deliberation. Gordon stepped over the stinking mound of guts, almost slipping in the spreading runoff of blood, and chased the monster down the row of folding seats.

Gordon leapt at the Bogey Man, hooked an arm around his throat, trying to drag or slow him down, but was only dragged along. Before they closed the distance to Shannon the lights came on, and the Bogey Man melted into the air with a howl.

Gordon thumped painfully to the floor, and a second later Shannon was next to him, kneeling down and giving him a shake.

"Are you okay?"

"Fine," he said, though he was still gasping for breath. "You?"

"Fine," she said. "Let's get out of here." They were alone in the theatre now, but not for long.

Shannon helped Gordon up and they ran toward the center aisle, avoiding what remained of the cop as best they could. When they reached the aisle, three uniformed men, Marquee uniforms instead of police, pushed through the door. They saw the splattered, hollowed remains on the floor in front of them and stopped. One ran back out of the theatre screaming, another lurched over, as if punched in the gut, and puked a mixture of popcorn and candy onto his feet. The third looked up at Gordon and Shannon, pointed an accusing finger, and said, "Stop right where you are." He was almost as big as the other two put together, probably outweighed Gordon by fifty pounds, all muscle.

Lying beside the bloody mound of guts and cop was Mr. Plain Clothes' service pistol. Gordon bent quickly and scooped it up, bringing the sight up to the center of the usher's massive chest. A second later the big usher was gone.

Gordon dropped the gun and ran toward the fire exit. He hit the door without slowing, bumping the release bar inward with his hands. The sound of the fire alarm chased them out into the back alley.

They didn't run to the car; there wasn't time. They didn't run toward the hotel room. By the time they made it there, the cops would be waiting. They ran without thinking and made it several blocks through the stretch of downtown alleys and into the industrial area before they realized they were most of the way to Feral Park.

Chapter 25

Dirty Dave heard them coming and pushed the Dumpster lid up just enough to see who it was. He thought it might be the cops again, trying to find the ones who had beaten him and run afoul of the kids at Feral Park. It wasn't. The cops were gone and he was safe for now. They passed within feet of his hiding place, and the afternoon held enough light for him to recognize them. These people had come before, separate and together. These two knew about the park and the kids in the playground. Their girl was one of them.

Most of the kids here were abused or unwanted, and beyond the initial searches and obligatory public outpouring of sympathy, nothing was ever done. Nobody really even knew they were here. People did know that Feral Park was not a good place to be, especially after dark, that weird things happened here. Dangerous things. And sometimes it wasn't only kids who vanished when they came here alone. No one but him had known about the kids, though. This was the first time he had ever seen someone come back for their child.

These people were different; they wanted her back. They cared.

"Hey . . . you!" His voice sounded alien to him. He didn't use it often, and never above the level of mumble or whisper. The sound of it startled him. The two stopped, turned back and saw him staring above the lip of the Dumpster. They traded questioning glances and started toward him. As they neared him, his sense of curiosity fled and the voice of self-preservation, his best friend all those lonely years, told him to hide. He let the lid drop back and burrowed deeper into the refuse. He whimpered when the father, a large man, pounded on the side of the metal box and said to come out. The lid opened all the way, pausing for a second as it stood vertical before falling with a wham against the back of the Dumpster.

"Hey." The woman's voice was soft, gentle, easier on the panicked creature he was becoming. "We won't hurt you," she said. "I promise, we just want to talk." Then with a motherly tone that gave him a brief, powerful sense of *déja vù*, she said, "I promise it will be fine."

It had been so long since he'd heard a woman's voice, longer since he'd heard one speaking to him, and nearly a lifetime ago since his own mother's voice had given that kind of blind, unquestionable comfort, like a drug.

He pushed the debris away from his face so he could see her, and when the beautiful woman with the kind but worried face put her hand into the Dumpster, he took it.

She helped him to his feet. "Did you call to us?"

Dave nodded. He tried to say, "Yes, ma'am," but it came out as a grunt. He kept a wary eye on the man until the woman, still holding his grubby hand, beckoned him back a step. This made Dave more at ease, and he was able to focus again on what she was saying.

"Why did you call to us?"

With his free hand he reached over her shoulder and pointed a grubby finger toward the park. "The kids," he managed, but his throat closed up again, denying him speech. He waggled his finger in the air for some kind of emphasis, squeezed his eyes shut, and concentrated on speaking past the lump in his throat.

"You know about them?" She sounded surprised, hopeful.

192

He nodded eagerly, almost bouncing in frustration at his stupid mouth, which had decided for the moment not to co-operate.

"What do you know?" She sounded urgent now. Her hold on his hand tightened painfully, but he didn't mind. Her skin felt good.

His finger shook more emphatically. She was starting to look worried—both of them were. The man standing behind her stepped up closer, and Dave thought if he didn't get the words out soon he would lose his chance. When they did come out, it was in a gush. "Don't go in there—they'll kill you!"

For a few seconds they said nothing. Their blank stares brought on the old crawling paranoia: a voice in his head that said they wouldn't listen to him—not because his words were insignificant, but because *he* was.

"My girl is in there." The man stepped closer as he spoke. The failing light made his face look incredibly long, tired. "I have to go back for her."

"We have to try," the woman said, and Dirty Dave knew he was right about these two. They were different from the parents of the other Feral Park kids. They would die trying to save a girl who was now probably beyond saving.

Beyond the industrial area a siren blatted, lasting just long enough to warn traffic away as it approached an intersection. Dave knew that in a few seconds he would see the nerve-freezing strobe-like flashes of blue and red, just like the night before, after the commotion from whatever madness had woken him in his den. He saw the fearful looks on the strangers' faces and knew he had to help.

"Help me out," he said, and was happy with how his voice sounded that time. Not the half-man grunt he had greeted them with, but something closer to the real Dave.

They didn't move. For a few seconds their collective gaze shifted between Dave and the direction of the siren. Another blast of the siren sounded, closer this time. There was no doubt about where it was headed.

"Help me out," he said again, this time with more force. "There's a place we can hide but we have to go quick!"

The woman tightened her grip on him, the man grasped his other hand, and they helped him from the Dumpster. He hit the pavement running, beckoning them to follow, and after another uncertain pause, they did.

He ran parallel with the park, up the slope to the top of the dike, and dropped down the other side to the tricky stone shoreline. He led them along the shore away from Feral Park, away from the sound of screeching tires in the parking lot and the spooky red/blue flash of cruiser's lights. They fell behind, unfamiliar with the terrain he crossed with the ease of practice; this had been his home for years, and he could run it in his sleep. He slowed for them, and they caught up.

"Where are we going?" the woman asked, winded, the man only slightly less so, and for a second Dave felt a fierce pride. At least in some ways he was superior to these *normal* people, whom he thought of as pets of the easy life.

"Almost there . . . follow!" He pulled ahead of them again, purposefully.

He knew one of the reasons they kept slowing down was to look down the shore behind them and along the dike above, to see if they were being chased. Dave knew they weren't. If the cops had known they were down here, they would have caught them by now.

Ahead was a chunk of large gray stone blocking the path. To get around they would have to drop into the water and wade around it.

In the failing light, and from a distance, the rock appeared

natural, but when they got closer they saw it for what it was—
the leaning and busted concrete wall of an old flood culvert.
Up close, there was no mistaking the rusted twists of rebar
that poked out in places. The culvert worked on the few occa-
sions when Riverside had enough rain to worry about
flooding. The leaning wall lay at an angle against its counter-
part, so there was no real danger of further collapse.

There was an arched opening near the spot where stone
met water. Dave dropped as he ran, like an animal running
on all fours, and scurried inside. A few seconds later, the
woman and man scrambled in clumsily behind him, and he
led them on.

Inside was near-perfect darkness. It would take a few minutes for his eyes to adjust to the radiant light coming from the
entrance, but he didn't need light to see where he was going.
The others were close behind him, their heavy breathing very
loud. *More than exertion now,* he thought.

Are they afraid of the dark? he wondered.

It didn't matter. His eyes adjusted just enough to see the
path ahead for a few feet. He stopped next to an adjoining
culvert, this one much smaller and narrower. He had to crawl
on his hands and knees. He reached inside, feeling around for
a second, and found what he was looking for.

He turned the flashlight on—the ray was feeble, the batteries weak, but it was enough.

"Almost there," he said, turning toward them. When he
saw their faces, raw panic turning to relief, he knew he was
right. They *were* afraid of the dark.

I'll be damned, he thought. *Look like a couple of lost kids
themselves.*

He led them through the narrow tunnel, moving much
slower than he usually did. Now he knew their fear and felt no
pleasure in proving his speed against them. In a few minutes

he would be home, and surprise of all surprises, for the first time in longer than he could remember he was about to entertain houseguests.

"If there's one thing I learned from the wild ones at the park," he said, "it's that when you're hiding, the best place to go is underground."

Chapter 26

Charity guessed the boy was four, maybe five years old. He wore a pair of dirty striped PJs, but his feet were bare. Thick bolts of red hair stood from his head at odd angles, his pale face and green eyes were expressive of his terror.

She stood beside Toni and watched the boy run screaming through a surrealistic kaleidoscope of scenes. His bedroom at one end, cluttered with dirty clothes and a few toys. The bedroom faded into a school playground, gravel and squeaky rusted playground equipment that creaked and squalled, set into motion by an unfelt breeze. The playground faded slowly into what looked like a big, open-air mirror maze, like a carnival funhouse. Beyond that, a vast, gray stone floor, crumbling at the edges into black nothingness, tapering toward the farthest end until nothing but a degenerating, plank-like appendage remained. After that was nothing, a straight drop into oblivion.

They stood just outside the dream in the inky nothingness above and beyond, watching with a bird's-eye view as the boy fled through the playground, toward the mirror maze. Behind him, lumbering from the boy's cluttered bedroom on four twisted wooden legs was a bed. Its sheets were askew; a single feather pillow lay ripped open at the headboard.

"Weird," Toni muttered, shivering lightly.

Amid the cloud of feathers that billowed from the torn pillow, severed fingers crawled like caterpillars. Eyeballs rolled and bounce from it like rubber balls, sets of biting, chattering teeth jittered around the mattress like dangerous toys; blood stained the pearly whites and smeared the bedspread behind them. Where the headboard should have been stood the body of a man: torso, arms, a thick, sunburned bull's neck, and a head with wild green eyes and a shock of greasy reddish hair as thick and unruly as the boy's.

"Get back here, you dirty little bastard. It's bedtime!" The voice of bed monster was huge, even from far away it made Charity's ears ring painfully. She winced, cupping her hands over them, but it didn't help.

"I'm going to catch you and put you to bed! Put you to bed forever!"

In the intervals between the Bed-Monster's grotesque shouts, Charity heard the boy shriek.

Charity knew it was a dream, and not even her dream, but she was scared anyway. She was scared for the redheaded boy. What if the thing chasing the boy saw them floating up there? Would it come for them too? *Could* it come for them? If it did, she could not escape by waking up, because she was awake.

They watched from above while the boy lost his way in the mirror maze and had to turn back, still screaming in his high, terrified voice. He found another path and ran down it. From above it looked like it might be the right one.

"Please please please," Charity breathed, unaware she was doing it.

The boy took another turn and went deeper into the interior of the maze; the Bed-Monster broke through the first wall of glass and waded in after him with its stiff gallop. It slammed through pane after pane, closing the gap while the boy struggled with the next dead-end. He backtracked, took another way, and screamed even louder as the thing broke through just behind him. He found another junction—right or left—picked right, and a few seconds later found his way out of the maze. Behind him the Bed-Monster crashed through and chased even faster.

"Put you to bed, boy! Put you to bed!"

"Help him," Charity pleaded. "God, can't we help him?"

Toni gave her hand a gentle squeeze. "We are."

He called to the boy then, and his voice moved through the dream like a wave, blowing everything away except for the startled boy.

"Jacob. Over here."

Jacob turned toward them, a look of wonder and relief spreading across his face, and Charity found herself in the center of the dream. It was a new dream, Feral Park. She recognized this dream; it was the one that had led her here.

It all began to fade as the boy approached, and she knew that he was awakening.

Toni's final words to Jacob, "Come to us, Jacob . . . we'll be waiting at Feral Park," followed Charity as the dream faded and the cramped walls of the tunnel came into view around her.

Toni was still standing next to her, the fingers of his hands crossed through hers, his torch in the other hand, burning their shadows into the jagged stone. He stood with his eyes shut a moment longer, as if sleeping.

"Tomorrow night," he said, then opened his eyes and stared at the long tunnel's dead end. "He's coming tomorrow night."

Later, she sat quietly, moodily, slouched forward in her seat next to Jenny's empty throne. She was alone there; Toni was in the group on the other side of the cavern. They all knew she wanted to be alone, so they let her be. She took the cell phone out again, turned it on; the display threw a green pallor over her grave face.

Gordon's cell #.

She had tried the number a few times, but to no avail. She supposed it was because she was . . . well, wherever she was. Finding her way back to the main menu, the glowing words *no service* confirmed that.

Back to the phonebook again, she found her dad's preset and punched it. Still nothing.

She turned it off, disgusted, frustrated, trying not to cry. She saw Toni approaching and shoved the phone in her pocket, wiped the moisture from her eyes, and tried not to look as miserable as she felt.

"C'mon," he beckoned. "It's time to play." As he said this, the others were on their way out, disappearing through the tunnel to the playground. A boy near the end of the line cradled the radio; a girl behind him, a large stack of CDs.

"I thought the batteries were dead," she said.

"My man Joey went into town today and lifted some."

"We can do that?"

"Yes," he said, favoring her with a cocky grin. "This isn't juvy, you know."

"We can go out anytime, no restrictions?"

"Anytime," he said. "No restrictions." He stopped, seemed thoughtful for a moment. "One restriction," he corrected. "You have to leave your flame in the playground. If you don't come back by sunrise the next day, we put it out."

Charity glanced down at her torch, burning at the foot of her seat, and felt suddenly very vulnerable. She had thought the only way it *could* go out is when you died, like Jesse's and Ginger's had. It scared her to think they could extinguish it while she was away, not that she could stay away long even if she did leave. She wouldn't last another night in the real world.

If the flame dies when you do, what happens to you when the flame dies?

The answer was obvious. Toni confirmed this a second after Charity thought it.

"We have to," he said with a shrug. "When you become one of us, it's forever. We're family now."

Charity finished for him, "And you can't let us desert the family."

Toni nodded. "If you leave us, the Bogeys will get you again, and you might tell them about us."

"I understand," she said, finally rising from her seat and plucking her torch from the ground, handling it with more care than previously. "You don't have to worry about me, though. I'm stuck here."

"The Bogey Man," Toni whispered, looking superstitiously about to see if they'd been overheard. They were alone. It was playtime.

"Yes."

Toni told her about himself while they walked to the playground, about a father who hadn't stuck around to see him born, and about a mother who started out nice, but had started sleeping with strange men for money, which she used to buy booze and drugs. She hadn't thought he knew, but he did. Eventually she started to hurt him.

"It's the way they are," he said. "That's why we call them Bogeys. A Bogey is a monster who hurts kids."

"Not all of them are Bogeys," Charity said, thinking of her dad and Shannon. They had tried so hard to save her. They had come back.

"Yes they are," he said. "All of them—even the ones who seem nice will hurt you if you give them a chance. We play with toys, and sometimes we break them. We're kids," he added, as if that explained it, and she supposed it did. Kids broke toys, even their favorites.

"We play with toys and they play with us, and even when they try to play nice they end up hurting us, like my mom hurt me. They can't help it."

Then he told her how he started dreaming about Jenny and Feral Park.

"There were only a few when I came; Jenny, Jesse, and another boy. That other boy is gone now—I don't remember him that well. I'm not supposed to talk about him. When they're gone they're gone, but I think I really liked him."

"What happened to him?" Charity asked, even though she didn't want to know. The whole conversation had a pre-planned feel to it, like a lesson. She thought maybe she was supposed to ask, because even if she didn't want to know, she *needed* to know.

"He left us." Toni deliberately looked away from her as he said this, and she had a feeling he wanted to talk about it even less than she wanted to hear.

"And you . . ."

"Yes?"

"How? How did you kill his flame?"

Toni jerked a thumb back over his shoulder, toward the abrupt wall of nothingness.

They put it in there, in the Never, she thought, and was chilled by the idea. *That's worse than being killed. That's being erased!*

They'd arrived—alone on the phantom trail one second, standing inside the playground the next. Toni joined the crowd at the monkey bars, at the other end of the park. The music was over there, loud enough to fill the entire playground and probably the park as well. There appeared to be some kind of game going on, a reckless junior version of the flying trapeze at a circus. A boy hung upside down from the topmost bars of the jungle gym, swinging to one end, grabbing the hands of the first kid in a short line, then swung them to the other side. He was a bigger boy, not quite as big as Toni, but close, and he was strong enough to make most of them fly. When he let them go, they either caught a rung, or skidded backside through the wood chips.

Next to the jungle gym, a handful of mostly smaller kids had the carousel spinning madly, each kid behind one of the rails that ran like arched spokes from center to edge. They pushed for all they were worth, grabbing on with both hands and letting the force of the spin carry them into the air, holding onto the bars for dear life, screaming in mingled terror and pleasure.

Toni slipped into the jungle gym and caught a flying kid right out of the air, like a football player making an interception, then carried the laughing kid over to the slowing carousel. He set the boy down, directed them all to the center, and started it spinning even faster.

Charity understood with a touch of anger that Toni was avoiding her. She asked too many tough questions, and he didn't want to answer any more of them tonight. She was glad he was away from her now, though; she needed a few minutes alone.

She watched them all for a few minutes, made her way slowly from the crowd, toward the exit. Remembering what Toni had said, about how she couldn't take her torch outside, she wondered what would happen if she tried. She didn't know, so she didn't chance it.

She pushed the butt of her torch into the dirt and stalked to the exit. All around the playground, as always, was darkness, unbroken nothing. Through the arched doorway she saw trees.

She stepped outside and the rest of the night appeared around her. Behind her, faintly now, she heard the noise of music and laughter, but it was like white noise from another world. When she turned, the playground appeared deserted. No one had followed her out. Quickly she stepped behind the big sign, *Feral Park*, glanced around feeling horribly vulnerable, and pulled the cell phone from her pocket. It was raining, so she hunched over it to keep it dry.

"Please work please work please work," she murmured, and when she turned it on the *no service* message was not there. She hunted down her father's preset, found it, and pushed Send.

It rang.

"Yes." A sibilant hiss of triumph.

After the third ring, a recorded message played; *I'm sorry, but the party you are trying to contact is outside the service area. Please try again later or leave a voice message after the beep.*

The phone beeped in her ear.

Reluctantly, and with a small voice, she spoke. "Dad."

Lightning flashed above, and a second later its booming thunder shook the ground.

"Dad, are you there?"

Chapter 27

Shannon heard that first great shock of thunder, not distant like the ones earlier, but directly overhead. The storm had officially begun and Shannon was glad they were under cover, even if it was with this strange, wild man.

They were somewhere under Riverside's industrial park, in the heart of an old network of tunnels and culverts. The man, Dave, had explained on their trip through the pipe how it was used to help control flooding before the Army Corps of Engineers built the dam up-river.

"It was before my time, but from what I understand it didn't work very well anyway. They built it to take excess flow and route it underground to the other end of this little peninsula."

They were inside a raised concrete recess off the main waterway, probably meant for a long-out-of-use maintenance crew. There had been no floods since the dam went up in the 1940s. What little water did make it into the tunnels was never more than a few inches. It ran swiftly to the river at the old tunnel's termination a few hundred feet farther down.

Dave had a fire burning inside a circle of large stones. Not for heat—it was only a little cooler down there than it was above—but for light. Sitting alongside the wall out of spark range was a stack of scavenged wood, a supply of cardboard, and plenty of old newspaper.

A few feet from the fire, a thick padding of filthy old blankets covered the concrete. A small table stood in the center of the blankets. On the table were an extinguished oil lamp and a small pile of magazines and paperbacks. There was a *Playboy*, which Dave had valiantly attempted to cover when he noticed it. What little of his face showed under the weeks-old dirt and bristly beard flamed in embarrassment. A *Soldier of Fortune*, an *Outdoor Life*, and a few tattered paperback novels. The novels displayed a surprising diversity: Plato's *Republic*, Charles Grant's *Symphony*, and a generic romance, a crotch ripper her father had called them, with Fabio on the cover.

I don't know what's more surprising, Shannon thought, *his selection, or that he can read at all!* She felt brief shame for the unkind thought, but couldn't help feeling it just the same. Dave *was* a man, but he was just as feral as the kids in the park. She had sensed that, even while reaching out to him in the Dumpster, had felt the wild animal heat in his touch. He had scared her, though she tried not to let it show. Was he dangerous? Crazy?

She didn't know, and that was all the more reason to be on guard.

But she had felt that he could help them, a touch of that old sixth sense maybe. She didn't know that either, but he did seem to know about the kids.

Dangerous or not, she decided, he was safer than being out in the dark, with *Him* searching for them. He had almost got them again, luck and timing saving them, but it probably wouldn't next time. Dave might be able to help them find Charity, or at least find out what happened to her, but he couldn't help with the Bogey Man. She didn't think anybody could.

There was a long silence after Dave's brief history lesson

on Riverside's underground. She and Gordon—who had remained utterly silent through the whole thing—watched each other nervously over the table. They sat in old chairs: she an old kitchen chair with green plastic upholstery that had been the height of fashion in the 1960s, Gordon on a splintery bar stool.

Dave sat alone by the fire, legs crossed, hands clasped in his lap, head down and staring into the jumping flames. After his story, he had gone eerily silent, withdrawn.

Shannon kicked Gordon lightly under the table.

C'mon, say something. I can't do this by myself.

Gordon jumped, startled. He turned to Dave, frowned, and after a few moments, spoke. "This place isn't so bad, you know." He grimaced when Shannon kicked him again. He gave her a desperate look, shrugged his shoulders.

Dave turned and regarded him with weary eyes. "It's okay," he said. "I know it's a shit hole." He paused awkwardly and added, "But you can't beat the rent."

That surprised a laugh out of Gordon.

Shannon tried to hide her own surprised smile behind a cupped hand. She was happy to see that despite everything, neither of them had lost their sense of humor.

Maybe this guy is okay after all, she thought, and barely a second later he rose suddenly, his beard bristling and eyes narrowed. He lunged toward them, a knife in his hand. Shannon couldn't remember him having it a few seconds before. There were plenty of places to hide it on his person, but he had pulled it so damn quickly!

Gordon jumped up as Dave rushed him. The old stool fell over behind him with a crack of wood on stone. Before he could run, Dave dove down, and Shannon lost sight of him behind the table. She heard the knife's rusty blade enter flesh, a wet ripping sound, but Gordon did not cry out. He only stared in wide-eyed surprise as Dave rose again, slowly, eyeing the small body wiggling and squealing on the end of the blade.

Dave ignored them, took his seat close to the fire again, and busied himself skinning and cleaning his kill.

A rat, a goddamn big one.

Warily, Gordon righted the stool and sat again. He did not attempt conversation with the wild man, and Shannon did not prompt him. She studied the walls, a gritty crumbling gray covered with moss and fungus. She studied the pattern of the ancient blanket that covered the floor. They read again the covers of Dave's magazines and paperbacks, but didn't dare touch them. When morbid curiosity at last drew their eyes back to Dave, the worst was over. The rodent was skinned and gutted, stuck on the end of the blade like a rabbit on a spit and turning slowly over the flames. Already the meat was turning a toasty brown. Shannon's stomach growled, and she turned away.

Above them, the thunder continued its heavy beat. Somewhere down the far end of the tunnel, Shannon thought she saw the brief flashes of lightning. The illumination was too faint to be certain and it might have been her imagination, but she didn't think so.

Dave ate his meal in silence, never once offering to share. Finally he belched and tossed the remains of his dinner into the fire. He sheathed the knife under his heavy shirt and turned to them, a sated look on his face.

"Why were you running from the cops?"

Shannon and Gordon looked at each other, then at Dave sitting on the floor before them, as attentive as a child waiting for a bedtime story.

They told him everything.

He's probably crazy enough to believe it, Shannon thought.

★ ★ ★ ★ ★

Gordon felt lost in the uncomfortable silence that followed the story, told in turns by him and Shannon. Shannon left after finishing the story, picking a corner of the alcove farthest from Dave and curling up in a parody of sleep on the filthy blankets. Though she seemed at rest, Gordon knew she wasn't. Her breathing was ragged, and he caught her sneaking glances at him and Dave every few minutes.

He knew it had taken all her bravery to reach out to Dave outside, to comfort him while he cowered in the Dumpster like an animal. Now, even as Dave regained his composure—the comfort of safe and familiar surroundings, Gordon guessed—Shannon lost hers.

That thing with the rat had not helped.

Dave sat where he had before at the edge of the shrinking fire, shaking his head. It was an unconscious gesture of disbelief. With each turn of his head small clumps of dirt and god-knew-what-else fell from his tangled explosion of hair.

"Far-fetched," he said, and scratched the chin beneath his matted beard.

At that moment he looked like a mad genius, Einstein's evil twin. He shook his head again, dislodging more debris from his hair, and seemed to fall into deep thought. Perhaps trying to nail down an inconsistency in their story, to explain it to himself. Or maybe he was studying the dirt under his fingernails; it was impossible to be sure. Maybe Gordon was giving him too much credit, but he thought he saw the ghost of a man Dave might have been once, a thoughtful, intelligent, social man. Maybe an important man.

Gordon sat at the edge of his stool, ready to move quickly if Dave's moment of sanity dissolved and the knife came out again. The grubby man was watching him.

"Sounds far-fetched," Dave repeated.

"Which part?"

"All of it," he said, looking away again. "I know about the kids in the park. I've seen your girl, but I don't know about any *Bogey Man*."

"It's true," Shannon said from behind her mask of sleep, making them both jump a little.

Dave looked at her, eyes narrowed slightly. "I want to believe you," he said. "I want to trust you, but it's hard." He smiled suddenly, craftily. Gordon didn't like the look of it.

"If he's so hot to kill the two of you, why doesn't he? Where is he now?"

"He's close," Gordon said. He could feel him in the dark around their pitiful oasis of light, waiting. Lightning flashed outside, lighting the far end of the tunnel briefly. Gordon thought he saw a shadow in the brief flash, but chalked it up to imagination. A second later thunder boomed. He could hear the rain outside too; it was coming down heavily now. Soon the main tunnel just a step down from their little concrete island would become a shallow river, flowing toward its confluence with the Snake River. "The light keeps him away, but he's close."

"What if I smothered the fire?" Dave asked, rising, facing Gordon. "What if I stomped it out, or pissed it out? Would he come then?"

Dave made to unlatch the buckle of his belt, more show than actual threat Gordon imagined, but the sudden heat in Shannon's voice stopped him.

"Stop!" It wasn't a plea—it was an order.

Dave let go of his belt, looked at his feet, his face flushed. "Sorry," he said. "My people skills are rusty."

From down the tunnel where Gordon had fancied the man-shape in the brief lightning flash, there came laughter.

They all heard him. They sensed him too, in every dark corner and dancing shadow. They moved closer to the light of the fire, and Dave fumbled in the woodpile for more scraps to stoke the flames.

"You can't hide forever," the voice said. "I'll get all of you."

Then he was gone. They felt his presence, rank and fever-hot, fade away.

Gone to feed, Gordon thought. And in the absence of the Bogey Man's sick heat, Shannon shivered.

"I was an executive accountant. I made partner at thirty-one, which was no small feat in that field, or in this market. I had control, focus. I was good." Dave sighed, smiled, frowned, and rubbed moisture from his eyes. "My professional life was full, maybe too full for a man my age, but my personal life was simple. I ate dinner every night at eight o'clock, and then I jogged before I went to bed. I jogged from my house to the park, watched the geese fight with the seagulls over breadcrumbs and hotdog scraps, and then I jogged home and went to bed at the same time every night.

"The park was almost always empty when I got here, just me and the birds. One night there was a girl there. She was alone. So instead of watching the birds, I watched her play. I was sure she shouldn't be there by herself but didn't know what to do about it. I thought maybe she was a runaway, and it turned out I was right."

They sat around the fire, Gordon and Shannon silent, attentive. Gordon couldn't tell if the story had any significance to them or was just the disconnected ramblings of a broken man. He almost felt it didn't matter. He felt where it was going, and this was, after all, the perfect night for spooky stories told around campfires.

"I decided to leave her alone. It wasn't any of my business. I started to jog back toward home when the little girl screamed." He closed his eyes, clenched them shut. The tears leaked through anyway. The expression that twisted his face was of emotional pain so strong it bordered on physical.

"I saw this guy, a really big guy, bald and wearing nothing but shorts and sandals. I don't know where he came from. He was holding her down in the sandbox, and the things he did to her . . ."

Dave went silent for a moment. He did not elaborate.

Then: "I was too scared to help her," he said in a low voice. "The guy was freakishly huge. He reminded me of a circus strongman. I couldn't run either, so I just stood up on the dike like a coward and watched.

"When he finished, I walked down to see if she was alive. I knew she wasn't, but I had to be sure. She was alive though. She couldn't . . . she couldn't talk. She just lay there, staring at me through more pain than a child should ever know, bawling like a hurt animal."

Gordon had heard enough. Shannon sat next to him, hugging her knees tight to her chest, crying. Gordon wanted to reach out and strangle Dave—for the craven, complacent self-pity in his voice, for sharing yet another nightmare they could have lived without.

"Why are you telling us this?" he said, rising and purposefully striding away from Dave, checking his impulse to kill the man. "What does this have to do with getting my daughter back?"

"Her name was Jenny," Dave continued as if he had not heard Gordon. "I read about her in the paper and saw her picture on the news."

Shannon's crying grew louder; the sobs shaking her body intensified.

"Shut up!" Gordon turned back to Dave, approached him with measured steps. *"You're upsetting her!"*

"Jenny never left the park. She never left me. I've been paying for my cowardice since that night."

"Shut up, damn you! This has nothing to do with Charity!"

"Yes, it does!" Dave screamed back with sudden violence. He leapt up, his previously slow, arthritic movements transformed to the pouncing grace of a cat. Before Gordon took more than one surprised step back, before he could raise a fist in defense, Dave seized him by the front of his shirt and threw him with scary ease against the wall. *"Your Charity is with her now!"*

"Stop it, you two," Shannon stared up at them, face pinched in grief, but Gordon saw the old resolve coming back into her eyes, the strength that had saved his daughter once, and hopefully would again.

Gordon righted himself, braced for another attack, but it didn't come.

Dave faced him, almost swelling with raw animal rage. His fists clenched and unclenched, and Gordon could see the right hand wanting to reach inside the fabric of his thick shirt, where the knife was. He didn't though; somehow Dave held the animal he had become at bay, and by short degrees regained his calm.

"Jenny never left," he repeated. "She stayed, and this place changed. Blackstone Park became Feral Park. She created her own world inside Feral Park, and she drew other kids, living kids, to it. She collected the unwanted and abused kids of Riverside and created a Never-Never land for them here. I keep an eye on them. I bring them food when I can, and music. They love music."

The image of the girl who had warned him and Charles away from the park suddenly came to Gordon, the naked, bleeding apparition, and Gordon understood that he had met the queen of Feral Park before.

The book, her book, *Where the Wild Things Are*, was still in his hotel room, if Winter and his cops hadn't taken it as evidence. Everything in the hotel room was forfeit—the money he had left, his clothes, everything. Even his car was likely impounded.

All he had were the clothes on his back, the meager wad of cash in his wallet, a bankcard he dare not use now, and the cell phone clipped to his belt. He remembered giving Winter his number, and wondered if the sergeant had tried to call it. He wouldn't be able to receive any calls down here, but he would remember to check his voice messages the next time he stepped out.

"How can I get her back?" Gordon said, his voice low, his energy spent in anger.

"I don't know," Dave admitted. "They come out sometimes, but they never leave. A part of them will always be there." He turned away from them again. "Maybe you shouldn't even try," he suggested.

"What?"

"What if you do rescue your girl from Feral Park? Can you protect her from, from *him?*"

That was a question Gordon didn't know how to answer.

Shannon did. Breaking her silence, she said, "We'll find a way."

She spoke with such confidence that Gordon almost believed her.

Chapter 28

Inside again, underground.

Charity lay curled at the foot of her stone chair, close to her torch, though it gave no heat. The cavern was neither cold nor warm. There was an absence of sensation, a sensory nothing that slowly pervaded the skin and worked its way to the heart and mind. She felt it working, and almost didn't care that it was changing her, making her more like *them*.

Her dad had not answered her call, maybe couldn't. She wondered if he was dead, or if he had maybe, finally, given up.

Shannon too?

The others lay scattered about the cavern, next to torches propped against walls or stones. Some had left the main cavern for the privacy of the tunnel and its regularly spaced cells, but most seemed to prefer the comfort of company. There were snores, and the occasional senseless word spoken from varied dreams and nightmares, but mostly silence.

It wasn't until she heard the whimpering of a small girl across the cavern that she realized she wasn't the only one awake. A handful of others lie in restful positions, but with eyes open wide and staring. Not at her though—they stared at Jenny. As she watched the growing horror on their faces, she heard Jenny crying again, as she had the night before.

Charity turned slowly, knowing she shouldn't, not wanting to but helpless to stop. She saw Jenny sitting in her throne, naked, mutilated, bawling like a tortured lamb.

Charity screamed, fell to the floor in an unconsciousness that wasn't sleep, but quickly blended in to sleep.

She stirred only once that night, despite the discomfort of the rough stone floor. They awoke all at once to a scream heard in the dreams of every child in Riverside and the towns just beyond. There was only one scream, then silence, and then the morning came, minus one child none of them knew and now never would.

She awoke the next morning, her vision of the horror from the night before little more than a foggy speck on her memory. Her memory of calling her father from outside the playground as the storm began in the real world was just as hazy. She still wondered if her father would come, but there was no emotional investment in her wondering. It was a curiosity, nothing more. She no longer cared if he did or not.

The morning passed as the last had before it, almost word for word, action for action, with the exception of her showdown with Ginger. Ginger wasn't a problem any more; she was dead and erased. It was almost as if she had never existed. In another day she might not remember the mean girl at all. Like the boy who had brought her here, a blond kid about her age, now nameless and faceless. His flame extinguished from their lives, his memory from the memory of the world in which they lived. Hadn't he just been a dream anyway? A figment of her imagination?

Charity couldn't remember.

As the morning passed, so did the day, the only difference then being her indoctrination with Jenny and Toni. Other than the absence of those events, it was all the same, like being caught in the same day forever and ever.

Their night would start the same too. At the appointed time, nightfall, they would file out of the cavern through the narrow stretch of dream, to the place where it had all started, and would start again, forever more.

Maybe her father and Shannon would come, maybe not. Tonight Jacob would come, the boy whose nightmare Toni and she had watched like a scary movie. As one of the three, Jenny's new left hand, she would go out to welcome him home. It would have to be quick, though, because whatever else she had forgot, and would forget in the days to come, she remembered the Bogey Man, and she knew he would remember her.

PART IV
King of the Bogeys

Chapter 29

When Shannon awoke the next morning, Dave was gone. It was just her and Gordon, lying stiffly beneath one of the dirty blankets, pressed so close she could feel his heartbeat and the mellow rhythm of his breathing. The fire was dead, smoldering coals and ashes. The oil lamp on the table burned dimly, the wick low to conserve fuel, turned up just enough to throw a pale flickering light over their surreal setting. What happened next happened without any thought, without any intention, or even concerns that Dave might be down the corridor watching them.

Shannon pressed closer to Gordon, feeling his heat and liking it, cherishing it in a way she had never cherished the feel of another body. She pressed her face into the back of his neck and inhaled his scent; a combination of sweat and endorphins, a residue of fear, and a scent that was indefinable.

He shifted against her in his sleep, and the action of that light friction brought gooseflesh and a shivering pleasure. When she moaned in his ear, a wholly unintentional sound, he awoke and turned.

Their lips found each other as if by instinct.

Some time later, as she sat riding him on the hard surface of their makeshift bed, she found the time to marvel at how swiftly it had happened, how in only two nights, emotional as they had been, she had fallen in love with him.

Then all thought was gone, and time followed. When they awoke again, he was still inside of her, their sleeping embrace so tight they might have been one instead of two. At length, though she didn't want to, she released him and rolled away. She found her clothes tossed with abandon from one side of the alcove to the other, one of her shoes so close to the cooling remains of the file pit, the sole had melted a little.

When they had both dressed, Dave had still not arrived.

Gordon found his flashlight, the one that had seen them through the narrow culvert to the main tunnel, took Shannon's hand, and led her down the corridor toward what he hoped was an exit. Sometime later, they found the end and stepped into the gray light of another day.

They walked along the river toward downtown not knowing where to go, not Feral Park, not Shannon's house, and certainly not the hotel room. Riverside wasn't big, but maybe if they were lucky they could stay lost. Gordon didn't think they would be suspects in the undercover cop's murder, but they were witnesses, and if Winter got hold of them, he wouldn't let go. Thinking of Winter, Gordon remembered his cell phone and wondered again if the sergeant had tried to call.

"Let's stop for a minute. I have to check something."

"Sure." Shannon sat down on the edge of an uneven boulder and rested.

Gordon paused for a second, looking at her, and felt a tremendous warmth.

You have gone and done it now, he thought. *Just when things couldn't get any stranger.*

He was not sorry about what had happened. It had been perhaps the only truly happy moment in the past six miserable years, and if they made it through this alive, he planned to make spending that kind of time with her a habit. He was worried about her, though; she had been strangely silent since finally pushing away from him.

"Shannon, are you okay?" He hated the way he sounded: needy, worried. In love.

"Yeah," she said, and smiled, the blank look leaving her face temporarily. "Just thinking."

"Thinking what?" More needy. He hated it, but couldn't help it.

"You know," she said. "About strange men in strange places, and not knowing what's coming next."

"Who you calling strange?" he said with mock anger.

"You, mister," she said, returning his playful glare. Then her face was serious again. "What next?"

Was that a question or just thinking out loud? he wondered. He took a chance and answered. "I don't know, but if we're lucky, we'll find out together."

"You, me, Charity," she said wistfully. She stared at the river, its flowing constancy seeming to soothe her. "That would be nice."

"Yes," he said. "That would be nice."

They stared at each other for a second. It took an almost physical effort to look away. She resumed watching the river. He stared at his cell phone.

Gordon knew what she was thinking. Thinking things could end the way they wanted them to was beyond optimistic, it was fantasy. But optimism was all he had, so he clung to it.

There were two voice messages, the first he had expected, from Sergeant Winter. The name attached to the second message almost buckled his knees. He stumbled backward, crying out in shock, dropped next to Shannon, and prepared to listen to a message from a dead man.

A message from Charles's cell phone.

★ ★ ★ ★ ★

Dad? A simple plaintive tone, spoken with a mixture of disbelief and hope. A crash of thunder interrupted, the night's reproving rebuttal. It rang painfully in Gordon's ears. He pulled the phone away cringing, and Shannon moved in closer to hear.

Dad, are you there?

He hadn't been, he had been hiding like a rat in the sewers, a cowardly rat. He had missed her, and just barely at that. It felt like the universe itself was conspiring against them, trapping them with circumstance and taunting them with near misses.

He groaned, closed his eyes, and rubbed at his temples with his free hand. Shannon pushed in closer. "What is it?"

He shushed her and stooped a little, moving ear to ear with her, the phone between them.

I guess not, huh? She sounded disappointed, but not surprised. Gordon guessed with all she'd been through, Charity was beyond surprise.

Shannon paled visibly, groped for him, and held onto his arm.

If you can, come back to the park tomorrow night. We'll come out after dark. In the background, beyond the drone of wind and falling rain was the laughter of children, and the rough rhythm of heavy metal music. Someone called her name.

Hide in the trees if you can, or on the path by the river. She was speaking quickly, almost frantically. Someone, a young boy, called her name again, and this time he sounded closer. *I have to go. Please come. I don't like it here.* There was a pause, and then she whispered, *I miss you, Dad. I miss Shannon. Please come for me.*

Then silence. A robotic voice followed, informing him that he could listen to the message again by pressing the

224

pound key, or that he could listed to the previous message by pushing the left arrow. Instead he pushed End, folded the phone closed, and slipped it back into the carrier on his belt.

They found an ugly piece of unused land closer to town. It was several feet from the shore, covered with thistles instead of stones, and shaded by a cluster of willows. The shade provided no relief from the heat, the air was heavy, laden with humidity and heat, but it gave him a feeling of privacy. A rise of the same barren land hid the city from them, and just beyond the rise, probably no more than a few hundred feet away, was the Riverside, and a room that might or might not be crawling with cops. He thought about sneaking closer, getting a look. Shannon's Chevelle might still be parked out back, but it wasn't likely.

"Don't even think it," Shannon said, and pulled him deeper into the tangle of trees. "Not until we know what he's thinking."

"You're right," Gordon said, sighed, then hunted for a clear place on the ground for them to sit. The signal was weak; for a moment he thought he *would* have to leave the grove to reach his voice messages, but the universe was feeling kind at that moment and the message came through.

Sergeant Winter's message was not what he had expected, dreaded. No angry demands that they turn themselves in, no telling questions or outright accusations. His message was tinged with a low-level panic, and what sounded like genuine concern.

Mr. Chambers? Ms. Pitcher? Are you guys all right? I just heard what happened at the theatre. Some anger did show through, but it was undirected, or at least not directed at them.

Goddamn, he almost shouted. *What are we dealing with*

225

here? The background noise of the station was a low commotion. He shouted for quiet and continued. *If you're alive, call me!*

That was it.

Gordon supposed he could be bluffing, trying to lure them back under false assumptions so he could lock them up, but he didn't think so. If Winter had suspected them, he wouldn't have let them go in the first place, and something about the man, maybe the directness of his words, or the way his thoughts showed so plainly on his simple face during their interview, excluded the possibility of a bluff. Gordon didn't think the man could bluff if he wanted to.

"I'm going to call him," Gordon said.

Shannon nodded, watched him anxiously as he pulled Winter's crumpled card from his pocket and dialed.

He picked up on the second ring.

"Riverside P.D.," he said gruffly. "Sergeant Winter speaking."

"Hello, Sergeant. It's Gordon Chambers."

There was a brief pause, maybe a moment of shock, or maybe enough time to start a trace on their location.

"I'm glad to hear from you." The tone was markedly softer, the gruffness gone completely. "I was sure you were dead. Where are you?"

"I'm not sure," he lied. "I don't know this town. I think I can find my way back to the Riverside." He glanced at Shannon, found her almost jittering with nerves, and gave her a quick wink, to let her know all was cool.

"Can you give me a landmark? I can have someone look for you."

"There's a Flying J truck stop," he said, remembering the place on his way through town. It was on the highway coming into town, probably five miles or more from where he sat. If

Winter was tracking the call he would know he was lying, and he would call him on it. "Don't bother, though. I don't want to stop moving, if you know what I mean. If I don't find my room, I'll find the station." Next came the important question. "Do you have anybody at the Riverside?"

"No. I lost three men yesterday. I don't have the manpower to stakeout someone who isn't a suspect now." Straightforward and without pause. If there was a bluff Gordon could not detect it. "I'm sending someone out for you, Mr. Chambers. Keep moving if you like, but stay on the main road so they can see you. I need to get you here, safe.

"I have a feeling there's more to this than I'm getting. You're going to come clean with me, Mr. Chambers. Another kid disappeared last night. His parents were butchered. If you don't come clean with me, I'll jail you for obstruction. You got that?"

"Yes," Gordon said. "I'll see you soon."

He hung up, looked at Shannon. "The coast is clear. Let's move."

Shannon drove west toward the park, onto the highway, and got them out of town without being seen. They'd found Gordon's car parked where they had left it the night before. A uniformed officer patrolling the area never strayed too far from it. Shannon thought this might be a good sign; if they were watching Gordon's car, maybe they wouldn't be watching for the Chevelle. Just outside of town they saw a state cruiser, probably out of Clarkston. Gordon slid down to the floorboard before they were close enough to see the driver, or for them to see him.

Shannon kept the speed at an even fifty-five as they passed, the state vehicle moving toward Riverside, she toward Normal Hills. She watched the cruiser in her rearview mirror, feeling a rush of panic as it slowed on the shoulder of the road and made a U-turn.

"Damn." She forced her eyes back to the road.

"Did he see me?"

"I don't know," she said. "I don't think so. We were too far away."

"What's he doing?"

"Following us."

"Damn," Gordon agreed. "Is he pulling us over?"

"No, just following. He's still back a ways. Maybe he's not following *us*."

"Just drive nice then."

Shannon's face reddened in frustration, tears of anger formed in her eyes. "If he doesn't pass us, I'll have to lose him in Normal Hills."

When she glanced in the mirror again, he was much closer, and closing the remaining distance quickly.

"Here he comes," she groaned. "God, what do I do?"

"I don't know. Damn it!"

"Maybe he's passing us," she said, and a second later the flashers came on. The cruiser closed the gap between them with scary speed, did not appear to be slowing. He swerved into the oncoming lane at the last second; giving them a warning blast of his siren as he passed them, then quickly vanished around the next corner.

Shannon exhaled.

Gordon climbed back into his seat wordlessly.

A few minutes later, she slowed and turned onto the rough tree-shrouded road to Crazy Ernie's place.

"Nobody comes here anymore," she said when the old house came into view.

Gordon nodded. "I believe it."

She drove the Chevelle slowly through the side yard and

parked in back. "This is where I hid Charity after he killed Jared," she said. "We'll be safe for the day."

"And tonight, after we pick up Charity?"

Shannon almost laughed at that, a kind understatement if she ever heard one. It sounded like they were *picking her up* from a girlfriend's house. She supposed it was better than *rescue,* which would have sounded hopelessly melodramatic. "If we make it this far, yeah. It should be."

He nodded, seemed satisfied. "But not for long. Just long enough to rest. We leave before morning."

"*We,* as in you and Charity?" She didn't realize how nervous she was until she felt the twinge of cramping muscles in her wrists. Even though they were parked, she held the steering wheel in a white-knuckle grip. She let go and let herself out.

Wind whipped the trees around the old house, warm but not as oppressively hot as before. The shade here was constant, its effect more enduring. Above, the sky had cleared, but that meant nothing. She had seen the sky to the north on their way here, the direction of the blowing wind. It wasn't promising.

She stood against the car, leaning into the wind and enjoying the brief comfort it brought. Gordon gave her an odd look as he climbed out of the Chevelle.

"Yes," he said. "Me and Charity, but I hoped you would come too."

For a moment she felt incredibly stupid; open mouth, insert foot. It wasn't the question, but her tone, needy, afraid, and reproachful, as if daring him *not* to take her with them. When he moved close to her and held her, the embarrassment departed. She was tired, scared, an emotional wreck. He understood.

"Will you?"

It was an obligatory question, protocol. She knew that he

knew what her answer would be. "I'm not letting Charity out of my sight again. Or you."

She led him down into the basement. The light was still on; she had left it on in her rush to catch Charity. She pulled the chain hanging next to the bulb and made it darker. The door was open, letting in enough light to see by. She couldn't handle full dark, might never be able to again.

She led him to the old couch where she had lost her virginity so many years ago, and they made love in the light of a calm blue day.

"How are we going to do it?" she asked.

"Quickly," he said. "In and out. We'll grab her and get the hell away. How good of a driver are you off-road?"

"If you're thinking what I think you are, then good enough."

"Good," he said. "Drop me off here."

She pulled to the side of the highway, parked at the end of a small graveled rest area, and killed the motor. "Gordon, I'm scared."

"So am I," he said, then leaned across the seat and kissed her neck. He took the keys from the ignition, climbed out, and walked around to the trunk. A few seconds later, the trunk slammed closed and he walked to her window with a tire iron in hand. He opened the door and handed the keys back. "Wait until the sun sets, then drive to the park. I'll have the gate open for you."

He started off toward the trees along the river.

"Be careful," Shannon called after him.

He turned, gave her a dismal smile. "I'll try."

It was a mile to Feral Park from where he started walking, and it was slow going over rough and uneven ground until he found the start of the trail. From there the walk went quickly, too quickly. He didn't know if he was ready for this, or ever would be. This was Charles's game, not his.

He came to the end of the trail, peeked through sagging boughs and the ugly green of heat-sapped leaves. It was empty, silent, but still felt haunted. He didn't go into the park, but up through the trees to the side of the highway, then walked to the entrance. The access road where they had all met by some strange chance, or fate, was still blocked—a long, swinging gate no more than a thick steel bar mounted to a swiveling post on one end, padlocked to a second post on the other.

Gordon pushed the tip of the tire iron through the U of the lock, and used the cement-mounted post as a pivot point. He pulled on the tire iron, twisting the chain until it was tight. He put all his strength into it, and when that wasn't enough, he threw his weight behind it as well. The U of the lock twisted out of shape, then let go with an interior snap of metal. He pulled the chain loose so Shannon could get in quickly when she arrived, but left the gate closed so no one would see it and wonder.

Then, slowly, as if moving that way would postpone the inevitable, he made his way back through the trees and picked a hiding place among them adjacent to the entrance of the playground. He waited, waited for what seemed forever; now that it was happening, it *would* seem forever.

He crouched behind the thick trunk of an old willow, and waited for the dark.

Chapter 30

Shannon waited at the edge of the river, watching the sun as it fell to the west, her dread growing as it edged into the horizon. She retreated to the safety of her car and the glow of its dome light before full dark caught her. She wondered how Gordon was, and how long he could remain in the dark until *He* sniffed him out.

Not long, she thought.

The drive to Feral Park was short and the highway devoid of cops. She shut off her headlights and coasted to a stop by the gate. She almost couldn't bring herself to leave the safety of the car. She couldn't feel the fever-hot presence of the Bogey Man, just a cold unfocused anxiety, like ice in her chest. It was the place. She was as scared of this place as she was of the killer who had chased Charity here.

Thinking of Charity and Gordon, hiding somewhere in the dark down there, she found the strength to move. She ran from the open car door, through the strange night, to the gate. It was unlocked as promised. She pushed it open wide enough to steer her car through and ran back. She guided the car inside without the lights, and parked at the edge of the willow wall, just out of sight.

There was nothing in the park, no movement or noise from the playground. So far so good. She regarded the open gate behind her, knowing if she didn't push it closed, a pass-erby might notice, maybe the cops or that state trooper.

Again she ran, letting her panic fuel her but holding onto a thread of calm, just enough to keep her from bolting into the night. She pushed the gate back into place, and almost screamed when she heard the voice.

"Sarge thinks they might come back," came a burly, irritated voice from the industrial area general parking lot.

"Here?" The other voice said. "What the fuck? I mean shit, I don't even like this place in the daylight."

The two cops walked along the edge of the park but did not enter it. A flashlight appeared, skimming over the overgrown grass briefly, and vanished. She watched them as they turned and walked back toward their cruiser.

She crept back toward the car, which they had miraculously missed, and as she did they vanished, there one second, gone the next, the first officer's voice cut short in mid gripe. "Beats the f—" and then there was nothing, and she realized with a kind of sick clarity that everything outside the park was changed. No city sounds at all, not even the chirp of a cricket. Even the images were muted somehow, foggy and unreal.

That's why they missed my car.

From somewhere inside the empty playground she heard the laughter of children, and the low, rough sound of their music. She saw a boy, younger than Charity, walking across the park toward the playground. She watched him as he walked around the playground, staring wonderingly at it from all angles, before stopping a few feet from the entrance. Then the music stopped, the laughter quieted, and they came out.

A girl, the girl who had taunted her the night she had found Charity here, a boy who could have been in his early teens, and Charity. As they approached him, something that seemed as out of place as contrails in the blue horizon of some spaghetti western, there was the sound of a cell phone chittering away in the darkness.

She sprinted the last few feet to the car and jumped in. In the second before she turned the key in the ignition and cranked the old Chevelle to life, she felt a rush of hot stale air, and heard *Him* laughing.

Gordon watched from behind a veil of green as they all stopped, looks of perfect surprise lighting their young faces. Charity stared at the bulge in her front pocket, a dreamy look of disbelief on her face, then slowly pulled the phone out, and after a quick search pushed a button and raised it her ear.

"Charity," he whispered, hoping they couldn't hear him, knowing the girl—the ghost—probably could. "It's me, your dad. Get ready to run!"

Charity said nothing. She held the phone to her ear, staring through the bushes in his direction with a growing smile. The older boy watched her, the look of confusion turning inward to wary distrust. The smaller boy, the new arrival, beamed at her.

"Awesome phone," he said. "Do you have a TV too?"

The ghost girl stood next to Charity staring into the bushes with a look of calm hatred. Charity could not see him where he stood, the cover was too thick, the interior too dark, but the other saw him clearly; he could see the recognition in her eyes.

For a moment all was silent.

From above came the sound of the Chevelle's engine turning over, the mechanical roar as it came out of hiding, and the blinding glare of its headlights, pinning the stunned kids in place. There was the grunt of metal on concrete as it jumped a barrier at the end of the parking lot and landed in the park, tires throwing dirt and dried grass in rooster tails.

The kids stood there as it rushed toward them, caught like deer in the glare. Shannon turned the beams to bright and held the horn in a long, loud blast, and they finally broke.

The tall boy grabbed the shorter boy's arm and fled to the playground, their forms turning to shadow as they crossed the arched entrance. The ghost girl (*Jenny, her name is Jenny, it's written in the book she left, when she warned you to stay away*) crossed her arms over her face and vanished with a surprised shriek.

Charity ran toward the trees, phone still clutched in her hand and the surprised smile widening. Gordon rushed through the veil and met her halfway.

"Daddy!" she screamed. "You came back!" She leapt at him, Charles's phone falling from her hand as she threw her arms open. Gordon fell to his knees in the dead grass and caught her. As her arms closed around his neck, the screams of joy broke into sobs, an all-out release of emotion that swallowed her whole. His arms closed around her, and he cried too.

"I'll never lose you again." He closed his eyes and leaned into her, weakened by the release. "Never, never again. I promise!" For a short time, seconds that felt like forever, they held each other, leaned on each other, supported each other in an embrace that denied the distance of time that had separated them, that defied a world full of monsters and circumstance that had tried to keep them apart.

It was Shannon's voice, its urgency a reminder of all that might separate them again, which brought him back to the moment. He opened his eyes and saw Shannon standing by the open driver's door. "Hurry." Her eyes, wide and fearful, turned toward the playground.

The kids were coming. They leapt over the edge of the blood-iron railing, poured like an angry, dirty river from the mouth of the playground. Each held a weapon of some kind—crude-fashioned broom-handle spears, great rusty butcher's knives, clubs. The tall boy broke through and led them toward the Chevelle, his hands resting on the butts of twin guns belted to his hips.

"Gordon, let's go!" Shannon screamed, then slid back into her seat, locking the door behind her.

The kids, the wild ones, Dave had called them, were almost halfway to the car. Gordon staggered to his feet and carried Charity to the car in great clumsy strides, her arms locked in a death grip around his neck. Shannon pushed the passenger door open for him, and he slipped in. Before he could close the door, Shannon stepped on the gas. Dried grass and dirt flew behind them; a stream of childish curses and taunts, then a hail of sticks, rocks, and knives followed them. Stones bounced off the hood and trunk. Some went through the shattered rear window and landed in the back seat. Something large and hard hit the back of Gordon's seat hard enough to bounce him.

Then the boy with the guns opened fire.

Chapter 31

Charity had given up, but they had not. They'd come back for her.

Charity sat in her father's lap, arms wrapped around his neck in a near chokehold. His cheek, scratchy with days of unshaved stubble, warmed her skin. He whispered little bits of nothing into her ear, disconnected words and sounds of comfort.

It was the gunshots that brought her back to reality.

Shannon cried out, almost lost control.

"Get down, baby," Gordon whispered in her ear and gently removed her arms from his neck. A second later she was sitting on the car floor, a familiar and comforting spot. Her father slid down and to the side, providing less of a target. She would have told him not to worry, she didn't think Toni could shoot well, but words failed her. She could only sit and watch him, trying not to blink lest he vanish the moment her eyes left him.

She winced as something pointy pressed her thigh. She pulled the scissors from her belt and held them to her chest.

There were more shots as they left the screaming mob behind, and there was a startling *pow* and a sharp lurch to the left as a tire exploded.

"Shit!" Shannon cried out in equal parts frustration and fear as their momentum slowed.

"We're almost there," Gordon soothed, but he didn't

sound hopeful. "Just get us out of the park and maybe they'll let us go."

Shannon stamped the gas pedal to the floor and grimaced at the sound the over-revved engine made. Their speed picked up a little, but the rear end fishtailed, and she had to fight the wheel to keep it straight.

"Hold on!" Gordon shouted, then placed both hands against the dash, bracing himself. A second later, Charity was jarred painfully as the car bounced over, then came to rest on, some unseen obstacle. The engine died, left them sitting at an odd angle. After a few calm moments Charity climbed back to the seat and dared a look behind them. The kids were gone.

They had made it out, barely. The Chevelle sat half in, half out of Feral Park, high centered on a concrete parking barrier.

In the silence, Shannon's eyes found Charity. She grabbed her, squeezed her in an embrace that was almost painful. "Don't you ever run away again," she scolded, though much of the force of her voice was lost in weeping. "Don't ever do it again."

"I'm sorry," Charity said, bursting into tears again. "I won't."

Gordon's long reach found them both, held them as they held each other.

Just like a family, Charity thought. She let her eyes slip shut and, dropping the Bogey Man's weapon to the seat, redoubled her grip on Shannon.

No, you're not, whispered a dissenting voice in her head. *You won't live long enough to be a family. You may have gotten away, but they still have a piece of you down there. If you don't go back, they will kill you.* Then, following that, *The Bogey Man's gonna get me, and he'll get them too.*

Chapter 32

They sat there for what seemed a long time, doors locked, dome light and headlights burning. Shannon was afraid to try the ignition, afraid the Chevelle might not start, afraid it would start but not move. She was also afraid of the battery running dry and leaving them defenseless in the dark. She felt *Him* near, his sick heat that pulsed around them like something infected.

She felt him waiting.

At last, her fear of the dark won out and she did try.

The Chevelle started and lurched forward with an ugly sound, a grinding of metal against stone, and when she tried to move the car, it only rocked uselessly for a few nightmare moments. Then the power wheels touched ground long enough to grab. The Chevelle's twisted frame groaned, then its tires found flat blacktop and the metal-against-stone sound ended. They crept slowly toward the highway.

They wouldn't make it to Crazy Ernie's on the flat tire, but they didn't dare leave the safety of the lit car until they were in a safer place.

As it happened, she didn't need to worry about the flat tire for long. Sergeant Winter waited beyond the gate with backup. Three city cruisers blocked the exit, but their lights were dark. He recognized the car—Jared's car—immediately, and nodded to the officers behind him as he approached them, gun pointed skyward.

"Don't like being lied to, Gordon." He peered through the windshield, saw Charity sitting between them, and seemed to relax. He even smiled a little. He motioned for the others to come down and holstered his gun before trying the door.

"Open up," he barked. "Let's get you guys safe."

A stone flew from the shaded grove to their left and smashed the driver's side window. Shannon and Charity screamed as glass flew around them. Gordon cursed and bent protectively over Charity.

"Turn on the lights," he screamed, then ducked as another stone bounced off the Chevelle's grill. A third followed, and one of the headlights shattered. Shadows previously held at bay leapt out and reached for them, the sickening heat grew, blowing like a wind through the car. Laughter followed, and Charity sank into her seat, groaning.

"Turn on the lights," Shannon and Gordon screamed.

Sergeant Winter and his officers ignored them. Winter's gun was trained on the shadowy jungle to their left. The officers inched toward it, their guns also leveled.

"Oh, my little Charity. My bad, bad little thing." It was the voice of the night, coming from nowhere and everywhere. "I can't stand it when you run from me, my precious little Charity. If only you knew how sad it makes me." The laughter that followed was cruel. "Now I have to punish you. Yes, I must punish you, and I think I'll start with her!" Another stone flew though the missing window, striking the back of Shannon's head. She cried out in pain and groaned as the world darkened for a moment. She felt the back of her head and her fingers came away tacky with blood.

"No!" Charity screamed and grabbed Shannon, holding her tight. "I'm sorry!"

"Turn on your fucking lights," Gordon screamed again, and this time Winter looked his way.

"It's not your fault," Shannon whispered in her ear. "Don't you ever think that!"

"Hit the lights!" Winter shouted. Two of the officers halted their slow approach to the willow jungle and ran for the cruisers. The third took a final step toward the shadows, and with a shriek that was half shock and half pain, was pulled into darkness.

"Fuck!" Winter took large strides around the front of the Chevelle. "Adams! You okay?" There were no replies and no more screams, just a meaty tearing sound followed by a wet thud.

The officers stopped at the gate, guns leveled into the darkness again.

A shot rang out, and the Chevelle's last headlight exploded.

"Get the fucking lights!"

Shannon couldn't tell if it was Gordon or Winter that time, but a second later the lights came on. Headlights pointed at odd angles down the slope and into the willows. Emergency flashers filled the world with unnatural pulsations of red and blue.

The sound that followed, an inhuman squeal of frustration, was like needles in the ear.

Sergeant Winter stood silhouetted, his shadow frozen across the Chevelle's blue hood. "My God," he moaned, then lurched forward and aired his stomach with a great, groaning belch.

Shannon looked out her window, then turned away, eyes clenched shut.

When Winter stood upright again, his face was pale and loose, sick with horror. "How about some help down here," he shouted at the two officers who only stood, staring at what was left of their partner. All of the bluster had left his voice, though.

241

They flung the gate open and ran unsteadily down the slope.

"Let's go!" Winter shouted, and Gordon opened his door.

Winter and his officers flanked Gordon, Shannon, and Charity, covering them as they sprinted up the hill. Seconds later they were sitting in the back seat of Winter's cruiser. Before shutting the door, Winter leaned in and gently touched Charity's shoulder.

"Sweetheart," it was the voice of a different man, a man who would forever sleep with the lights on.

Charity lifted her gaze from her lap and Shannon saw something spark between the girl and the crusty old police sergeant.

"Was he the one who kidnapped you?"

Charity nodded, then looked back at her hands, folded primly in her lap.

"We'll get him," he said to her. "I promise."

They were moving slowly away from Feral Park and toward town. Charity looked up from her lap again, gasped, and Shannon followed her gaze out the window. For a second she saw the girl from the park, standing alone along the edge of the road, glaring up at them. Then she was gone.

Chapter 33

Several hours under police protection, or guard, which was more like how it felt, and nothing happened. It was down time.

Dead time.

Sergeant Winter was not among their keepers; he was out with what remained of his dilapidated force searching the park area. Gordon wondered how many of them would be coming back. Their protection that early morning consisted of two off-duty police, watching late night television and drinking endless pots of coffee, and a state trooper making endless circuits around the hotel.

By midnight the fearful anticipation they felt had melted into exhaustion. They simply lay on the motel room bed, the long-separated father and daughter, and Shannon. Sometimes they stared wordlessly at each other, sometimes at the television, though none could concentrate on what it had to offer. Sometimes they stared through the walls at nothing, living and reliving their private horrors of the past few days and projecting those horrors into an unforeseeable future, a bleak one.

By one o'clock in the morning nothing had happened. As their bodies and brains began to shut down only an intangible dread remained, and that dread followed them all into sleep, a sleep that each secretly believed they might never wake from.

At three o'clock the next morning, Gordon did awake, still tired and scared, but feeling more like himself than he had in days.

One of the off-duty cops slept, sitting upright in the stiff-back hotel chair while the other watched the TV, giving Gordon only a cursory glance as he rose.

Shannon looked peaceful, beautiful, perhaps dreaming of better days, or maybe nothing at all.

Charity looked pale, sickly, somehow diminished in a way that not even the stress of her terror could explain. She tossed and turned violently on the bed, whimpered and moaned in her sleep.

Shannon awoke a few minutes later, but Charity did not. Her sleep had become more restful, but she looked worse than before. Not just gaunt, but transparent.

When they tried to wake her, shaking her gently by the shoulders, she only groaned softly. She rolled like a rag doll in their shaking hands, all loose joints wrapped with a thin, pale skin. Gordon began to fear that something had happened to her down there in the place of the wild ones, something that might take her away from him again before the Bogey Man had the chance to.

Sometimes, Charity remembered, if she thought about a person or a place hard enough before sleeping, she could go there in her dreams. She had always thought this was something the Bogey Man did to tease her, but the Bogey Man wasn't here with her, and she was out of his control. She was surprised to find herself standing inside the rusted iron bar walls of the playground. No sooner had she awakened to her surroundings, or at least become aware of them, than Toni appeared, a handsome but gangly teenage gunslinger in a heavy metal shirt.

"Welcome home. I thought you might come back," he said. He looked mad, but also relieved. "Jenny wants to see you. She's pretty pissed." He didn't give Charity a chance to respond. Hefting his torch, he led the way through the path to the real Feral Park. He was silent, his demeanor serious, grim.

The long walk felt more like a prisoner's march than a homecoming.

He doesn't understand, she thought. *He thinks I'm really here.*

I am here, though, or part of me is. My body is somewhere else but I'm still here. I'm here the same way Jenny is. I just hope part of me is enough.

As she thought about what she needed to do, there was an unexpected spark of understanding, and she had to fight to keep her consciousness. She felt her hold on this place slip. Her senses seemed momentarily doubled. She felt the sensory nothing of the air around her, the strange but implacable ground underfoot, but she also felt the stiff hotel bed mattress under her back, a loose button poking her shoulder uncomfortably, and she felt hands on her shoulders trying to shake her awake.

Her father's voice reached her as if through a bad phone line, his words garbled, panicky, without meaning. She heard Shannon too, though her voice came through weaker. Perhaps because there were no blood ties between her and Shannon. Given her revelation, this made sense. It was all in the blood.

The Bogey Man didn't want her; he wanted what was in her blood, her talent; the thing that made her *special.*

He wanted to keep her until she was older, so he could marry her and have kids with her, kids with her blood and her talent. Kids who could send not just their shadows, but their very self to the farthest of places with a thought. Kids who could go places and do things he could not.

"Quiet, they're all sleeping." He stopped and turned toward her. "I'm happy you came back," he said. "I would have missed you."

"I had to come back."

"I know. I'm still glad."

She stopped beside him, and when he grabbed her hand, she fought hard not to acknowledge the sudden spark between them, or the quickening of her heart. She supposed this was what they called a crush, her first crush. She never had a chance to have one before, and it felt good. The good feeling was soured with an unhappy sense of regret. It was unfair that it had to happen in this time, this place, where she knew it could lead to nothing else. But the spark they shared drove away the strange doubling she felt in her body and head, and she was able to draw some courage from it.

Holding her hand, Toni led her through the veil and into that strange land of ghosts and maniac kids.

It was the same night all over again. Kids slept in the same spots they had before, in the same positions. She overheard the same mumbled conversation in the background. She felt the strange magic at work, the things that stole thought and memory, slowed time, and kept them forever young. The only thing different this time was her.

Toni led her to her seat beside Jenny's, the queen's, throne. Jenny, like before, was nowhere around.

"Sit," Toni said. "She'll be back."

Charity sat and watched Toni as he took his seat on the other side. Before her, burning like a physical incarnation of her very spirit, was her torch. It was her tie to a place, an anchor. She picked it up, felt its energy, her energy, surging back into her.

"Goodbye, Toni," she said, then closed her eyes and thought of her dad and Shannon, waiting for her on the other side.

She heard startled gasps, alarmed cries echoing through the cavern, Toni's the loudest, but it was faint. Their echoes faded quickly, and when she opened her eyes again she was in the hotel room, staring up at her dad and Shannon. For a second she could still feel the hardness of the torch in her hand, then that too was gone, and the fire was back inside *her*, where it belonged.

She was free.

Now she had to keep her freedom, and something occurred to her, a hint of an idea and the memory of something Toni had said to her the night they had met.

Motherfucker doesn't have a clue, he had said.

We have the power in there.

Shannon watched the sleeping girl, her fear turning to amazement as the sallow face and strangely diminished body seemed to fill up. It was like watching a cup fill with water, except she was filling up with life. Charity, a picture of death only moments before, was all color and energy, a force so strong it was coming from her skin like a radiant heat.

She opened her eyes, smiled at them.

Beside her, a nearly hysterical Gordon had fallen silent. One of the off-duty cops gasped and crossed himself. "Grant, hold up for a second. I think she's better now."

The other cop held a two-way radio, was about to call for an ambulance. He set it on the lamp stand next to his chair and approached the bed. "I'll be damned," he said, and a smile of intense relief spread across his homely face. "Young lady, you had us scared half to death." He gave Charity's shoulder a brief, gentle squeeze before returning to his watch.

The cop who had crossed himself gave her another uneasy look before following his partner to the window.

"Charity, what was that?" Gordon spoke quietly, like someone asking a secret. "Where did you go?"

Charity pushed herself up and leaned in close to her father. She gave him a look that was at once adorable and frightening, a strangely adult look. "I'm sorry," she said. "I had to go back for something." Then she moved closer still, grabbed them both by the arms, and brought them down to her level. More secrets to share.

"I know why he wants me." Her strange adult-like composure seemed to shimmer, but she kept control. She did not cry.

Shannon listened with growing revulsion as she told them.

Gordon found himself remembering, almost reliving, the dream he had on this very bed only a few days before. Charity had been in it, not just his image of her but her very essence. She had been there as sure as she was here now, and he recognized the locket she wore, the one with a picture of Shannon's family inside, as the one she had worn in the nightmare. The Bogey Man had also been there, and he had made his intentions clear to Gordon. He remembered the vision of his little girl's swollen belly, completely out of proportion with the rest of her. She had been pregnant. His fear was suddenly overshadowed by a rage for Charity's monster the likes of which he had never known. Rage for what the monster was planning to do.

The rage exhausted itself quickly though, and the fear returned in growing waves.

They might last days or weeks against her monster, months or even years if they were strong and smart, but they could not last forever. Eventually *he* would get to them, and he would get her back.

Eventually they would lose, because in the end, the Bogey Man always won.

The two-way radio squawked repeatedly, mostly startling bits of static and short bursts of communication between the field and dispatch. An hour after Charity's strange awakening it squawked again, and Officer Grant took it outside while his partner stayed behind to baby-sit. A few minutes later he returned. Gordon and Shannon met him anxiously at the door.

"It's over," Grant said. "They caught your psycho at the dike, a local guy known as Dirty Dave, been around for years. He's dead."

Gordon noted Shannon's expression at the news, a mixture of emotions, chiefly disbelief.

"I've met Dave," he said. "Psychotic, I'll buy, but he's no killer."

"He was covered with blood," Grant said. "It wasn't his blood. He pulled a gun on Sergeant Winter. It was Adams's gun." Adams was the officer who had been ripped open earlier that night, left to cool on the blacktop while they made their getaway. "A lot of kids have disappeared around that park over the years, and based on what we've seen in the last few weeks, we have good reason to think it was his work."

"What did he look like?" Charity had come from behind while they spoke. She grasped Gordon's right hand, Shannon's left, and stood between them.

Grant looked down at her, an almost pained expression on his face. Gordon understood from that look that Grant had children of his own, and that he had, knowingly or unknowingly, put his own children in Charity's place. He hoped

Grant and his children would never have to experience what he, Shannon, and Charity had.

"He's a little bigger than your daddy, taller too. Long scraggly hair, dark colored, and a thick beard."

Charity considered this for a moment, and nodded. "Yeah, that's him," she said, then walked back to her bed and lay down.

Minutes later, Grant and his partner said their goodbyes and headed home. Their job was done.

Gordon and Shannon sat next to Charity. She shook her head. "I just want to go," she said. "Can we go home now?"

Chapter 34

Shannon walked the few blocks from their room to where Gordon's car sat, still parked from their night at the movies. The streets were well lit, but the spaces between streetlights were ripe with shadows. Darkness lurked between buildings, under awnings and inside storefronts like something ready to pounce. She passed them with a gawking, nervy anticipation that never wholly departed. The morbid anticipation she felt as each approached was the worst. It was like walking towards death's open arms.

They could have waited for dawn—Gordon said they should—but Charity wanted to leave, now, and Shannon was ready. She wanted to go wherever Gordon and Charity would take her and never look back.

She tried to hold to the voice of reason, the voice in her head that said she was in no danger. Any danger that the darkness still held for them was back at the room with Charity, and that she was right in insisting that Gordon stay behind to guard Charity while she went for his car. There was no reason for them all to go out and risk the open dark, she had argued, and to that Gordon had agreed. The voice of reason, she now knew, was as afraid of the dark as she was.

Even as she shied away from those shadows, her focus split between their impenetrable darkness and Gordon's car. It sat alone at the curb a few blocks away.

Then there was a loud moaning grunt and the shadow she

skirted (but, oh God, she was still too close!) shot out and reached for her arm. She saw something shine with reflected light from the closest streetlamp, saw the open blades of those deadly scissors coming toward her in an arc, and screamed.

Then she read the label; Thunderbird.

"I heard a shot," the old woman said, stumbling from the shadowy mouth of an alley. Hair like the pelt of a road-killed dog fell from beneath an old pink scarf, her face was pock-marked, ruddy, her nose a shining map of busted capillaries, her eyes a great expansive nothing. She lifted the bottle to her mouth and drank deeply, then yanked it away with a spastic motion, barely holding onto it.

She was crying.

"They killed Dave," she bawled. "Why did they do that?"

Shannon ran the rest of the way to Gordon's car without looking back, not daring to breathe until the doors were closed and locked behind her.

She made a U-turn on the deserted main street, and was unable to help looking into the alley as she passed it. The old woman was gone, swallowed by the shadows.

Gordon packed his bags in a clumsy rush, wadding up clothing, clean and dirty alike, and shoving them in fistfuls into a large suitcase and plain gray duffel. Under the edge of his bed amid a nearly forgotten pair of socks he found the books: *Where the Wild Things Are* (his autographed "Feral Park" edition) and the library book, *Legend of the Bogey Man*. He shoved them in without thinking and pulled the zipper shut over them. It didn't take long; he had learned to travel light over the past few years.

In the bathroom, the shower ran. He would wait until Charity was done before collecting his toiletries. She was a big girl now, not a baby, and as much as he hated to let her out of his sight, she needed her privacy. She had had none for the past six years, all that time under the constant watchful eye of a fairytale killer who turned out to be real. Whatever else the kids got wrong in their uninformed, stumbling exploration of life, they were right when it came to the Bogey Man.

And he didn't want to scare her by knocking to be let in; he never wanted to scare her.

With nothing else to do but wait for Charity to finish her shower and Shannon to bring his car, he sat in the chair by the nightstand and counted the seconds. There were too many of them, and each that ticked past gave him more leisure to imagine, and to fear. But as the minutes passed, those imaginings and fears became less and less immediate. The hard-won peace was so soothing, so inviting. His eyes slipped shut and he dozed.

Awareness came back like a blow to the chest, a physical manifestation of every intangible anxiety, and the fever hot presence that brought beads of sweat to his brow like blood from an open wound. He couldn't breathe.

When Gordon opened his eyes there was darkness, broken only by weak moon glow, shrouded by gray clouds and pulled curtains. In the center of the darkness was a darker shape, a glint of bloodstained steel, the scissors Charity had left in the Chevelle, and a shark's grin.

"I always knew I would come back for you, Gordon, my dear boy. Your fear was far too sweet not to taste again."

Gordon tried to rise, to dodge the coming blow, but his strength was gone, running from his open chest and pooling in his seat. The open blade found its mark again, digging deeper into the hole in him and slicing downward toward his lap as if through paper.

"I'm glad I waited, though," the monster said through his shining Cheshire grin. "Because you gave me Charity, and you will never know how much she means to me."

Gordon tried to scream, a warning to Charity, his baby, a curse against the monster who would take her away from him again, but it came out in a warm, choked spray.

He heard Charity (*Daddy?*) in the bathroom, frightened and at the edge of tears. He saw that Cheshire smile widen and turn away from him.

And that was all.

The lights had failed them in the end, as they always did. Lanterns break and burn out, the campfires always sputter and die in the wind, electricity falters. They could hide from him, surround themselves in light, but in the end the nightlights would always burn out. The hand of darkness always knows where the switches are, and when it tires of waiting it pulls them. The darkness always wins.

"Charity, my sweet," he crooned, moving toward the closed door at the other end of the room. He heard her behind it, crying because she knows she's been a very bad girl, knowing that even though he loves her, needs her, she must be punished. "Charity, my darling, my baby, my love."

"Daddy!" she shrieked, and it pleased him to finally hear her lose her everlasting, precious control. It made his old soul feel very good. Hers was the sweetest fear of all.

He heard her pound a fist against the door, heard glass shatter as she hurled something against a mirror. What a temper this one had.

"Open the door, Charity. It's time to go home." He spoke in his kindest, softest voice, the voice that never failed to bring the most frightened of little lambs to him on their own feet, but it did not work on her now. She was growing stronger, stronger than even he believed she could. When the voice of love failed, the voice of power was needed.

"Charity!" he roared. *"Open that fucking door and come out!"*

Nothing from the other side; her raging and crying had stopped. The door did not open.

He rushed the door, arms outstretched, and the thin wood shredded into a million hair-fine splinters. They settled around and over Charity's still body.

She had dressed hastily, as best as she could in the dark, not bothering to dry herself. Her hair lay around her head in a wet fan. Water pooled on the floor around her. Her face was gray, sunken and sallow. She looked diminished, not dead; he could see her chest rise and fall almost imperceptibly. She was vacant.

She had discovered her gift, the thing about her that he loved and needed, and she had learned to use it.

"You little bitch." He lifted her body from the wet floor and tossed it over his shoulder. She might have been strong, but her body was weak. It wouldn't last long without her, and if this body died, she would be lost to him.

He closed his eyes, reached out with his will, and found her.

Not far, he thought. Then he was gone; folded into the darkness with her body over his shoulder.

The Riverside was in Shannon's sight, the blue fluorescent glare of its sign stood high above the parking lot entrance like a beacon. Then the building went dark. The gaudy blue light of the sign, the overhead parking lights, the motel front and lobby—all dark. The edgy relief she felt died with the light, and suddenly she couldn't breathe for her terror.

Then she heard Charity scream. The sound exploded behind her eyes, pulsed with her heartbeat, jackhammer quick. She answered the scream with one of her own, part pain and part sympathy, and jammed on the brakes. She skidded and came to a jouncing halt against the curb. Slowly the echoes in her head receded, taking most of the pain with it, and another sound slipped neatly in to fill the space between her ears. She groaned and pushed herself off the steering wheel, and the blaring of the car horn silenced. Her vision cleared and she focused again on the motel—still dark.

"No!" She slammed her fists against the wheel, setting the horn off again in twin bleats, beating out her frustration and trying desperately to hold back the tears. Despite their best try, the darkness had come. Something had gone wrong and the darkness had come for them, for Charity.

"Daddy's dead."

The voice was strange and thin, almost not there, like a whisper in a dream. It wasn't in her head this time; it was in the car with her. Shannon looked around, down on the floor, in the back seat, but she was alone. Then something touched her arm, cool, thin fingers stroked the back of her hand, and Charity was sitting in the front seat next to her.

"He knows where we are." Her face was solid enough to be real. Shannon felt a semblance of solid flesh when she reached out and touched her cheek, but she could see through it into the night beyond. It was a calm face, but serious, urgent. Charity's voice was emotionless, like a clever imitation.

"He's coming for the rest of me," she said. "We have to go now."

Shannon felt the girl's calm take her, like a dose of mental painkiller. The rising panic, the terror, and grief for Gordon that tore at her, faded into that dark corner of her mind where her Alicia's voice would always live. She knew those things would come back, every grief she could handle and more, but for now they were gone and she was in control.

Or is it Charity in control? she wondered, locking away her pain and shutting down all but the vital functions while the girl worked her as nimbly as a puppet master.

"Yes," Shannon agreed numbly. "Time to go." Operating on pure motor memory she pulled away from the curb. Her feet worked the pedals independent of her will, her hands worked the wheel without consulting her, turning right at the intersection, bringing the car on a familiar path.

Feral Park.

"Where are we going?" But Shannon knew where they were going, a place of destiny, both cursed and blessed, because even if her waking nightmare that dreadful night had heralded the greater horrors to come, she had found something good there: Charity, a girl who Shannon, after only four days, thought of as a daughter. She knew where they were going; the real question was *why?*

Charity did not answer. She didn't need to. The answer, both terrible and awesome in its implications, was plain. It was where it had started, for her anyway, and for good or bad, it would end there tonight.

"Turn the light on," Charity said, pointing toward the dome light as she opened the glove box. The glow from the open glove box was feeble, but it filled her transparent form like a bright smoke.

Shannon turned on the dome light, and jerked her hand down, cringing as something large struck the hood. The cab flooded with that fever heat, thick and sickly as clear puss. Something, a darker shape in the darkness above, *Him,* flew past them holding a small rag doll form in its arms. It flew up, away from the twin cones of halogen light. It turned in the air above them and circled the car.

"You loved my daddy," Charity said, not a question, but an observation.

"Yes," Shannon said, and felt the cool touch of unreality leave her, running away from her like water. Those hidden things, the undead grief and horrors in the back shadows of her mind came forward. Not hateful, hurtful things, she now realized, but lost things, scared things, needing only direction.

He passed overhead again, close enough this time for Shannon to clearly see Charity's limp body hanging from one hooked arm. He howled in triumph, teased again by touching down on the car, jolting it, nearly making her run off the road.

"I'm back, my little Charity!"

"Do you love me?" Charity asked Shannon, and this time there was just a hint of emotion in her words.

"Yes, I do," Shannon said, and smiled. "I love you very much."

The ghostly image returned the smile, then faded. "I'll see you soon then," she said. "You know where to find me."

"I'll come for you," Shannon said, but she was alone again. Charity was gone; the dark thing in the sky was gone.

Chapter 35

Feral Park sat empty, a place on the edge of two worlds, the civilized and the wild, a wasteland of thistles and refuse. No laughter, no music, no playing. There was no movement but the shifting of shadows in the playground, a swing tossed by a light breeze, the rhythmic rocking of the rope bridges. Those shadows seemed things full of rage.

The children were pissed.

Charity felt them very near, seeing her and moving toward her in this place between worlds. She stood just outside the playground with her back to the entrance, feeling them behind her, feeling him but not yet seeing him as he drew near to her. One nightmare behind, ahead another. Soon they would meet with her in the middle. If she could not escape, there was always the final escape of death. She could simply refuse her body the life it needed, and slip away as it died.

Why are you teasing me? It was Toni. She gave no reply, aloud or silent. Only waited.

Why did you come back? It was Jenny, she was angry. It was the first time Charity had sensed any emotion in the ghostly child. *Stay or go, but do it quick. I won't save you from them.*

There were shouts of approval from the others, angry sounds that weren't quite words.

Charity faced forward, silent, ignoring them. Waiting.

As one they rose up behind her, she felt them; it was a hot, violent aura like the Bogey Man's.

Then with a collective gasp of shock, they vanished.

He fell from the sky and came for her, his sandpaper laughter breaking the silence. Eyes that burned like black suns promised pain; his razorblade smile pledged submission if not death.

"Run Charity, run, as fast as you can. You'll never get away from the Bogey Man."

"You're not all that scary," she said flippantly, favoring him with a sly smile, and when he rushed her, she fell back from him, into the playground.

He tossed her dying body to the ground and followed her inside.

Once inside, he could not see her, could not even feel her presence.

"Come to daddy, you little bitch. If you don't come to me this instant, I'll make you suffer far worse than your mom or dad." He walked deeper into the playground, feeling odd and somehow weak. There was something about this place he didn't understand or like, but he would not leave until he found her.

"When I catch you, I'll do things to you can't imagine, and I'll make you live through them. You will suffer like no other has suffered before, and then I'll take you, ready or not."

Still nothing. If she was here, her fear was somehow masked. Or perhaps she wasn't afraid of him at all.

Impossible!

Behind him, a rusty swing squeaked, as if nudged by the wind or an unseen hand. To his left, old wood groaned. Something moved before him. A shadow that hadn't been there seconds earlier snaked across the wood-chip–covered ground toward him. Deep, primal fear, an emotion he had never felt in his long life, drove him back from it.

Hey mister! A soft young voice, faint but clear, as if someone had come unnoticed behind him and whispered in his ear.

He spun around, the razor edge of his weapon slicing the air, finding nothing *but* air.

Something touched his ankle, wrapped around it like a tentacle.

Then the night exploded inside his head, a raucous noise, laughter and music, the kind of wild stuff the kids seemed to like these days. He sometimes heard it in his head like this as he devoured them, but never this loud, and never this frightening. He turned and faced a boy, something only half-flesh.

Boo! The boy shouted in his head, then laughed at him.

The Bogey Man roared and stabbed at the boy, but the boy became shadow once again, and when his weapon pierced that shadow the scissors were pulled away. He drew his arm back with a cry of pain; there was a bloody stump where his hand should have been.

Blood!

A long broom-handle spear jabbed at him, pierced his leg, and withdrew. His howl of pain became surprise as the shadow tentacle tightened on his leg and yanked his feet from under him.

Then he saw them, standing in a circle around him, staring down with death in their eyes. Charity stood among them watching smugly, lips pressed tight in a grimace of satisfaction.

"I give you the King of the Bogeys."

Then they were gone again, and in their place the shadows, moving liquidly, merging, growing. As he struggled away on legs that didn't want to hold him, it rushed like a great black river.

The King! someone shouted.

Catch the Bogey!

Kill the Bogey!

Then it was on him, oozing over him with excruciating slowness, and the horrible brats began to devour every fiber of him.

"No!" He dug in with the palm of his left hand and the stump of his right, pushed himself an inch closer to the exit. "Let me go, you little bastards!"

Shut the fuck up! A hand reached from the living shadow, a small, prissy hand, and honked his nose.

Arooga, arooga!

Laughter. Mocking laughter.

A lone shape stepped from the shadow, stared down at him: Charity. In her hands was his weapon, still dripping with her father's blood. She fell to her knees and drew the scissors over her head with a howl of rage, then plunged them into his face.

Something was terribly wrong. He felt the pain as the blades broke through bone and pushed into the soft stuff beyond. Something had turned the laws of his world inside out and given his power to the sheep, and they were slaughtering him.

Shannon approached the playground. The sound of the kids' chanting was huge. It filled the park, actual physical voices, as well as the ones in her head.

The King is dead! The King is dead!

They ignored her as she approached the entrance. Inside the playground, all was still, no movement, no activity, but the voices and the chanting never stopped. Music played, the wild stuff that Jared used to love, but it was a low background drone, overpowered by the Feral kids' gleeful song.

The King is dead!

She found Charity exactly as she had before, a still, collapsed form lying in the dust and wood chips at the playground's arched entrance.

The Playground of Dreams.

Feral Park.

Gray skin stretched thin over a gaunt face, lit by an apologetic moon. Listless. There was no sign of movement under her parchment eyelids, no gentle rise and fall of the chest, and when she picked up Charity's too light body, there was no heat.

Shannon cried silently, as not to disturb the wild ones—*the King is dead*—and carried Charity away from Feral Park.

Epilogue

Shannon heard her name called softly in the night and rose to answer it. She was still somewhere between dream and reality, and in her mind it was Alicia's voice. She was always fearful upon opening her eyes on the almost perfect blackness her shade provided, but when she pulled it from her eyes, the light flooded in and filled her with comfort. Inside her bedroom all the lights burned brightly, the overhead fixture, two bedside lamps. The lively glare of the television, silently proclaiming the virtue of Ginsu knives. The infomercials didn't bother her like they used to; the secret to not letting them bother you, she had discovered, was to keep the sound off. They provided that much more light, that much more life.

She made her way into the hall. Her belly preceded her by several inches. She was seven months pregnant, and walking had become a chore akin to weightlifting.

"Mommy!"

"I'm here, Charity." She pushed into Charity's room, instantly on edge. Something was not right; the room was too dark.

She found the problem almost instantly. One of the bulbs in the overhead fixture had burned out.

"Oh dear," Shannon sighed. "I'll fix that."

"Thanks," Charity smiled, but held her blankets firmly under her chin. She was better, but wouldn't be comfortable until it was fixed. "It must have burnt out while I was asleep."

A stepladder lay folded against the inner wall of the closet. A carton of new bulbs sat on the shelf above.

It took Shannon several minutes to change the dead bulb. Her balance had gone to shit in the past few months, heights of any kind made her nauseous, but she felt better when it was finished. She stowed the ladder, tossed the dead bulb in the trash bin beneath Charity's desk, and gave her girl a clumsy hug and goodnight kiss.

" 'Night, Mom," Charity said, then pulled her shade over her eyes.

" 'Night, girl. Don't let the bedbugs bite."

"Shut up about the bedbugs, would you." But she smiled as she said it.

Shannon stood in her doorway and watched until she slept again. As she turned to leave, the nightlight caught her eye. Charity had forgot to turn it on.

Shannon bent and turned it on, with a final appraising glance at the room: closet light—check, ceiling lights—check, desk lamp—check, and nightlight. All burned brightly, killing every hint of shadow that might surface in Charity's safe place. She left Charity's bedroom door open—more light from the hall flooded in—and waddled to her own room, yawning.

Beside Charity's bed, low to the floor to illuminate the darkness under her bed, the small nightlight bulb flickered, popped, and went dark. A small tendril of smoke, whisper-fine, drifted up and dissipated.

That was all.

About the Author

Brian Knight lives in eastern Washington state with Shawna, his wife of seven years, and his three children: Chris, Judi, and Ellie. His single author collection, *Dragonfly*, has garnered critical acclaim from such respected names as Douglas Clegg, and was recommended for the Bram Stoker Award for 2002. Visit Brian Knight online at www.brian-knight.com for news and fiction.